IS THIS THE FUN PART?

AN ANTHOLOGY

by Wayne Berry

authorHOUSE®

AuthorHouse™
1663 Liberty Drive, Suite 200
Bloomington, IN 47403
www.authorhouse.com
Phone: 1-800-839-8640

First published by AuthorHouse 1/12/2009

ISBN: 978-1-4343-9926-7 (sc)
ISBN: 978-1-4343-9927-4 (hc)

Printed in the United States of America
Bloomington, Indiana

This book is printed on acid-free paper.

ALSO BY WAYNE BERRY

The Beatification of Shirley

A Play in Two Acts

For my sister, Jean Smith, who thought my ramblings were interesting enough to encourage me to continue rambling.

IS THIS THE FUN PART?

HERE'S TO YOU, MR. ROBINSON   1

A FEW GOOD MEN?   39

CINDER EDDIE AND THE WICKED
     STEPMOTHER: NOT A FAIRY TALE
     FOR CHILDREN   91

THE MIRROR   119

THE LAST ROSE OF AUTUMN   204

THE ENTITY   266

FEAR IS A BIRD   284

HERE'S TO YOU, MR. ROBINSON

DWIGHT LOWERY GREW UP in the most loving environment any child could ever hope to have. He wasn't aware it was anything special. It was just the way things were to him. True, he noticed some of his friends had problems with their parents, siblings, extended families, but he never really examined just what the mechanics of their troubles might be, or why he didn't seem to suffer from anything similar. He simply grew up enjoying his life, his mother and father, whom he respected and adored.

His childhood was unremarkable other than it was not marked or marred by over-protective parents, overly strict and disciplinarian parents, overly permissive parents, or overly religious parents. His parents were none of those things, rather a uniquely tempered and pleasing blend of all those things. Dwight benefited by their temperance and moderation. He never had free rein, but always had a say in matters involving his affairs. His parents would listen to his ideas and suggestions, as if they held some weight, and would make decisions accordingly. Dwight never felt ignored, abused, or belittled. He never questioned final decisions regarding his welfare because he always had adequate input and felt the ultimate verdict was fair and balanced, if not always exactly what he would have preferred.

Such an idyllic upbringing had molded him into a success story any parents would have given just about anything to achieve. Dwight hadn't an inkling that anything of a deceitful nature, a little capricious nature perhaps, but definitely of a devastating nature, were it ever to have been found out, had occurred long ago. Something that could possibly have had a hugely negative impact on his life, could certainly have altered its course entirely, thus, making him someone quite different from who he had become.

****

CAROLYN LOWERY WAS COMPLETELY in love with Grant, her new husband. Each had been aware from the moment they met that there was something extraordinary about the other. It was a feeling of completion like few couples ever truly experience. They fit together physically as well, when they merged on the dance floor. Their heights, weights, and proportions seemed to indicate they'd been purposely fashioned as a set, a pair. Even total strangers commented on the uncanny effect they created as they took the floor and began their expert moves to whatever piece of music the band happened to be playing.

It was the 40's and the sound was big and bold. Swing was in and each band boasted its own chanteuse. Melody was everything. Lyrics followed, but with heartfelt messages always expertly rendered by an attractive female singer decked out in something soft and appealing. Carolyn and Grant loved the dance floor and the dance floor loved them back.

No one was the least bit surprised when they announced their engagement. Many were surprised they'd dated for so long before making their final commitment. Everyone was pleased with the decision, his parents, her parents, and all of their friends. Since they'd dated for some time before the big announcement, they chose not to make it a long engagement. Both were sure of their relationship and saw no reason to wait for months or years for a wedding.

They wanted a traditional ceremony with all that went with it, but nothing huge or lavish. There would be no gross expenditure of money. Carolyn made her folks promise to keep things simple, tasteful, and small. Her parents baulked at first. They certainly had the funds to throw a wedding that could have been the social event of the season, but Carolyn forbade them to do so. She also begged them not to get overly creative with the invitations, just immediate family and friends; no reaching out to extended family or friends all over the country, including distant aunts and uncles, great or otherwise, cousins many times removed, best friends from long past college days, no matter how important or influential they might be. Her parents reluctantly complied.

The wedding took place on the most brilliantly magnificent day September could have provided. There was not a cloud in the sky. Just a hint of a cool 70's breeze stirred the now brightly coloring leaves as they donned their fall raiment, a promise of things more spectacular to come. The Groom was beaming, the Bride radiant. It was as perfect a wedding as anyone could have wished. No one could have predicted that within months this new adventure would face a challenge and a detour, unseen just over the horizon.

Carolyn's parents, since they had been denied the pleasure of lavishing gobs of money and gaggles of people upon the couple's nuptials, opted instead to spend as much as they could by sending the pair on a dream honeymoon to Hawaii. The two week getaway was to be five star across the board. Nothing but the finest hotels, the best restaurants, and the most extensive of sightseeing excursions, would be good enough for their little girl and her new husband. Neither Carolyn nor Grant voiced a single complaint on that score, happy to accept graciously this more than generous beginning to their life together.

The honeymoon proved to be more than they could have imagined. The islands were, without a doubt, jewels, boasting a diversity of culture, landscape and beauty, neither had been quite prepared for. This trip would forever remain seared on their memories, especially in light of what was about to transpire there.

Grant and Carolyn had hardly had time to settle themselves into the routine of their new life together before all hell broke loose. The Hawaiian Islands they had barely left were under attack by The Empire of Japan. Pearl Harbor had been devastated and the country was suddenly at war. Grant had been well aware of the conflict in Europe; Hitler and his minions marching across the continent in all directions, gobbling up neighboring countries like hors d'oeuvres on some continental buffet. He found it disturbing but certainly far from a major sphere of concern for him personally. Europe was apparently dealing with the threat, as well they should.

Now the conflict had suddenly been interjected into his personal sphere of concern, The President declaring war and thousands of his fellow citizens were flocking to enlist and defend all that they cherished and held dear. Grant felt he owed his country nothing less than all those others already being trained and sent off to show The Japs and Krauts just who they had messed with.

Grant was loath to leave his new bride so soon in their marriage, well aware of the danger in which he was voluntarily placing himself, as well as their future together, but compelled to act none the less. Carolyn was beside herself with fear and trepidation. She had never faced a day in her life without a hefty support system backing up her every waking moment. She wasn't at all sure she was going to be able to cope with this sudden void opening up before her. Her parents assured her they would be right there, whatever a now murky and nebulous future might bring. Grant's father-in-law was absolutely behind Grant's decision and would have even gone himself had he been young enough to do so. Carolyn had no alternative but to accept the inevitable and try somehow to get through it all, praying fervently for a swift and positive conclusion to the global insanity she perceived all around her.

****

THERE FOLLOWED A LENGTHY period of darks days, lonely nights, and overwhelming uncertainty for Carolyn. There was one bright spot, at least she strove valiantly to make it a bright spot, when she learned she was pregnant. She wrote to Grant the moment she'd learned the news. She was most adamant that he know as soon as possible. He must be aware of this new development and make it a reason for him to take care of himself at all cost, not do anything foolhardy just to prove a point or exact revenge on an enemy who would like nothing more than to deprive Carolyn of her husband. At least she looked at things in that light. She saw the country's enemy as personally after her and out to put an end to her happiness in particular. She wasn't thinking as clearly or as rationally as she might have. On some level she had to know the war was about something bigger, much more important than her own personal comfort, hopes and dreams.

****

CAROLYN WOULD GIVE BIRTH to Dwight Lawrence Lowery without the comfort of knowing her husband was nearby. She made a vow to her infant son, as he squirmed and squealed in her arms, that he was going to have the most amazing childhood, free from fear, bathed in encouragement, loved and supported, hopefully by both his parents. Carolyn would keep her vow and get her hoped for return of Grant, but not before an unseen enemy exacted a heavy toll.

****

AS GRANT LAY in a hospital bed somewhere in England, his son was thriving even without his presence. Born early in September, he was now three month's old and growing rapidly. He already sported a full head of thick dark hair and was teething. Carolyn was afraid by the time Grant got to see his son, he'd be walking and talking, totally unaware of who his father was. It was then she received notification that Grant had been injured and was receiving medical treatment in England. Grant wrote that it was quite possible he would soon be coming home and Carolyn's spirits soared. They would take a nosedive when she saw her husband upon his eventual return.

****

GRANT HAD LITTLE MEMORY of just exactly what had happened, it had been so swift, and loss of blood had rapidly plunged him into severe shock. He had been fortunate that medics had been nearby, able to render immediate first aid and arrange for evacuation to a more suitable care facility, necessitating air transport to Britain and an Army hospital. Army surgeons had labored for hours over Grant's extensive wounds. Enemy fire had nicked a femoral artery and, had medics not been close by, he would most probably have bled to death quickly. His lower extremities had taken several hits and later reconstructive surgery might be necessary. Major muscles had been damaged with some circulatory compromise which would plague Grant the rest of his life. That was not the news the surgeon feared would impact his patient's future most drastically. Grant's groin had resembled hamburger when he arrived for advanced surgical care. Unfortunately both Grant's testicles were unrecognizable as distinct organs and could not be saved. He would not be fathering any future children. The surgeon was most sympathetic and consoling when he broke the news to his patient once anesthesia had worn off and he was certain Grant was alert enough to comprehend the ramifications of the disturbing news he was about to impart. Grant received the information with a stony silence. The surgeon proceeded to add the good news that Grant would not be totally impaired as a male and husband. Although his penis had been badly lacerated, they had been able to save it and the surgeon was optimistic normal function would be restored, even if the organ would be a little worse for wear. The doctor pre-warned Grant not to expect his injured member to look like it had previously, and that he might find it somewhat disturbing, even ugly now. Grant also absorbed this news with another stony silence.

****

GRANT POSTPONED the inevitable as long as possible. He returned home to a hero's welcome and several rounds of addition surgery before discharge and a real homecoming could be contemplated. All the while he kept his most private of misgivings a secret from his wife and from their families. He had instructed his physicians to withhold the sexual facets of his injuries from everyone until he had the opportunity to address it himself at a time of his choosing. He was seriously contemplating never addressing the subject at all, if he thought he could get away with such a deception. He had a healthy infant son. He could make himself be content with that. Could he expect Carolyn to be content with Dwight as their only child? He decided that he would play it by ear, only revealing what he found it necessary to reveal as Carolyn and he attempted to resume their lives together. He would certainly make Dwight the best father he could possibly be, since he was not going to get a second chance.

****

CAROLYN FELT WEAK in the knees when she saw Grant back in the States in a hospital bed awaiting the final reconstructive surgery before he would be allowed to come home. He was emaciated, pale, and she might have passed him by had the nurses not directed her to his bed when she entered the ward. She had been briefed on the damage to his legs, both muscular and circulatory, and was aware that he would probably walk with a limp and have problems with his circulation, possibly for life, as well as extensive ugly scarring. She thought she could deal with that. She would make herself deal with that. She was unaware of Grant's other injuries and he would keep it so for many years to come. At some point she was bound to see the scars, but Grant was prepared to minimize their importance as long as he was able.

****

GRANT WAS RELIEVED and encouraged by the homecoming he received once he'd recovered from his final surgery. His wife and both families were overjoyed to have him back alive, if scarred, and he was thrilled to be able to hold his not-so-infant son for the first time. Dwight looked a lot like his dad. He had the same shock of dark hair and the ice blue eyes with which Grant had always been happy he'd been blessed. From the moment he held Dwight in his arms, he knew things were going to be fine.

Despite his injuries, Grant was determined to find employment, not sit back and try to live on disability, which he would be receiving and justly deserved. He wanted more than anything to make his life as "normal" as possible, and that included becoming the bread winner for his infant son, his wife, himself. His family. Somehow he would manage that no matter how difficult such an undertaking might be.

A country, grateful for the sacrifices made by countless men and women, certainly would have a place for him to prove his metal. And it did.

****

BEING AN ONLY CHILD, Dwight was precocious, as many only children are. He had a most inquisitive nature and being around no one but adults, his parents and grandparents, he matured rapidly into more of a little person than a child. Neither Grant nor Carolyn were sure that was a good thing, but they were proud of his growing intellect and comprehension of matters beyond his years. At the same time they avoided spoiling him by giving him everything he wanted, or everything they would liked to have given him. They reprimanded all the grandparents when they tried to do just that. As a result, Dwight was not the spoiled little brat he might have easily been when he began school.

****

DWIGHT WAS MUCH MORE prepared for the learning experience than many of his classmates but he was not a show off, did not lord his superior abilities over lesser, slower classmates. He had been taught well at home that such behavior was unacceptable. He had been counseled wisely to offer the benefit of his knowledge to others having difficulty by being supportive and assisting them in any way he could. Such affirmative action earned him many friends and praise from over-worked and harried teachers as well. He would breeze through grade school at the top of his class, as well as the most popular, well-liked student the school had seen in some time.

****

ABOUT THE TIME Dwight reached the fourth grade, his family moved into a new home. Grant was having difficulty with stairs and his doctor had thought the solution would be moving into something on one floor, a ranch style home, saving Grant the aggravation of steps and possible injury from a fall. Even Dwight liked the new arrangements better. He especially liked the services available at the new place. Even into the 50's life was much different than it would become once the 60's and 70's rolled around. Mom and Pop stores abounded. Only in the heart of big cities would one find huge department stores. There were no mega-groceries in which to shop. Even those were family owned affairs. Grant and Carolyn shopped in one such store. Dwight often went with them. He really liked the family that ran the store and hand cut any meat they might need for their meals. But at their new house they even had milk service. Very early in the morning, a milkman actually left whatever they ordered on their doorstep. They also had bread delivery. They didn't need to shop for bread or milk, pastries or any dairy products. It all came to them. Dwight thought that was really neat. Carolyn always let him choose what he wanted from the assortment of doughnuts and pastries in the array of tempting goodies in the bread man's basket, if he was home when the delivery was made.

****

THE REST OF DWIGHT'S schooling went just as well as his parents had expected and knew it would. Dwight had an innate thirst for knowledge, soaking up facts and figures like a gigantic sponge. He seemed to possess an unlimited ability to store, recall, and use every scrap of information that came his way. His parents and grandparents were understandably proud, but kept their praise to a minimum, lest they create a monster with a head so big it wouldn't fit through their modest doorframes. Graduating from high school with honors, he earned a scholarship for college and was excited about the prospects. At the same time he was nervous about being out on his own for the first time in his life, and leaving his parents alone for the first time. His parents assured him, he was going to be just fine and they would be as well.

****

DWIGHT *WAS* JUST FINE. He had to study harder than he'd ever done in the past, spending more time on assignments and doing much more research than required. There was a great deal more work to be done and less time to do it in. At least it seemed that way. But Dwight was determined to take full advantage of everything offered him. He wanted to finish his education with the tools necessary to land him a great job with excellent pay, so he could show his appreciation to his parents for all their hard work and support by helping them out financially. Grant had had to cut back on his work schedule. He was beginning to have increased problems stemming from his old injuries. Carolyn had taken a part time job as soon as Dwight had left for college in order to help out.

When Dwight graduated from college, he was able to obtain a first rate position with a starting salary above the norm, for which he was very grateful. The entire world had changed a great deal from that he'd known while he slaved away within ivy-covered walls. Just the years he'd spent in college saw sweeping new ideas and industries popping up on the horizon. The days of family owned Mom and Pop stores had all but disappeared. Huge chain stores were being built everywhere, putting small businessmen out of business. Gone were small personalized services and mass production with discount prices had taken center stage. Gone were the home delivery of milk, dairy products, bread, and pastries.Dwight wasn't sure he liked the changes but there wasn't a thing he could do about it. He would find himself becoming a part of it whether he liked it or not. This new progress would be his bread and butter. It would assist him in assisting his parents when they needed it most.

****

HE HAD HARDLY BEGUN subsidizing his parents income, trying to convince his mother she didn't need to work any longer and encouraging her to stay home and take care of his dad, when Grant became gravely ill. It was fairly sudden in its onset. He became extremely weak and was unable to work at all. Carolyn was forced to do as Dwight had suggested, quitting her job to care for Grant. As a Veteran with a purple heart and some lingering disability, Grant had been receiving some disability payments which had always come in handy, but he was also eligible for medical care which now was necessary. The coverage offered by his employer was vastly inadequate for what Grant was now facing. He was fortunate he had his VA benefits to fall back on at this critical time. After many tests and consultations they got the bad news. Grant had a virulent form of leukemia. They instituted every treatment available at the time with little results. Grant was not doing well at all. The only other option was experimental bone marrow transplantation. It was risky, of unproven benefit, but had induced remission in some recipients. It was also outrageously expensive. Dwight hadn't the slightest qualms about what he wanted done. The bone marrow transplant had to be arranged. Then came the major stumbling block to scheduling such a procedure. They had to find a suitable donor, and that was difficult and often took a great deal of time, while the patient's condition worsened. Many patients had died while awaiting treatments that were costly, experimental, and not covered by insurance companies. Dwight didn't want his father to be one of them.

****

GRANT'S DOCTORS EXPLAINED to Dwight that the most likely place to find a donor match was somewhere within the direct family, brothers, sisters, parents, offspring. Grant had no siblings, but Dwight was sure his grandparents would not hesitate to be donors if either were found to be a match. Dwight, being an only child, was himself more than willing to be tested as a candidate in an attempt to save his father's life. Unfortunately, neither of his grandparents were an acceptable match. They were understandably distressed to learn they could be of no help to their son, now in dire straights and needing anything medical science could offer, and soon.

****

THE MOST UPSETTING and confusing news was revealed to Dwight when his test results showed not only was he not a match, he wasn't even Grant's son. The totally unexpected and mind blowing announcement from lab reports left Dwight reeling. He was sure there must have been some mistake. The samples had gotten switched. There had been some kind of mix up or contamination in the lab. So positive was he of the lab's error, he insisted they draw new samples and rerun the tests again. The repeated data was no different from the original, leaving no doubt, at least in the mind's of the technicians and doctors, that Dwight Lowery was definitely not Grant Lowery's son.

****

DWIGHT WAS UNDERSTANDABLY devastated and perplexed by the unnerving revelation that Grant was not his father. The question then became, who was his father? Why had he not known about this before? Why should his mother keep such information secret? How could she have been so deceptive all these years? As a young man of twenty-six, he no longer knew who he was. His entire life had been a cruel ruse and he found himself angry at his mother. Only Carolyn Lowery knew the truth. He had no choice but to confront her.

****

CAROLYN LOWERY WAS TOTALLY unaware of the firestorm of emotion and betrayal about to unleash itself upon her with Dwight's next visit. She had not heard the disappointing results of Dwight's test results. She had been appraised of her mother- and father-in-law's unsuitability as donors for their son's bone marrow transplant. Now she would come face to face with a situation which she had ignored, convinced herself was just a silly fear from the start, indeed, had completely dismissed from her mind, so sure was she that she had been mistaken some twenty-seven years earlier.

****

WHEN DWIGHT APPEARED at his mother's door, she was immediately aware something terrible must have happened. The first thought that entered her mind was that Grant was dead.

"Dwight, what is it? You look awful! What's happened. Is he dead? Oh, no. He died. He died didn't he? I wasn't there. I should have been there. Why didn't they call me?" she began to sob uncontrollably. It was a fortuitous misconception. It softened Dwight's anger toward his mother. It was obvious she loved this man, Grant Lowery, just as much as Dwight had always observed. Their devotion to each other had never been in question. It pained him to have to sit down and question it with her now. There had to be some rational explanation and he wanted to hear it.

"No mother. Please don't cry. Dad's not dead. He's still very, very ill, but hanging in there. But we have another serious problem and I need to talk to you about it. Please dry your eyes and sit down," he tried to console her, as he handed her a box of tissues.

Carolyn visibly relaxed at the news that her husband was not dead. She sat, drying the tears now dripping from her nose and chin, as Dwight took a seat next to her. Now Dwight was having difficulty gathering his thoughts. He sat silently for a time as Carolyn dried her eyes and blew her nose. He was pondering now just how to proceed, how to begin what was bound to be a painful, perhaps embarrassing encounter. It had all seemed very straightforward the moment he'd gotten the most disruptive piece of information in his life. He had planned to march into his mother's house and shout out the most pressing question in his mind, "Who's my father?" Now it didn't seem quite that simple. Once his mother seemed to have composed herself, he had also gotten his own emotions under control and realized an attack mode was not going to help the situation in the least.

"I'm afraid I do have some bad news. I'm not a match for dad's transplant either." He let the news slowly register on his mother's face, but it wasn't the reaction he'd expected. She was visibly disappointed, but there was no hint of horror on her face that some deep, dark secret had suddenly come to light.

"That's terrible. So, what do we do now? Does this mean some long wait on a long list of suffering people? We don't have anyone else in the family to turn to," and she began to sob once more. Dwight put his arm around her shoulders.

"I think that's the only other option for now. I hate to make things worse, but it doesn't look good for dad. His condition is grave and donors are few. The chance of one presenting itself quickly seems slim." He let Carolyn absorb and deal with the news thus far for as long as he could before proceeding with the real reason for his visit.

"I'm sorry to have to give you yet more disturbing news, but I really have no choice." Carolyn looked at him questioningly, no hint that she had the slightest inkling what he was talking about. "The tests that they did on me not only showed that I wasn't a match, they indicated I wasn't Grant's son." Carolyn stared at him dumbfounded. There was no break down, no obvious sign she'd been found out. Dwight thought she still seemed totally in the dark about what his announcement actually meant.

"That's absurd!" she said. "Of course he's your father. What's wrong with those people?"

"There's no mistake mom. The lab ran the tests twice on two separate samples and they were absolutely positive there's no way dad is my father. Not my biological father anyway."

Carolyn just stared at him in disbelief for some minutes. Then her expression began to change, very slowly at first. Then some dawning realization, long repressed, began to show itself as her composure began to crumble and she looked like she was about to implode, suddenly seeming much smaller, frailer, defeated. No sobs this time, just a steady flow of tears welling up and rolling down her cheeks with no attempt to stem them or wipe them away.

Dwight waited patiently. Slowly, with many fits and starts, Carolyn began to relive something she had all but obliterated from her memory.

****

IT HAD BEEN 1941. Grant and Carolyn had just enjoyed the most wonderful honeymoon at her parent's insistence, with no resistance from the newlyweds. It seemed they'd hardly begun life in their new home when the country was viciously attacked at Pearl Harbor, a site they'd visited just a few months before. It had made the attack more immediate for them, having just been there, and Grant had felt compelled to run off and enlist, leaving her alone for the first time in her life. Both her parents and his had supported his decision, leaving her the only dissenter. Before she knew it, he was gone. Although her parents were not too far away, she still felt very alone and ill at ease. She had been prone to periods of depression and lethargy the minute Grant left. She cried sometimes for hours, alone in the house, not wanting to call or see her parents or his. She blamed them somewhat for his absence, although she knew he would have gone anyway even had everyone been dead set against it. She was positive her life was over. She was sure she would never see Grant again. It was in one of her deepest moments of despair that she received a visitor.

****

IT WAS DELIVERY DAY for bread and the like. The doorbell rang and she forced herself to the door, resembling what her grandmother had always referred to as, "The Wreck of the Hesperus."The delivery man stood on the doorstep with his ample basket filled with bread, doughnuts, and pastries.

"Mornin' Carolyn. Gee, you look all done in this morning. What's happened? Somethin' bad happen?" he asked her, concerned.

"No, Blake. Nothing bad. Come in," she invited as she opened the door wide and he entered, carrying bread and the tempting treats with him. She knew she needed some bread, but was afraid none of the confections in his basket were going to be any consolation for the despair and loneliness she was feeling. As she removed a loaf of bread from his basket, and a box of chocolate covered doughnuts after all, she burst into tears for some unknown reason. She'd been doing that a lot lately. Before she knew what was happening she had her head on his shoulder sobbing away.

Blake leaned toward her as she sagged his direction, putting an arm around her in a comforting manner. Blake had no ulterior motives in mind when Carolyn's head hit his shoulder. He didn't even know this woman well. He'd only been delivering bread at this address for several months. The couple had barely moved in.

He knew her husband, who he'd only met once, had enlisted and that she was not happy about it. They were a good deal younger than he, and now here he was consoling this distraught woman not quite sure how to do that.

"My husband's left me. He's never coming back. I just know it," Carolyn sobbed.

"Come on now. Things aren't that bad. Everything thing is going to be alright. You'll see. Your husband isn't going to be gone forever. He'll be back soon. This war is putting a strain on just about everybody, but he will be back. You've got to believe that," Blake attempted to calm her fears. Blake was an extremely attractive older man. In fact he resembled Grant in more ways than one. He could have passed for Grants father. He had the same dark hair, now flecked with silver, giving him a most distinguished air. He had the same piercing ice blue eyes. He was tall and strapping for his age, just like Grant was. Carolyn felt very comforted on his shoulder. She didn't know it, but Blake was experiencing some marital difficulties of his own, and before long his platonic motives would take a decidedly more personal turn. Carolyn might have avoided what happened next had she heeded Blake's advice and gotten a hold of herself and her emotions. But she hadn't. And now she experienced full recall of the moments which followed that fateful morning.

****

BEFORE EITHER OF THEM were fully aware of what was happening, Carolyn's overwhelming need to be held more closely and Blake's long overdue needs unmet by his wife, they would find themselves comforting each other more passionately. Clothing was hastily shed and the two soon found themselves naked, intertwined, and writhing in an ecstasy neither had anticipated when the doorbell rang. It was one of those things that happened more frequently than admitted, in many places, in many families, all over the country. It would not happen again for Carolyn and Blake.

****

CAROLYN WAS SO EMBARASSED, if not completely comforted by this handsome, Grant look-alike bread man, that she decided she could not remain in the house alone, and moved immediately back home with her parents, there to remain until Grant's return home. She never breathed a word of the underlying reason for her sudden return. Her parents were well aware of her depression and loneliness, that being reason enough for them. It would be scant weeks before Carolyn discovered she was pregnant and every fiber of her being was certain it was Grant's. The timing of his enlistment and leaving for training was consistent with it being his child. Carolyn had never been particularly regular in her female cycles. The fleeting thought that this child might possibly be other than Grant's was dismissed. Now she had been given a reason to hold on, wait for Grant's return and raise his child with him by her side. She would also give Grant a reason to take care of himself, take no foolish chances, and return to raise this child with her. It had been her reason for wanting Grant to know of her pregnancy as soon as possible.

****

NOW SHE KNEW she had made a slight miscalculation. It had only been a matter of weeks, days perhaps, but it had been enough to make the difference. She had had only the slightest and most momentary pause when she'd first learned she was pregnant. She'd consulted her calendar to allay that slight suspicion, and once she'd done that, there was no longer any doubt in her mind. Grant was going to be a father. She gave not another thought to Blake and their indiscretion, until now. Well, that was not entirely true. There had been the move they'd made to this, the ranch style house, for Grant's convenience when Dwight had been in grade school. The house they'd lived in before Dwight was born had been sold as soon as Grant returned home, and a place in her parent's neighborhood purchased. Carolyn had never really liked their first house anyway, and Grant's employment, once home and recovered, would have necessitated him traveling quite some distance for work. Dwight had grown up in their new home until Grant began having real difficulty with the stairs. Grant was able to obtain a transfer, and they moved into the one storey house nearer his parents. That house happened to be on Blake's bread route. Carolyn hadn't seen him since she'd suddenly fled to her parents before she even knew she was pregnant. She barely recognized him. He'd aged a great deal. Now wispy white hair was all that was left of the dark hair flecked with silver. He was much thinner and age lines crossed and re-crossed his face. It was the eyes that gave her a start the first time he came in with his bread basket. She hadn't given the slightest hint that she remembered what had happened so long ago, and neither did he. It was obvious he had not aged well. He surely was not as old as he appeared. He wouldn't have still been working had he been. Carolyn remembered now that Dwight had been allowed to choose whatever he wanted from the goodies Blake always had in the basket. But Blake had only worked a very short time before someone else took over the route. Eventually, home deliveries would stop. That bread company would go out of business completely. There had never been any further contact between Blake and Carolyn.

****

"SO, JUST WHO WAS this person, mom?" Dwight pressed her for details she really didn't want to give. What possible good could it do now? She just wanted to put it all back in the little sealed compartment she'd convinced herself years ago wasn't even there.

But Dwight would not be content with the little she'd shared with him as she dredged up things she'd rather not have. "I'd really like to know who my real father is. I think I have that right, painful as it may be for you."

"What about your father? What is this going to do to him? He doesn't deserve this," she lamented as she began to cry once more.

"There's no reason he has to know about any of this. If he hasn't known all these years, or even had the slightest doubts, I don't see the harm in saying nothing now. The fact I'm not a suitable donor is all he needs to know. But I need to know more."

****

THEIR CONVERSATION was interrupted by a phone call from the hospital saying they should come immediately. Grant's condition had worsened. They got to the hospital in time to say their final goodbyes before Grant died. He never received the information about Dwight, neither his donor status nor his paternity. All that was now moot. He had lived and died believing Dwight was his son, and that was just fine with Carolyn. It was also fine with Dwight. They would put any further discussions on hold until after the funeral. But Dwight was not about to let the matter rest for long.

****

ONCE THE SERVICES were over, Dwight allowed his mother a week to grieve before revisiting their interrupted conversation. Carolyn knew it was coming. She wished Dwight would just forget it, but knew he would not. She could tell by the look of determination on his face when he stopped by a week after Grant's funeral, that she was going to have to reveal everything.

"I don't mean to cause you undue pain, mom, but I'd like to finish what we started. You remember? You know what I mean?" he pressed her, as he tried to ease back into the uncomfortable topic.

"Yes, Dwight. Unfortunately, I do," she began. "What more can I tell you?" she begged, still hoping what she'd already revealed would be enough.

"I want to know exactly who he was. Where is he now? I know it's still embarrassing for you, but it's very important for me. I can't even put it into the right words. I'm so very grateful for the wonderful life you and dad provided for me, but now that I know there's someone out there responsible for my even being here, I have to know who he was."

"If I must." She took a great deep breath, then let it out slowly before continuing. "You met him when you were small. I'm sure you don't even remember him. Oh, dear this is just dreadful," she paused to sigh and collect her thoughts. "Do you remember when we moved into this house and how we all liked it so much?"

"Sure, mom. I've always loved this house. It's the greatest. It was nice to have everything on one floor, and being close to granddad and grammy. I liked having the milk and things left for us in the morning. I also liked being able to pick out whatever I wanted when the bread man came, even if it wasn't good for my teeth, as you always reminded me! I kind of miss that still today."

"You remember all that?" she asked, surprised he'd come up with all those detail so quickly.

"Of course I do. Why? What does that have to do with my real father?" Dwight asked in return.

"Well, I'm pretty certain that your real father was the man who delivered your bread and doughnuts," she let the final piece of the puzzle fall into place. "His name was Blake Robinson."

"The old guy who delivered bread for the first few months after we moved in? But mom he was so old!" Dwight thought his mother was pulling his leg.

"Well he wasn't as old as he looked. And he looked much younger when I first knew him after your dad and I moved into our first house. We'd only been there a few weeks before World War II started and your father left to fight. I was devastated and depressed. Beside myself with visions of widowhood. Your father never coming home. Blake came by one morning when I was an absolute basket case. I have to admit that he bore a striking resemblance to your father back then. Older, and with some grey in his hair but now that I think about it, the similarity was unmistakable. Maybe that's why I felt drawn to him that morning. He could have been Grant's father or older brother. I was looking for some solace and I think I may have come on too strong. Solace turned into more, and that was that. I felt so bad I moved back with your grandparents and never saw him again. That is until we moved here to this ranch style, and there he was looking so much older, still carrying his bread basket. I hardly recognized him myself. We never said a word about what happened. At that time I didn't believe you were anything other than Grant's. He'd only been gone a short time. I don't even think it was two weeks when Blake and I lost all sense of…. . I'm so sorry." Carolyn simply hung her head. All the tears had been shed now.

"But what happened to him?" Dwight was still pushing for more.

"I have no idea. There wasn't any reason for me to stay in touch with him. I hadn't seen him in years anyway and then he retired, at least I guess that's why the younger man took over the route. I really don't think Blake was well back then. I don't know what happened to him. If I'd really thought he was your father I might have done differently. Who knows now? I can't tell you anymore than that." she finished. "You're going to look for him aren't you?" she asked.

"I have to," Dwight answered.

****

DWIGHT THOUGHT he might be able to get some information from employment records, but the company Blake had worked for had long since ceased to exist. There was no Blake Robinson listed in the phone book. He called the Robinsons that were listed and came up empty. No one knew or was related to a Blake Robinson, no wife, no siblings, no children. The man had simply vanished. That wasn't possible. Dwight wasn't about to give up. He very possibly could have moved when he retired. Many people did that. Where might Mr. Robinson have retired to? Florida was a good bet. How was he going to canvas the entire state of Florida for one person? He wasn't even sure Florida was where he'd gone.

Perhaps the postal service could be of help. He wasn't sure how long they kept that kind of information, or if he could get it if they did. Then he had another thought. He might be dead. If he retired when he was 65, he'd be 88! Dwight thought he'd looked 80 when he'd brought the doughnuts, but then he'd thought everyone was old back then. Lots of people lived to 88. His grandmother was 95.

Maybe he wasn't 65 when he retired. Not everyone retired at 65. Some people retired early. His mother said he'd not been well. He could only be in his late 70s, early 80's. There were hundreds of thousands of people that old! He remembered the old guy had been very friendly. If he was as friendly with everyone else, as he probably had been, maybe one of his other old customers might remember him. It certainly wouldn't hurt to ask around the neighborhood. Many people still lived here from when Dwight had been a boy.

****

DWIGHT PROCEEDED to canvass the neighborhood, talking with anyone he remembered who still lived there from twenty years ago. There weren't too many, but more than he had expected. He had just about given up hope when he remembered Mrs. Edgeworthy. She'd probably be in her 90's if she was still alive. Her tiny house sat way back off the street and looked deserted, but he knocked on the door anyway. No one answered. He was just about to leave when a curtain parted and a white haired woman peered out at him through thick glasses. He waved at her and smiled.

"Hello, Mrs. Edgeworthy. I'll bet you don't remember me," he said loudly, fearing her hearing might not be so good.

The curtain fell back into place and there was a rattling of the lock before the door opened slightly. "Who is it?" the old woman asked.

"It's Dwight Lowery, Mrs. Edgeworthy," he said. "I used to cut your grass."

"Dwight! Lawd ha' mercy! You done growed up fine. I ain't seed you in 'coon's ages," her withered old black face wrinkled in a welcoming toothless smile. "Come on in here an' visit. I doan see nobody 'tall anymore." It would be Dwight's lucky day. Mrs. Edgeworthy knew where Mr. Robinson was. "Mr. Robinson. He was sutch a nice man. Had lot o' problems he did. Health problems. Looked old afore he time. Laws! He looked as old as I was and I knowed he weren't. Quit his job early, he did. He an' the Missus took off for Florida. Warmer weather. Get a Christmas card from 'em ever' year. Well not this year. Let me see wered' I put that las' card?" She rummaged through a nearby drawer before finding what she was looking for. "Here it is! Boynton Beach! Tha's the place."

Dwight gave Mrs. Edgeworthy a big hug. "You don't know how happy this makes me!" he hollered, as he left her standing confused but pleased on her doorstep.

****

DWIGHT HAD NO DIFFICULTY finding the Robinson's house. Once he'd found it, he didn't know what to do next. He couldn't just knock on the door and say, "Hi, Mr. Robinson! I'm your son!" It might be too much of a shock. What might the Mrs. Robinson think? He hadn't even thought of that. She certainly wouldn't be pleased. He decided to take his time and approach the whole thing slowly. He watched the house, trying not to look like a criminal planning some mischief. The place was awfully quiet. There was an old car in the driveway. At least someone still lived there. The card Mrs. Edgeworthy had come up with was fourteen months old. Thank goodness she was one of those people who saved old Christmas cards.

After several hours with no activity evident, Dwight decided to go find some nearby lodging and try again later. After a quick lunch he returned, parking way down the block so he wouldn't be noticeable from inside the house. He certainly didn't want to scare them. After just a few minutes, the mailman passed down the street delivering some mail to the house he'd been watching. No one came out to get it. After another half an hour he got out of his car and walked nonchalantly toward the mailbox. Not a soul was visible on the street. All the shades were down in the house. Could he sneak a peak at their mail without getting caught? He'd risk it. He opened the mailbox and the sun fell directly on the name and address stamped on the envelope on the top of the pile. It read: Mr. Blake Robinson.

****

DWIGHT RETURNED to his car, excited that he'd found the man responsible for giving him life. He was still pondering how best to approach the Robinsons. As he sat thinking about that, a short, plump, grey-haired woman emerged from the house to retrieve the mail. She moved slowly and used a cane as she made her way to the street and back. About fifteen minutes later she appeared once more, this time to get into the old car parked in the drive.

She drove off leaving Dwight with a decision to make. Should he go and ring the doorbell now? If Mr. Robinson was at home, he'd most probably be alone and that would give Dwight the opportunity of introducing himself without his wife's having to know. Only Blake could judge what effect Dwight's sudden appearance might have on her.

Dwight rang the doorbell feeling anxious and now foolish, standing there waiting to tell this complete stranger he was his son. No one came to the door. He rang twice more and waited again. There was no answer. Perhaps Mrs. Robinson had gone off to pick up her husband. Maybe Mr. Robinson was an invalid and couldn't answer the door. Whatever the case Dwight decided to go back to the room he'd secured and return in the evening when both the Robinsons would most probably be in.

****

AFTER HAVING an early dinner, Dwight returned once more to the Robinson's house and went up to the door, this time more composed and prepared, even though Mrs. Robinson would probably also be at home. The same woman he'd seen collecting the mail, then driving off, answered the door.

"May I help you young man?" she asked with a friendly smile.

"I hope so," Dwight began, now nervous once more. "I'm looking for a Mr. Blake Robinson."

The face fell as the smile faded, a look of sadness replacing it.

"I'm sorry to say Mr. Robinson died four months ago." She paused, confused. "Did you know my husband?" she asked, wondering why such a young man should be on her doorstep asking about her husband.

"Yes, I did," Dwight's disappointment evident in his face and voice.

"Where are my manners? Please don't stand there on the porch, come in. Come, let's sit in the kitchen. I don't get many visitors anymore. My husband was the social one. Sit, sit. I was just about to have a cup of tea. Would you like some?" Mrs. Robinson talked away as she led the way into a cozy kitchen and busied herself fixing tea for the two of them. "Tell me how you knew my husband," she finished as she placed the tea on the table and sat down opposite Dwight.

"Well, to tell the truth, I didn't know him all that well. I was just a kid way back then. Your husband used to deliver bread at my house and I used to have my pick of all the other goodies in his basket, if I was home when he called. I always thought he was such a nice man and a friend of mine said he lived here. I just thought I'd stop in and say hello. I'm so sorry to hear he died. He probably wouldn't have remembered me anyway. He must have delivered things to hundreds of kids like me."

"Oh. The bread route. So that's how you knew my Blake. My husband always was the most engaging man. He had a way with people I never had and couldn't understand at all. And that bread route. It was a source of contention with us, I hate to admit. My Blake was a brilliant man, but he never took advantage of his gift. He was top of his class in high school. Graduated *cum laude* from college. He could have made quite a name for himself, I always thought. I thought the job delivering bread was beneath him. He thought otherwise. It's what he wanted to do. He loved being out and around people without having some overbearing boss type constantly looking over his shoulder, telling him what to do. He tried that when we were first married and hated it. And don't be too sure he wouldn't have remembered you, young man. He knew everyone on his route by name. I sometimes thought I must know them too, the way he'd tell me about them. What was your name again"

"I'm sorry. Dwight Lowery."

"Lowery. Lowery," she searched her memory for something. "Oh yes. I even remember that name. Blake came home upset because the Mrs. had completely fallen apart over her husband's enlistment for the war. What an awful time that was for a lot of people. My Blake was a little too old for that, thank goodness. He said she completely disappeared after that. Hadn't a clue what happened to her. I can remember that very well because we were having some major problems ourselves back then. We both wanted children real bad and we just weren't having any. I got pretty upset and I think I blamed it all on Blake. I still feel regret over that whole time. Found out later, quite by accident, wasn't his fault at all. Was mine. Almost ended our marriage over it. But we reconciled. Things were much better after that. Then Blake started having health problems of his own and we thought it best to give it all up and move here. Try to enjoy the time we had left. A lot of good years here. But we never had any children. It would have been nice now to have children and grandchildren around." She lapsed into silence, lost in a world of could-have-beens, as Dwight sat dumbfounded at the information he'd just heard.

Pieces of a puzzle even his mother had had no insight into. And dropped into his lap without the slightest prying.

"I'm sorry. Where was I? There was something else I was going to tell you," Mrs. Robinson was back from her reverie. "Oh yes. Now I remember. He said the same woman was back on one of his routes. Her husband had come home alive, but had suffered some sort of injuries in the war, and they had a darling little son. That's got to be you. Dwight Lowery. How sad he isn't here to see you. He'd have been so pleased you stopped to see him. You know you gave me a little start when I saw you at the door. You remind very much of my Blake when he was young."

"I look a lot like my dad," Dwight decided to do some damage control before it was needed. "My mom says my dad and your husband looked a lot alike when they were younger, could have been brothers. My dad died just recently too. He'd been very ill and there wasn't much they could do for him. I miss him very much. He was a wonderful dad," Dwight finished with tears now welling in the corners of his eyes.

"How tragic for you. Your dad couldn't have been very old. At least my Blake had a good many years. I'd have liked a few more though. How's your mother doing? She must be devastated."

"Yeah. She's pretty broken up still." Dwight's disappointment at finding his real father deceased was just not an acceptable end to his quest. He wasn't yet satisfied with his search and determined to go yet one step further. "Mrs. Robinson, I wonder if it wouldn't be too much for me to ask where your husband is buried?"

"Certainly not. I'm flattered that you would even care. I even kept some of the notices they printed in the paper. I thought I'd send them to people, and then I realized I didn't have many people to send them to. But now I'm glad I saved a few."

****

DWIGHT STOOD at Blake Robinson's grave for quite some time as he mentally painted the picture of the past. He put the jigsaw puzzle together in his mind, down to the last piece. His mother's overwhelming sense of loneliness and abandonment. Blake's sense of guilt and emptiness as his wife blamed him for a childless marriage. Carolyn's probable subconscious attraction to this man so like her husband. Blake's natural tendencies to be outgoing and compassionate. No mystery there. No real betrayal. Just a fateful meeting of two people dealing with circumstances beyond their control at a time the whole world seemed out of control. And Dwight's looks now no mystery either. He looked as much like his dad as he did his father. And the intellect. No secret where that had come from. Grant Lowery had been a terrific man, but by no standards brilliant. By Mrs. Robinson's accounts, her husband could have done much more with his talents, besides delivering bread, had he chosen to do so, but then Dwight wouldn't be standing, head bowed, on Blake's grave now.

****

FROM THEN ON, every year, on Dwight's birthday, he had a delivery made. At Blake's gravesite, a beautiful arrangement of flowers would appear, and the card would read simply:

HERE'S TO YOU,
MR. ROBINSON.

A FEW GOOD MEN?

It was the 60's. Viet Nam loomed large on the horizon. Barry Hanley's world was in somewhat of a turmoil. He'd finished high school with honors and gone straight off to college with a work scholarship and financial support from a family friend. Barry's family, sad to say, hadn't a pot to piss in.

College was quite a shock after the nurturing atmosphere he'd experienced from his teachers back home. All of them had made themselves available for assistance whenever needed. His professors were aloof and detached; present during lectures, totally absent afterward. It was completely up to him now to keep up with the work load, finding whatever help and assistance he required whenever and wherever he could find it. It was not the walk in the park he'd expected. Not that he was lacking in intellect, he just wasn't prepared for the hands-off approach to learning which seemed to permeate the new environment.

Perhaps he'd chosen too heavy a course load to begin with. He'd always opted for the most difficult, challenging and advanced classes he could fit into his daily schedule before. Now it seemed he'd bitten off more than he could chew. Now he had to make some drastic decisions in order to survive. He would have to drop some classes, while he was still able to do so without penalty, to stay afloat and expect to do well in all those remaining on his plate.

Once he'd accomplished the downsizing of his expectations for his Freshman year, he found himself in a more tenable position. His studies were paramount. He had never given a thought to college as an opportunity to party and carry on irresponsibly, as he noticed so many of his classmates were doing. Basically he was your run-of-the-mill nerd, long before nerdism would become the fashion with the advent of the computer, and nerds would become geeks making millions before they were thirty. He kept his eyes always on what was most important, education, while working as many hours as he could on the work-scholarship program without jeopardizing his studies. Social activity was not in the picture and, as such, he was branded an outcast among classmates, ridiculed for not joining in the fun.

The fun was often just what one sees in many movies about the college experience, *Animal House* being a prime example. Barry would not be having any such experiences. While classmates were off partying and jockeying for nominations to Sororities and Fraternities, Barry was deep into his books in the dorm room alone and not feeling the least bit left out.

His Freshman year would deal him a major hiccup with an emergency appendectomy, a post-op staph infection, and several weeks post-hospitalization stay in the college infirmary. Although he tried to catch up with studies missed during the downtime, he wasn't able to pull off his usual stellar performance, failing to regain top of the class standing upon his return to the classroom. It put a major damper on his psyche as a whole. He wasn't acquainted with anything but perfect attendance and perfect grades. Without any help from professors, who couldn't have cared less if he got the material or not, and classmates, who would have been perfectly thrilled to see this odd, introverted misfit fail and disappear from their midst, Barry was on his own and floundering for the first time in his life.

It scared him to think he wouldn't succeed where he always had in the past. His academic success was all he'd ever thought he had to offer his family for validation, for approval, for acceptance. Without that attribute, how would he hold his head up?

You see, Barry harbored a deep and shameful secret. At least it was assuredly deep. Perhaps only shameful in light of the time and the background from which he came. The 60's were a little early to reveal a secret of the kind with which Barry was grappling. His family and his church would be embarrassed, appalled and mortified. They would mount an immediate campaign, intervention, or perhaps even an exorcism to eradicate this most unacceptable of perversions. In his short life this malady was never even alluded to in its most graphic of terms. From the pulpit it was always, "The Abomination," "The Perversion," or the unspeakable, "Sin That Dare Not Speak Its Name!" At that point in the service Barry was certain he had a neon sign attached to his forehead which immediately lit up with glowing red letters, flashing the message to the congregation and his scandalized family in terms more specific and colloquial. "Faggot!" "Queer!" "Pansy!" "Homo!" There wasn't room on his forehead for the complete, technical, and dictionary definition, "Homosexual!"

But nothing like that had ever occurred. However, he was sure he'd felt a surge of blood to his face, a reddening which would have given him away just as efficiently as his imagined neon sign might have. The service ended and he escaped once more from detection, vowing to squash his innermost feelings before they destroyed himself and his family. There were times he toyed with ending it all. But that was probably a worse sin. He wasn't exactly sure, but wasn't about to ask for guidance as to which was the most serious infraction of God's Law. He muddled on.

He was an exemplary student. He was never sited for the kinds of teenage infractions and rebellions that seemed to go along with that rite of passage. Instead, he labored long and hard at presenting himself as normal in the only other way he knew how. The award winning report card.

Now he was in his late teens and still struggling internally with the problem he'd had since his earliest memories, his attraction to members of his own sex, as opposed to those of the opposite. He'd tried dating many times with many girls, but never found the slightest spark of physical attraction or chemistry with any of them. In fact, he experienced just the opposite. His feelings leaned toward aversion. No matter how hard he tried or how many dating experiences he put under his belt, no bonds ever emerged, not even the slightest stirrings of physical desire would show themselves. His equipment remained dormant. Actual physical contact with prospective mates only enhanced the dormancy of his manhood as it shriveled up to almost nothing. However, the sight of an extremely good looking athletic boy or man sent pulses of electricity through his entire body and the manhood, shriveled by feminine softness and wiles, was awakened by masculine power and the manly hardness of muscles. Even a picture was enough to provoke a response. He certainly wasn't about to do anything about those feelings except battle to extinguish them.

So Barry lived in a limbo between the sexes, concentrating all his time and effort on the cerebral, squashing the carnal. He did without feminine company because it was unfair to any girl and merely a ruse, and without masculine company because he simply couldn't trust himself to remain totally hands-off indefinitely, while being petrified of rejection or retaliation should things move towards hands-on.

When Barry received a letter from the family friend paying his tuition informing him that, due to a slight dip in the stock market and some miscalculations or mismanagement of assets, his tuition payments might soon have to be curtailed, Barry took it as a sign for him to move on. He could not afford to pay the tuition on his own. The work-scholarship helped, but he could not engage in yet further gainful employment and maintain his studies at any level acceptable to him. He dropped out of college, earning only half the credits he had expected to receive for his time and toil.

Return home was painful. He wasn't the success he'd planned on being and had little to recommend him in the employment market. Minimum wage doing a boring job seemed the deadest of dead ends. He was well aware that soon his number was about to come up for the draft, and being sucked into the Army seemed an even worse fate. His father had been in the Army and his stories were grim and gruesome. Barry usually tried to shut off auditory pathways whenever his father's conversations wended their way in that direction. He'd let his mind wander off somewhere else, missing the bloody and graphic descriptions of battles fought and won.

He opted instead to enlist in the Navy. "Join the Navy and See the World," seemed to call out to him. He aimed at getting some topnotch training and he even liked the uniforms. His family seemed pleased enough that he was enlisting. Serving your country was a tradition, an honor, and an obligation they strongly supported. The fact that Barry's service wouldn't be taking the same path as his dad's was not considered crucial.

The paperwork involved in getting into the Navy proved a little tricky for Barry. It was decades before the, "Don't Ask. Don't Tell," policy. It was currently a, "We Ask. You Lie," type deal. At least you'd lie if you wanted to be accepted, serve your country, and receive some excellent training while doing so. If it was your intent to shirk your duty, you could be truthful and be rejected, or you could lie, answering "Yes," to be rejected. Barry answered "No" to all questions dealing with sex of any nature! He didn't feel particularly guilty about doing so. He felt it was none of their business and it wasn't going to affect how he functioned, or the caliber of job he would do during his years of service. In that, he would turn out to be absolutely correct. He was accepted without further ado.

The crude introduction into Navy Boot Camp possibly made Barry rue the day he'd made the fateful decision to enlist. Upon arrival at the training facilities, hundreds of new recruits were herded into an enormous drill hall, a cavernous space crowded with austere metal bunk beds as close to each other as possible, leaving just enough room to maneuver between them and get in and out without kicking those in neighboring beds in the head. It was a surreal atmosphere to feel so cramped in such an overwhelmingly large space. Barry noted with some trepidation that the accommodations were far from comfortable; mattresses at least an inch thick, and privacy would be nonexistent. His resolve was about to be sorely tested. Perhaps he had made a huge mistake after all. Maybe Canada would have been a less daunting choice? Too late now. He would have to make the best of it somehow.

Lights out came early, and a good thing too. The wake up call came before the sun had even thought about rising. The pitch blackness of the drill hall was suddenly illuminated by blinding spotlights and a cacophony of noise, unearthly in its quality and deafening in its intensity. Immediately, the air was blue with curses and language Barry had never heard in his life! Perhaps he'd died during the night, and this was Hell!

Rough, deep, demeaning voices filled with authority and disdain screamed out at the top of their lungs.

"Drop your cocks and grab sox, you sorry excuses for human beings! Let's move it Muthafuckers! We ain't got all morning to whip you pussies into shape. I've never seen such a collection of sorry-assed, pimply-faced cock suckers in my life! Let's go ladies! Are you deaf as well as ugly?"

Barry's face burned with embarrassment. His first morning in the service and these total strangers were already accusing him of the very thing he'd been fighting his entire life to suppress. How had they found him out? Now they would berate him in front of hundreds of these other strangers. Life as he knew it was over.

Then he was totally awake and aware that he was not the sole target of the invective flying throughout the drill hall. It was a collective indictment of them all. Everyone was in a panic, jumping from their racks, bumping into each other, not knowing what was happening. Their tormenters were laughing uproariously at the recruit's confusion.

"Now girls, if we could have your attention, we're going to tell you how this is going to go. We're going to tell you what to do, and you're going to do it double time and without question. Are we understood?"

A smattering of weak responses, barely audible, could be heard squeaking from frightened, constricted throats.

"Yes," weak and timid.

"OK," fearful and high pitched.

"Yush," an unintelligible assent.

"Jesus Christ! Do you believe this shit? What giant rock did this motley pile of whale shit crawl out from under? What disappointing gathering of princesses are we blessed with here? I don't think there's a man in the entire lot!" the lead captor yelled his disapproval of this latest batch of captives. "What do you think?" he addressed his co-captors.

"I don't see a one!"

"Not an ounce of backbone in the lot!"

"I don't see nothin' but twats!"

"I've never seen such an ugly bunch of women in my life!" came the assessments from their other captors.

The lead captor resumed control once everyone had had their fun at the recruit's expense. By now everyone was completely awake, many trembling uncontrollably. One had even wet himself. Unfortunately for him, he was in the tormentor's direct line of vision.

"Oh, my god! Will you look at this sorry fucker, guys," directing all his henchmen's attention to the now wet and embarrassed recruit. "This scum sucker's pissed himself! Peed right in his pants! I don't think we want a sorry-assed bed wetter!" he ratcheted up the recruit's discomfort as he strode forward, grabbing him roughly by the arm and propelling him toward one of his assistant jailers. "Get this goddamn retarded reject out of my sight!" he bellowed as he thrust the petrified and miserable recruit into the waiting clutches of one of the guards, who escorted him from the drill hall with such force the recruit couldn't keep up, and the guard ended up having to drag him from the premises.

"Now ladies, let me tell you how this is going to go from now on! If my instructions are not followed to the letter and immediately, you will be sorry you were ever born. Don't test me on that!! You will not speak unless spoken to! If you are spoken to, your response will be immediate, forceful, and respectful. Every response will be preceded and followed by SIR! When I ask you if you understand these instructions, your response will be, 'SIR. Yes, SIR!' Do you understand?"

A weak, "Sir. Yes, sir," echoed from some of the assembled inductees. Their tormentor was not amused.

"That was the most pathetic response I've ever heard from any recruits in my entire life! Drop and give me ten!"

There was no response from the group.

"Ladies, get down on the fucking ground and give me ten push-ups right now!!" he screamed, his face crimson with rage.

Everyone dropped and attempted to give him ten. Many had never ever given anyone even one! It was a pretty poor showing and everyone knew it. They were in for the ruing of the day they were born now for sure.

"That was the weakest, pansy-assed excuse for ten I've ever seen. Maybe we should just throw this whole bunch back in the cesspool they were bred in. What do you think, guys?" he asked his cohorts.

"I don't know what else to do with them."

"It's a lost cause."

"Sorriest thing I've ever seen."

"Rejects, every one!" they all agreed.

"Gentlemen, and I use that term loosely, let's try this once more. And if I don't hear some improvement, some significant improvement, you'll drop and give me twenty. God help you! It might be the death of over half of you on the spot! Let me just refresh your memories. We seem to have an over abundance of dunce heads here! When I ask you if you understand my instructions, you will reply immediately, forcefully, and with all due respect, 'SIR. Yes, SIR!' Do you understand?"

A much more rousing and enthusiastic, "Sir. Yes, Sir!" emanated from hundreds of throats. Not exactly a roar, but considering the newness of it all, promising.

"Well. What do you know? We have a few live pansies at least. Before we kill half of you off with twenty, let's try that once more and I want to hear some goddamned, unbridled enthusiasm! Do you understand?"

A loud, reverberating, "SIR! Yes, SIR!" echoed throughout the hall. The tormentor was pleased. He smiled.

"That's more like it!"

The recruits were then given the detailed agenda for the day. They would be issued all their Navy gear. They would be broken up into companies and assigned specific barracks which would be their home until basic training was completed. They would meet and be given further instructions by their Company Commanders, some of whom were now standing in front of them, though the recruits didn't know that as yet. Daily routines would be delineated, from which there would be no deviation.

With each new pronouncement and instruction there was an obligatory and enthusiastic, "SIR! Yes, SIR!" They were given thirty minutes for their morning ablutions before they would be marched off to the mess hall for chow.

Thus began the most difficult, challenging, and rewarding experience of Barry's life so far. As he rushed to use the bathroom and throw some cold water on his face, he hadn't time for much more, he was so unnerved by the morning's rude wakening that he barely noticed he was in the presence of hundreds of young men, many of them unabashedly walking around naked after their hurried showers. He was completely absorbed in just the physical act of trying to use the bathroom with dozens of others in the same open room with him. He closed his eyes and tried to pretend he was in his own bathroom at home, but the noises around him belied the pretense. Dozens of recruits used the facilities and left while he was still attempting to do so himself. As a result of his delay, there was only time for the splash of cold water on his face before they were being instructed to form up outside for the march to the mess hall.

Barry would soon discover that he was the most senior recruit, an adult at twenty-one. All the others were by and large seventeen and eighteen, newly graduated from high school, and just as nervous and fearful of this strange new environment, perhaps more so, than he was. It occurred to Barry that for the first time in his life he might hold the key to getting the upper hand, taking control of his own fears while helping to allay those of the younger recruits around him. He made the decision to become the recruit's voice just as adroitly as the lead captor had controlled his band of merry tormentors.

The results were astounding. The moment he spoke up, those around him deferred to his council and advice. He became the one person to whom anyone could come with any problem and Barry was quick to offer assistance, even go before their Company Commander, if necessary, on their behalf. He took it upon himself to offer tutoring to those having difficulty with any aspect of the training they were undergoing. Barry seemed to grasp the essence of everything required quickly and was anxious that those around him grasp it too, not fall behind or fail in their attempts to master the material at hand.

He once more determined that whatever needed doing, he was going to do it best. If a recruit next to him had a little more spring in his step, Barry added even more to his own. If someone exhibited an ounce more of snap to their drill routine, Barry added two to his. Their Company Commander was soon singling him out before the entire company as the example to which all of them should aspire.

"Hanley!" their Commander would bellow, "Get up here!" Barry would be trotted in front of his assembled company. "Now I want all of you to watch Hanley closely and do this drill exactly as he's been doing it!" The Commander would call out the commands as Barry snapped and turned, his every motion crackling with precision and exactitude.

"Let's all try this once more and for Christ's sake put some fire into it!" The repeat drill was more to his liking but it would take five or ten repeats before he would concede that the recruits had made some measure of progress.

Barry survived his training. Not only survived, but excelled. He was completely overwhelmed when at the conclusion of basic, his fellow company members voted him Company Honor Man. He would be presented with a commendation in front of the entire graduating assembly. Dozens of companies would stand at attention in front of the base staff, their Company Commanders, and recruit's friends and families as each company's designated Honor Man received his commendation.

But the most important and biggest honor of the day would be the presentation of The American Spirit Honor Medal to the sole recruit in all the graduating companies who most deserved such an accolade. To Barry's utter disbelief, he was to be that honoree. The Company Commanders, Drill Instructors, and Classroom Teachers had selected their candidates for that honor. Each had had a lengthy interview with the Base Commander and his choice had placed that honor squarely on Barry Hanley.

The medal was quite hefty and engraved. The commendation that went with it into his permanent service record was something he had never imagined could possibly happen to him. And although he was humbled yet exhilarated by the honor, his most rewarding honor was the fact that all those guys in his company had chosen him to represent them as an example to which they all aspired. They were all total strangers such a very short time ago.

They came from such different backgrounds, races, and religions that Barry still had difficulty grappling with how he had even managed to relate at all with any of them. His own background was so judgmental, unforgiving, and divisive, that he knew, had he encountered these men back home, he would never have been able to communicate with them on any level. And yet here they were honoring him as the person they most looked up to. It actually brought tears to Barry's eyes whenever he thought about the unlikelihood of such a thing ever occurring.

Barry's triumph was not without one glaring defeat. He had managed to complete his training without learning how to swim! A Navy man not knowing how to swim? The Navy never knew. He was quite content to let that little fact remain a secret only he was aware of.

Barry was well aware that he was not fond of the water, did not know how to swim and had no burning desire to learn. The Navy was on a collision course with his reticence. The big day was approaching and Barry knew it. He had no idea how he was going to pull off a monumental victory in the face of his being petrified of drowning and desperately afraid of water, especially the kind that went over his head. He cringed every time he thought about the looming swim test. He knew he couldn't swim, would not likely be able to learn to swim, would fail miserably, be dismissed from the Navy as unacceptable, disgracing himself and his family.

On the big day hundreds of naked men were marched into the gymnasium housing an Olympic-sized pool. As they filed in, the swim instructors made an announcement that struck even more fear into Barry's heart.

"All those of you who do not know how to swim, please fall out and form a group on the opposite side of the pool.

For all swimmers, please proceed to the base of the four towers on this side of the pool and line up behind the stairs to the top of the platforms above."

Barry's heart skipped several beats. He was being instructed to separate himself from the group and stand facing hundreds of recruits, naked and exposed, the object of judgment and securitization, all his "inadequacies" in plain view for all to see and ridicule, which he was certain they would do. Memories from high school came rushing back as he remembered his shame and embarrassment from gym classes.

"Hit the showers, guys!" the gym teacher would shout. Barry would try to dress without hitting the showers. He certainly didn't want his classmates to see how little Mother Nature had regarded him when she had passed out the masculine equipment. It had not escaped his notice, as classmates paraded naked into the communal showers, how very generous she had been with others. "Barry, I said hit the showers," the teacher would catch him before he could scoot out the door, skipping the dreaded shower. He'd slowly make his way to the shower room wrapped securely in the largest towel he could find, hoping everyone had finished and he would have the place to himself. He was never quite slow enough to accomplish that, but at least his exposure was limited to a very few.

Now he was being instructed to parade his privates in front of hundreds. He kept in step with everyone else, approaching the towers, lining up, prepared for defeat in front of everyone. He noted that the non-swimmer's corner remained empty. Apparently he was the only one who didn't know how to swim. At least that's what he thought.

"Form four lines, one line for each of the four towers," the instructors began. "When we begin, the first four recruits will climb to the platform and wait on the edge. The next four recruits will climb behind the first four and wait at the top of the stairs. The next four recruits will ascend halfway up the stairs and wait there. The last four recruits will position themselves on the bottom step of the tower. We will have four recruits in those positions at all times and as each recruit on the platform jumps into the pool, the three behind him will move upward to fill the vacant position in front of him and a new recruit will assume the bottom step. Please keep the flow moving each time we call out 'Jump!' When we indicate the first four recruits are to jump into the pool, they will cross their arms over their chests, hold their noses closed with the fingers of one hand and jump feet first into the pool. They will then surface and swim to the opposite side of the pool and climb out. We have hundreds of recruits to process today and must keep the pace as brisk as possible. Are all the instructors in place and ready to begin?" The instructors indicated their readiness.

"Will the first four recruits at each tower take up the positions I've described." They did so and the day's entertainment began as the voice over the PA system ordered, "Jump!"

Each set of four plunged into the pool and swam across to climb out as the PA called, "Jump!" for the next set of four. When it was Barry's turn to jump, he crossed his arms, held his nose, and prepared to drown. He hit the surface in a panic, sure he would never see the light of day again. Miraculously, he did surface, but not for long. His arms flailing, he immediately went under again, taking in a good deal of water. Choking and sputtering, he came up several more times before an instructor had to dive in and pull him out, directing him to a growing group of embarrassed, coughing, naked men, their secret now exposed as well as their "inadequacies," now even smaller after emersion in the cold water.

As those who had passed their swim test with flying colors, and were on their way to get dressed, filed past the failures, Barry stealthily infiltrated their ranks without anyone noticing and never looked back as the rest of the failures squirmed nakedly on the sidelines. He had successfully "passed" his test.

At the conclusion of Barry's training he received a battery of aptitude and proficiency tests which were designed to determine how he would be assigned and what specific job he might best be qualified for, or in which he might receive extensive training to optimize his service to the Navy. His tests indicated a high level of ability in the mechanical fields. Barry couldn't understand how he'd scored such marks since he was baffled by a wheelbarrow. Mechanics simply stymied him. He begged for inclusion in some field or job involving science and biology. The Navy was hard pressed for Corpsmen and Barry was sent on to Corps School. He couldn't have been more pleased and relieved.

Corps School was more like school than Navy. There were still lots of rules and regimentation, but the pace wasn't as rapid and grueling. Most of the time was spent in the classroom and they were truly like a regular classroom. The instructors were Navy Nurses. Subjects included Anatomy, Physiology, Pharmacology, Medical and Surgical Intervention, Emergency Medicine, and Patient Care. Barry was back in his element once more. He flew though all his classes, ending up with the highest grades in his graduating class and receiving yet another commendation to be entered into a now impressive service record.

He did so well so easily in all his classes that he had a great deal of spare time to once again assist fellow students with their studies and problem areas. He also began to form some lasting friendships with a number of his fellow classmates with whom he felt a special bond, and he now had the time to nurture those friendships. Basic training had simply been too hectic and rushed to allow enough free time to really get to know any of his fellow recruits very well. Corps School may have been the first time in Barry's life that such close relationships had ever been possible. There had been no time in high school either. There had been much too much to learn for him to find the time to form any friendships. He was very much the outcast there as he had been in college. Education had always taken every minute and all the effort he could muster. He found it a welcome change now to have the opportunity to make friends as he'd never done before. For some reason he'd been able soak up the curriculum like a sponge and retain every drop of it for future use. He ended up with exactly what he'd hoped for and more. He had acquired a large body of knowledge, excellent hands on training, and was leaving not only with that, but some true friends as well.

Along with Barry, three of his friends, Lewis Ford, John Tierney, and Alfred Lorenzo, received orders to the same duty station. No sea duty aboard ship for them. Not such a bad outcome, considering Barry still didn't know how to swim. All four would be serving at a Naval Hospital. They were all excited over their good fortune.

After a brief leave for each of them to visit their families, they reported to their new duty station eager to go to work. They would find a great deal of work waiting for them. Casualties from Viet Nam had already begun to clog the med-evac pathways to every Naval Hospital in the country. Barry was assigned to SOQ, the Sick Officer's Quarters, the top two floors of the hospital. The view was quite spectacular and the duty was choice. No wards on the SOQ. Each officer had a private room. His three friends were assigned elsewhere on enlisted floors taking care of orthopedic, surgical, and neurological patients. No one was complaining about their assignments. The Navy Nurses were wonderful to work with and the Navy Doctors went out of their way to give additional pointers and training to all the corpsmen working for them and their patients. Barry took advantage of every opportunity, observing procedures and treatments with an eagle eye and even assisting whenever any doctor required it or asked him.

As weeks of hospital work turned into months, Barry and all three of his friends would not be as thrilled with their assignments as they'd been initially. As more and more casualties from Viet Nam poured into the facility, each of them would have their own horror stories to relate and their own private qualms and nightmares to deal with.

Lewis was on the surgical floor and he had witnessed first hand the damage that could be wrought by flying shrapnel. His floor would receive those servicemen who had had major soft tissue and organ damage.

"Going up to the ward is becoming a real bummer," Lewis announced to the other three as they shared dinner one evening. "We have three guys right now that look like hamburger. The wounds are so extensive and they're going to need a great deal more surgery and extensive skin grafts. I don't think any of them will ever be normal or have much of life from now on, if they survive. One has lost almost all his large intestines and a lot of his small. God I hate colostomies. Another had his balls, penis and bladder blown away. All his urine has to drain into the urostomy bag which will be a permanent fixture, glued to his side for the rest of his life. He definitely won't be having any family. Can't say I would want to have to deal with what he's facing. Another's lost both kidneys and will have to survive on permanent dialysis treatments. Maybe he might get a transplant if they ever get good at that. He also had major disruptions throughout his abdominal cavity, but is maybe luckier than the other two."

Alfred had a few awful experiences as well. "Well, I hate to squeal on myself, but I almost fainted today. One of our orthopedic patients needed to be put in traction in order to align major fractures in his thigh. The doctor needed to drill a hole through the bone to insert a pin that would hold the traction weights. I was asked to hold the patient's leg as the doctor drilled completely through the bone. God, the vibrations coming up through my hands as I steadied the patient's leg were so creepy that I suddenly felt light headed and started to see spots before my eyes. Thank goodness the drill popped out the other side before I lost it completely and dropped to the floor. I've never felt anything like that before in my life and don't want to ever again. We have another poor young man who, it's been rumored, shot himself in the foot in order to get out of Viet Nam. All his toes look like beef jerky. I swear if you went up and pulled on them, they snap off like burnt toast! He's definitely going to lose all of them. He's in constant pain and has been getting lots of morphine. I don't know why they're waiting so long to amputate. Maybe they're punishing him for having shot himself in the foot. Seems pretty cruel, but I don't know."

"Well, I've just about had it, if you have to know," John told his share of tragedy. "I have a ward full of vegetables. So many laying around with such severe brain damage. It's sickening. There's no one in there anymore. For some the lights are on but the house is empty. For others the property's just been plain fucking evacuated! We just tend them like some human garden. There's no communication possible. We talk to each other, that's about it. What a silent patch of roughage!"

"I'm really sorry you're all having such awful experiences," Barry had to weigh in. "We all are. Me too. Can't say too much because, though I can't speak for you, this is what I begged for once I'd finished boot camp. I wanted to be useful and get some expert training I could put to use later. You know, when I'm out of the service. Well, I'm getting it! They brought in a very young, good-looking officer yesterday who's had his spinal cord severed. He can breathe but that's about all. It's heart wrenching and sad to see such promise cut down like a stalk of wheat. And he'd just gotten married before deployment. The wife is a basket case! He's still got his balls, unlike your poor bastard, Lewis. Maybe it'll be possible for him to have children, but he won't be on the working end of it, if it happens at all. He'll have a Foley in his pecker from now on. Don't know if this wife will have the fortitude to face the rest of her life with a husband who is basically only a head on a pillow." It wasn't the most enjoyable of dinners.

It wasn't all work for the four friends. There was liberty to look forward to. Having dinner off base at a real restaurant was always a welcome change. A night out for a movie at one of the many ornate theaters in town, also a welcome break. None of them had ever seen such show places at home, each being from small towns with a theater, but nothing to compare to the size, grandeur and comfort of these mega-movie houses. Barry, however, did not see as much of his three friends as he would have liked. They did make plans for dinner and a movie when they had days off once in a while. But many days when Barry was off, and he knew his friends were also, he was unable to find them anywhere in the barracks. He'd then content himself with going alone. It was never as much fun as having company, but he hadn't made any new contacts on base other than the three who'd come there with him from Corps School.

Although he felt comfortable with all three, somehow he felt there was a barrier of some kind between them and himself. Sometimes when he'd approach the three deep in conversation, they'd suddenly curtail whatever they'd been talking about and seem a bit flustered before they were able to fit Barry into the flow of conversation as it resumed.

"Let's meet at The Crossover around midnight," Barry overheard his three friends talking in the hallway late one afternoon. He waited for one of them to include him in the evening's plans, but the invitation to join them never came. He was confused and couldn't understand why they'd obviously slighted him by going off without him. Had he said something to offend them? He couldn't remember doing so. He knew sometimes they looked bored with his offerings to their conversations, but was he really that boring? He could just forget about it and say nothing, but it really bothered him. Perhaps they weren't the good friends that he'd imagined. He knew where The Crossover was. It wasn't that far from the hospital. It sat next to a major overpass on a through town interstate, thus the name. He'd never been there, but had heard it was very popular and open 24 hours. It was a real Blue Plate Special, 50's type diner, reputed to serve excellent home style cooking. No cuisine there, but who could afford it anyway on what the Navy was paying them. He decided he'd just show up there uninvited after midnight, as if he'd just felt like going out for a late night meal. They couldn't accuse him of following them. He'd just do that and watch closely to see what their reaction would be. If they seemed truly annoyed that he'd dropped in on them, he'd know his assessment of the closeness of their friendship was flawed.

Barry entered The Crossover shortly after midnight and surveyed the booths and counter to find his friends had not yet arrived. The place was about half full at that late hour. He chose an empty booth with full view of the door so he would see his friends the minute they came in. He found he really was hungry and gave the waitress his order for a hot turkey sandwich with mashed potatoes and gravy and a coke. The fare really was very good and he finished his entire plate, keeping his eye all the while on the door. Still he didn't see anyone he knew.

"Can I get you anything else, Sir?" the waitress asked him as she removed the empty plate. She was very friendly and extremely attractive. Long curly red hair flowed around her shoulders with the prerequisite Dixie Cup waitress cap perched on top. If Barry had been interested in the opposite sex, he would have pounced. Perhaps she was looking to be pounced upon? It didn't really matter, there wasn't going to be any pouncing going on tonight, at least not from him.

"Would you like some pie, Sugar?" she smiled sweetly at Barry, flashing an amazing mouthful of sparkling, even white teeth. "We bake all our own pies. They're really good," she pushed desert.

"What kind of pie do you have?" Barry asked. *Might as well have some,* he decided. It sounded good and still his friends hadn't shown up.

"Apple, Blueberry, Peach, and Lemon Meringue. I think there might be one or two slices left of the Coconut Custard. What's your pleasure, Hon?" *Is she coming on to me? No!! She's just being a waitress,* he thought.

"If there's any Coconut Custard left I'll have that. If it's gone make it Lemon Meringue. Oh, and a cup of black coffee. Thank you."

"Comin' right up," and she hurried off with an extra little wiggle in her hips Barry couldn't help but notice. *She is coming on to me!*

"There you go Sweetie. Enjoy!" she leaned down as far as she could as she sat the pie and coffee on the table.

Damn! Cleavage with my pie! Barry thought. *Poor girl. She's wasting all that on me. I'll leave her a big tip.*

Barry finished his pie and coffee. He'd been there over an hour. He'd have one more cup of coffee, and if no one showed, he was out of there. No one showed. He left. The tip he put on the table was the same amount as the bill. His waitress did not miss the gesture and perhaps mistook it's meaning.

"Come back and see us, Darlin'," she cooed and smiled at the same time as Barry made his way out the door.

What had happened to his friends? Could he have misheard? He didn't think so. In truth, he had not misheard, but he would not know that for five years. The conversation he'd overheard had gone exactly as he'd thought. The only problem was his interpretation of it. He mistook The

Crossover as the diner near the hospital, when in fact The Crossover his friends had been alluding to was a gay dance club in the heart of the city. They were out dancing and having fun while Barry was sitting having pie and coffee, probably being hit on by his waitress. Indeed, his friends had had secrets. Five years later he'd find out what they had been.

Barry never said a word to his friends about his stakeout at The Crossover. He let it pass. He didn't know where they'd gone, but let them go off without him if they wanted. He wasn't about to make a federal case of it. They acted as if nothing had happened the next time he saw them. Strange, but so what.

They would soon lose one of their members. John was about to have a major melt down. They should have seen it coming. He'd given off enough vibes with his disgust at having to care for dozens of what he sometimes called "The Living Dead." He showed up for duty one morning wearing a sun bonnet and carrying a watering can.

The charge nurse was livid. John was adamant.

"We have to water these vegetables. Tend to our little garden like the expert gardeners we are," John spouted, as he pranced down the aisle between the rows of beds sprinkling water as he went. "Yes, indeedy! What a fine crop! They'll be ready for picking any day now!"

"Stop it this instant!" the charge nurse screamed at him as she ran to grab the watering can from John's hands. "You just stop it this instant!"

John sidestepped her and she went sprawling to the floor. "Oh, but you don't understand, Missy! We have to get these babies to market before they rot!!" John shouted at her as she rolled to face him, her face crimson with rage. "We can't afford to lose this plump juicy crop!"

"Call Security!" she screamed, trying to get up.

"Oh dear. You're looking a little wilted, Missy. Me thinks you need a watering," and he proceeded to liberally spray her with his watering can.

"Get Security! Now!!" she screamed even louder, as she took in some of the life-giving water John was aiming toward her face, making her cough and sputter. "Get this idiot in a straight jacket!" she managed to get out before lapsing into a fit of uncontrollable coughing.

Security arrived. It took four of them to subdue and cart John away. The news was all over the hospital in minutes. Barry, Lewis, and Alfred listened to the news with great sadness. John was in big trouble. He was probably on his way to the loony bin as they heard the disturbing story of his break down and outrageous performance as "the nutty gardener on the neurology floor."

Barry would learn that John was placed under military arrest, charged with endangering patients' wellbeing, assaulting an officer, and dereliction of duty. He would, however, receive a full psychiatric evaluation to determine his level of competency at the time of the incident. None of the remaining three would ever hear what became of John.

Not long after the disappearance of John Tierney, the three friends, Barry Hanley, Lewis Ford and Alfred Lorenzo would receive the decidedly questionable good news that they were all being reassigned. All three were being transferred to The Marine Corps! Barry would be leaving first. Lewis and Alfred would follow several months later.

Barry was shocked and panicked. He had never for an instant thought about becoming a Marine. When he could clear his head enough to contemplate this new wrinkle, all that came to mind was, "Very doubtful!" "Not likely!" "Are you out of your mind?" Now he was not being given a choice. He was definitely going to now become a Marine! He had to admit to himself that he thought it a very bad idea, if not a cruel joke. Of course there was the matter of those extremely attractive full dress uniforms. What was he thinking? Dress uniforms!! This was insane. He'd never make a Marine.

Maybe so, but he soon found himself back at boot camp, only this time with Marines. Camp Pendleton, in Oceanside, California, was a huge and foreboding place, with platoons of uniformed men marching, running, sweating, and chanting constantly with no apparent purpose other than to remain in motion. Could he survive this? Possibly not! But he was going to give it his best and hope that was good enough.

Soon he would be expected to become proficient in firearms! That was a very dangerous thought. Barry couldn't quite see himself in the possession of a firearm, let alone actually firing one. He'd never handled a gun in his life. Now he was going to be expected to shoot one without injuring himself or any fellow trainees. Lying flat on the ground with earplugs and a headset in place, the gunfire began. He closed his eyes and squeezed the trigger, nearly dislocating his shoulder. All his shots went wild. Unfortunately, he put more holes in the targets of those flanking him than in his own. A very useful skill if the enemy suddenly dodged to the left or right, but not much consolation if they charged straight at him. He'd have to do better than that. His instructor was not amused. Next time he tried to keep his eyes open and make some attempt at aiming. He scored a few hits. If he had a few hours before the enemy closed the gap, it was possible they might bleed to death. He felt his chances of coming out on top of this assignment dwindle.

To Barry the entire brunt of the training seemed to be a rush to get somewhere so you could turn around and get right back. He was constantly marching, running, jogging to and from a destination that seemed totally irrelevant once it had been attained. The breakneck pace never slowed for any reason during the long days. Meals were an exercise in speed eating and Barry nearly starved. The first person to get served had the most time to eat, which was scant minutes at best. The last person to be served, which Barry often was, was lucky to get a seat before the company was ordered to fall out and form up for yet another rush to somewhere. He could never finish even half a meal and was unable to master the art of swallowing everything whole. Bathroom breaks were also few, far between, and just as rushed. He never acquired the knack of peeing double time. His bladder was often threatening to burst on those grueling runs to nowhere and back. Bottom line, he was not enjoying this experience.

All the new trainees were required to learn how to find their way to a designated rendezvous after successfully completing night maneuvers using only the stars and a compass. Each group was to complete the assignment, all meeting at the assigned location within the allocated timeframe. Barry was lost! If someone in his group had not been able to figure it out, he'd likely still be wondering through the foothills of Southern California. That was one of the longest, most daunting of nights in Barry's entire training period. He found himself in a confining pup-tent, which he and his assigned partner pitched themselves. Barry had had so much experience camping as a child that he could have pitched it with long rehearsed precision on his own! No! Make that, Barry had never been camping or pitched a tent in his life, and if it had been up to him he'd have just spread it out on the ground and slept on top of it. His partner was not impressed with Barry's lack of experience or enthusiasm. That night Barry found himself pressed up against a strange man who smelled bad and snored a lot. He prayed they would not be joined by any roaming spiders, snakes, or scorpions looking for warmth and company for the evening.

Barry made it through the training period, whether because he actually passed, or they just couldn't afford to flunk anyone, the need was so great on the frontlines, he would never know.

All those finishing their training in preparation for deployment to Viet Nam were granted a generous leave before they were required to catch their flight out of Vallejo, California, north of San Francisco. Barry was not in the mood for a visit home. He'd never been to California and it seemed an excellent opportunity for a leisurely trip northward, sightseeing along the way.

One of Barry's fellow graduates, Ronald Berg, had been a familiar face at the Naval Hospital, although he'd never really gotten to know him there. Ronald recognized Barry as well and Ron now proposed they travel together to Vallejo. Ron had family in Los Angeles and Barry's old pastor from home was now ministering to a congregation there. They decided to rent a car and do some visiting as well as sightseeing along the way before leaving the States. They stayed with Ron's relatives once they reach L.A., visited Barry's old pastor, and enjoyed as many tourist sites as they could in the time they had. Disneyland, of course, was first on the list. One day wasn't enough to cover it all and they had to return for a second. Knott's Berry Farm occupied another whole day. Then it was time for the Hollywood tours. A walk down Hollywood Boulevard. A visit to Graumen's Chinese Theater to inspect the hand and footprints of famous stars. A showing of the smash movie hit, *Who's Afraid of Virginia Woolf?* with Elizabeth Taylor and Richard Burton at the Pantages Theater.

In the few days remaining, Barry and Ron would take a leisurely drive along the coast highway to San Francisco. They'd ride a cable car and visit Fisherman's Wharf for some seafood before reporting to Vallejo.

As the fresh troops reported in, they were all housed at the Marine Corps' expense in a first rate motel. There was a pool for their convenience and all meals were included. Their flight was to be a commercial Continental Airlines jet charter and it was late arriving, delayed by needed maintenance and repair. For days, everyone "languished" poolside and ate the most expensive items on the menu. When their flight finally arrived, everyone reluctantly boarded, saying goodbye to the States as they flew over the Golden Gate Bridge on their way to The Orient. Within an hour they were saying hello to the States again as they once more flew over The Golden Gate Bridge in the opposite direction. The plane was headed back to Vallejo for yet additional repairs. The temporarily reprieved were forced to endure more time poolside and more good meals. There wasn't a complaint to be heard. The second departure was a success, with a layover in Hawaii for refueling and a maintenance check before moving on to Okinawa.

Once Barry arrived on Okinawa, he would see little of Ronald Berg. He was once more thrown into a sea of soldiers coming and going from the frontlines. Many were there on R&R from their units and, knowing they would soon be rejoining their units for yet more brutal punishment in the steamy jungle terrain, they partied like wild men, drank excessively, and were more than willing to pay for the sexual favors readily available almost anywhere. Those just arriving were more reticent, restrained, and fearful of what it was they were about to face. Stories from those who had already been there didn't lend much encouragement or incentive for newbie's to look forward to imminent deployment themselves.

Barry was required to store his entire sea bag, including the gorgeous dress uniform, exchanging everything for the jungle gear he would be wearing and using from now on.

For two weeks he would be laboring in the medical clinic every day. Occasionally he would see Ronald, who was also put to work as soon he arrived. Ron was assisting in the section of the clinic treating veteran frontline soldiers who needed medical attention for a variety of reasons, many of them venereal, but a smattering of other maladies as well. A lot of those on R&R had picked up some of the endemic pathogens, many of which could give a body quite a jolt.

Service in the war theater required a hefty number of inoculations against diseases prevalent there. Barry was assigned to administering Gamma globulin in large doses, necessitating two separate dosage sites. For two weeks it was full moon, all day, every day, as he injected two shots, one in each cheek of the behinds of the men soon to be on the frontlines. It was an assembly line like no other. The mechanics of the job soon transformed the behinds bared to his full view into nothing more than the oranges he'd practiced on so many times when learning how to give an injection. Soon it would be Barry's turn to bare his own behind, turn both his other cheeks, in preparation for his own journey to Viet Nam.

Barry's flight was packed with both newbie's and those returning to their units. Upon touchdown in Da Nang, those returning were met by transport from their units and whisked off quickly. All the new troops were singled out and marched off for initial processing and assignment to the units with which they would be serving; in Barry's and all other medic's cases, the units for whose medical care they would soon be responsible. Barry was listed with a number of other newly arrived medics, Ron Berg not among them, loaded on a truck and transported to his unit. The truck would end its journey in a very large encampment just outside a very old and poorly maintained town that appeared to Barry a sad affair, swarming with peasants who looked bedraggled and undernourished. The Marine encampment was headquartered in what had been a French fort and plantation of sorts, left over from the French occupation of the region back when it had been known as Indochina.

Barry was of the opinion that one of the reasons he was there now, stemmed from the abuse of that occupation when a colonial attitude prevailed in more than one backward country of the world, and large powerful nations were want to strip smaller, weaker ones of their resources if they could get away with it. Rubber had been the gold standard, while its demand remained the driving force and an economic plum for those controlling it. Local inhabitants hadn't really benefited a whole lot from the partnership.

The enlisted men's encampment was spread out around the officer's quarters in the largest, most impressive of the plantation's buildings. Even that was looking a bit worn and dilapidated. The entire encampment was set on a rather prominent hill with a goodly view of the surrounding territory.

During the day it was quite lovely; the mountains in the distance a blur of lavender and purple, the nearby landscape a blanket of intense greens, peppered with bright flowers. Moist and oppressive heat dominated; the gear Barry was wearing, most constrictive and annoying, producing a copious, never-ending sweat.

Barry lined up with all the other new arrivals to be issued the final pieces of gear they would need and be responsible for. Barry was handed a mess kit, a most important tool for any soldier. He would have to keep track of it at all times. All his meals would be served in it and he would be the one to see it was sterilized in boiling water once the meal was eaten. Unfortunately, Barry's mess kit did not include any eating utensils, and there did not seem to be any extra ones lying around. Barry would spend the rest of his time in Viet Nam eating with his hands, positive he was introducing every local pathogen into his digestive system every time he ate a meal.

Further down the supply line he was given his inflatable "rubber lady," and not the kind they sell in porn shops! Barry would be sleeping on this inflatable mattress from now on. It would be sticky and uncomfortable at best, and he had no access to designer sheets to improve its comfort.

Unfortunately for Barry, even his rubber lady was defective. Yes, she had holes! She wouldn't hold air for more than a few hours before he would feel rocks and stones poking him in the ribs, unable to keep her up and unable to sleep.

Barry's final and most disturbing insult would occur with the issue of his 45. Medics were issued one to protect themselves and their patients in the event of attack in the field. The Marine issuing the weapons handed Barry his sidearm with head down, not paying particular attention to the proceedings. Barry looked at the weapon and knew instinctively, even though he was far from a weapons expert, that something was amiss.

"Where's the ammunition for this," Barry questioned the Marine.

"Sorry. We're out of ammunition," the Marine replied nonchalantly, as if it were common practice give out guns without the ammo.

"Well, that's just great," Barry fired back. "What am I supposed to do with this thing? Wait until the enemy gets close enough for me to hit him over the head with it?"

"Move along! Wiseass!" the Marine barked.

Welcome to war, Barry thought.

At night the camp was transformed into something quite different. With the setting of the sun, the tropic night descended like a black velvet curtain, enveloping everything in its blackness within minutes of the sun's disappearance below horizon of the distant western mountains. Somewhere out there in the blackness, artillery and gunfire were audible. There really was fighting going on out there. The reality of where he was and what he would soon be expected to do, hit Barry with a sudden force that almost took his breath away. Somewhere out there in the dark, men were shooting at each other. They were being injured, maimed, and killed as he sat on his deflated rubber lady and pondered the predicament now facing him. He had already seen in graphic detail, over and over again, the ultimate results of what he was hearing with his own ears scant miles away.

During the day Barry had noticed a very strange, large, white object, much like a bed sheet, tacked to two poles on one of the highest elevations of the camp. He hadn't a clue at the time what it was, but with sundown, he now realized it was a makeshift movie screen. They were presently showing, *The Brides of Fu Manchu!* It looked to Barry like an excellent target, so he removed himself, along with his trusty but defective rubber lady, to a spot as far from the screen as he could get. He assumed any incoming would get the theater goers before they got him.

Probably one of the most scenic views in camp was from the latrine. It too was on a higher elevation, an eight-holer, four holes back to back and screened-in, so one could enjoy the view while one relieved oneself. The vista dropped off dramatically over terraced rice paddies, local peasants toiling in the ankle-deep water with their little straw coolie hats. They waved a good-natured good morning to Barry and his fellow occupants as they sat with their trousers around their ankles, butt cheek to butt cheek with the person behind them. Next the native cooks arrived by the truckload to begin preparing the camp's meals, giving Barry and everyone else their hearty salute as they whizzed past, while Barry and entourage just whizzed. This was not exactly what Barry had envisioned back when he had first received the good news of his redeployment.

It was inevitable that this idyllic existence could not continue indefinitely. After all, there was a war that had to be attended to. News was soon rampant throughout the camp that change was on the way and soon. The unit was scheduled for advancement to some trouble spot ahead where, as Barry envisioned it, they would engage the enemy and they would be ours. Fortunately for Barry, and every single new medic that had arrived with him, they would not be engaging the enemy and they would not be theirs.

Before the unit moved forward, all the new medics needed to complete some necessary paperwork. Barry wasn't privy to exactly what it was they'd be required to sign or fill out, but he had a suspicion it might have to do with a Last Will and Testaments or some such thing. Neither he nor his fellow medics would ever put pen to paper before their tour of Viet Nam would come to an abrupt and horrifying conclusion. That abrupt conclusion would, unfortunately, spell disaster for all those departing medics who were packed and awaiting transport back home. Those orders would be rescinded, and when the unit moved out, the departing medics would still be there moving out along with it. On the way to complete that final paperwork, Barry and the entire truckload of medics would be blown sky high by a mine.

The road had been swept for mines that morning and deemed safe for traffic. But someone had managed to place the lurking mine after the minesweeper had passed. Riding along in the back of the truck, all of the new medics were unprepared for what was about to happen next. Naked children ran along the roadside, waving and smiling. Barry waved back. Suddenly, he was flying through the air, tumbling over and over, his brain not having caught up with or yet comprehended what had just occurred in a nanosecond. He was totally conscious, but confused. Flying through the air was a very exciting and exhilarating feeling, like an amusement park ride. But this was no ride. There were no lights, music or amusement car beneath him. There was nothing beneath him holding him up, or propelling him forward. As Barry tumbled, he saw the guy who'd been sitting next to him, a good hundred pounds heavier than he, above him in the air. Then they began to descend and Barry knew exactly what had happened. If the guy above him landed on top of him, he would be in a world of trouble. All that weight would squash him flat, but there wasn't a thing Barry could do about it.

Barry landed face down in a muddy ditch and the other guy landed face up right next to him, as only an arm flopped down across Barry's back. He became aware of a sudden flourish of activity as a unit that had been on patrol nearby rushed to set up a perimeter around the truck and medics that had fallen from the sky. As Barry and the medic next to him lay in the muddy water, he could see the two Marine drivers, apparently unhurt, circling their truck.

"Jesus! Look at that truck!" one said.

"We're really in deep shit now!" the other added.

Apparently they had forgotten about the passengers they'd had in the back of their truck as they continued to bemoan the catastrophic damage in front of them. The cab was intact, but the rear was in shambles. The rear axle had been snapped in two and propelled upward through the truck bed. Barry and his fellow medics were lucky the truck had been an open one with no canvas covering, and no metal support arches enclosing it. Any one of them might have been torn in two by those metal braces had they soared through such a roof.

One of the nearby Marines approached Barry as he tried to keep his nose out of the stinking soup of mud and water in which he was lying. As the soldier crouched down beside him, he began to feel an overwhelming nausea envelope him and he emptied the contents of his stomach, adding to the already disgusting stench of his surroundings.

"Don't try to move. Just lie still. I'm a medic," the soldier informed Barry as he quickly assessed Barry's condition. "There's a chopper on the way."

"Oh, I'm a medic too," Barry weakly admitted. "How convenient you were so close by. I don't feel too well," he finished, as his head began to spin.

"Let me have your sidearm," the medic requested.

"Go right ahead and help yourself," Barry was more than happy to relinquish his useless weapon. "But, I don't have any ammunition. Never did. Never did."

The medic swore but took the gun anyway. The chopper arrived with a great downdraft and cloud of swirling dirt and debris, filling Barry's eyes before he could clamp them shut. All the wounded medics were loaded aboard as the two Marine drivers continued to survey their damaged truck, still oblivious to the passengers they'd been carrying. On the way to the field hospital Barry was relieved of much of his clothing, as those attending him continued to examine him for the extent of sustained injuries.

"Is it alright if we have your clothes?" they asked. "It looks like you won't be needing them for some time."

"Help yourself," Barry readily agreed. He really wasn't thinking about clothing or how he might look right then.

He arrived at the field hospital in just his underwear. That too was quickly removed and spoken for.

"You people must be in dire need to take someone else's underwear," but he was not as coherent as he'd been earlier. "I've got a tremendous pain in my back and I can't feel my legs." Naked except for his dog tags, Barry was sedated with morphine and x-rayed, which showed a number of spinal fractures. The morphine was doing its job. Barry wasn't feeling any pain but he wasn't liking what he wasn't feeling.

"Help," he croaked weakly. "I'm dying. I'm not breathing. I can't get any air. I don't feel anything. Something's really wrong."

"Relax," the nurse hovering over him tried to calm him down. "That's just the morphine. If you weren't breathing, you wouldn't be talking. Just take it easy. You're going back to the States!" she finished with a bright smile.

Barry wasn't quite sure he'd heard her properly, but he was dozing off and left any questions about what he thought he'd heard for later. Barry wouldn't see Viet Nam again. He would never retrieve any of the clothing he'd left on Okinawa, including the dress blues that he'd found so appealing. He hoped that all the clothing stripped from him on the trip from muddy ditch to field hospital x-ray would serve whoever got them well.

Before leaving Viet Nam he would have one last brief and memorable encounter. While lying in the field hospital ward awaiting med-evac, someone passed down the row of beds with something that looked like a picnic basket, from which they were handing out Purple Hearts as if they were Santa Claus passing out candy to children. Barry didn't think it was Christmas, and he sure as hell knew it wasn't any picnic!

Barry would soon find himself at the first stop on his way home, Clark Air Force Base, in the Philippines. To his amazement, the Air Force Nurse assigned to his care lived only a mile from his home. He'd attended high school with her younger sister. He took her presence as a good omen. The next day a severely injured marine was admitted to the other bed in his room. His name was Petor Wolinski and he looked like death warmed over. It occurred to him that that could easily have been him. Perhaps luck had been with him when that truck met its match. He was now overwhelmed with the feeling of relief, knowing that he was on his way home. That relief had a momentary lapse late in the afternoon when he was visited by none other than General Westmoreland himself.

"Just stopping by to check on all my people. You're doing one hell of a job. Your country is grateful and I'm very proud. You're doing just fine. Nothin' to worry about. You'll be back with your unit in no time!" he said as he shook hands and gave Barry his widest and brightest smile of encouragement. Barry was much more encouraged when he learned from the day shift's charge nurse, Ben Weinstock, that, in fact, General Westmoreland's take on his condition was in direct opposition to that of his attending physician's. He had already been scheduled for med-evac later in the day.

It would take Barry two weeks to make the trip home from Viet Nam. It was arduous at best with many stops along the way, many stays in many facilities, all of it becoming a blur. It was a series of hops; Viet Nam, The Philippines, Hawaii, California, Texas, Illinois, New Jersey, and finally Pennsylvania. He was flat on his back on a stretcher the entire time, transported in huge, noisy cargo planes with many other patients, all stacked four to five deep. The flights were long and meals consisted of box lunches containing a sandwich and an apple. Nothing was more welcome than the crisp white sheets of a hospital bed and the friendly faces of many of the nurses he had worked with before leaving on his Marine Odyssey.

Barry found himself on the orthopedic ward, the very same ward where his friend, Alfred, had nearly fainted assisting a doctor place a Krutchfield Pin through a patient's femur for traction purposes. The ward seemed even busier than ever. The charge nurse who greeted him attested to that.

"I knew we'd be seeing at least one of you back here again. We just didn't know it would be this soon. As I'm sure you've noticed, this place is a zoo. We never have enough beds for the number of casualties coming in, and we've had to open up an overflow way the hell out almost to New Jersey that we're using for the most stable, or those who need the least treatment or attention," she caught Barry up on the curent woes of her own private war. "I can't keep a trained corpsman more than a few months before the Navy swoops in and carts him off for Marine duty, just like they did you. Seems all I'm doing anymore is training new corpsmen for nothing. I'm tearing my hair out here, trying to provide the best care I can for those coming in from Viet Nam only to have them snatch my trainees away as soon as they know what they're doing. Then I have to start all over again. I can't give the kind care these men deserve. But don't you worry. You're one of our own and I'm going to make sure you get the best if it kills me! Corpsman!" she screamed at the nearest staff member. "Hell! They come and go so fast, I can't even keep up with their names," she confided in a whisper. "Corpsman," she continued as the flustered new corpsman joined her, "this is one of our very best men who worked here when you were still wet behind the ears, and I want you to know he's to get special attention at all times. You let all your cohorts in on my orders. You understand me?" she asked the new boy with a mean look in her eye.

"Yes, Ma'm," he answered meekly. Barry saw that his name tag read, Aldrich.

"If I receive as much as one little complaint from this man, you'll all be very sorry! Do I make myself clear?"

"Yes, Ma'm," he answered with more enthusiasm, as she stomped off looking for new prey. "Jes'! What's wrong with her?" Aldrich asked Barry, confused.

"Don't get too flustered. I'll try not to make your life any more miserable than it already seems, but I think she's suffering from a major staffing problem."

The next opportunity Barry had, he asked anybody who looked familiar about his three friends. No one seemed to know what had happened to John Tierney, although even people who'd never met him were familiar with the now infamous "Garden Incident" on the neurology floor. He discovered Lewis and Alfred had already left and were most probably at Camp Lejune. He didn't want to lose touch with them and wrote to see how they were doing and let them know what had happened to him.

Barry's recovery, including extensive physical therapy, would take six months. During that time he would receive lots of encouragement from his Navy Nurse care givers.

"Take your time. There's no rushing these kind of things." one would say.

"Don't push too hard. A relapse wouldn't do you any good," said another.

"Just slow down and tell them you're in lots of pain," the charge nurse advised him. "They can't prove you're not, and if you snap back too fast, they'll send you right back to Viet Nam!"

Barry listened to all his doctors and tried to follow the advice the nurses were imparting as well, but soon he was unable to take the snail's pace his recovery seemed to have taken. He worked harder and did more, and was eventually up on his feet helping the overworked staff with some of the lighter duties he was able to perform. The newly arrived orthopedic department nurse supervisor took notice of him.

"What's that patient doing passing out water to everyone?" she asked the charge nurse.

"He's just helping us with little things we don't have time to do that add to our patients' comfort. We're much too busy doing treatments and medications to pass out water. If you haven't noticed how understaffed we are, take another good look around." she informed her supervisor with a "and what if he is?' inflection in her annoyed tone. "He's one of our best corpsmen, blown up in Viet Nam. He's recovering slowly and we're grateful for any little thing he does for us here." she looked her straight in the eye, daring her to make trouble.

But trouble she was bound and determined to make. Each time the supervisor saw Barry doing anything that slightly resembled work, she made a note in her book.

When she had made a number of notations to that effect she pounced.

"It's my opinion that Barry Hanley is now in a position to return to active service and I'm reporting such to the administration, recommending him for orders at the Navy's earliest convenience. We must remember that we serve the needs of the Navy, not the needs of your ward!" she delivered her decision with great relish.

"Well, he's not going anywhere until the doctors say he is. Who elected you God?" the charge nurse fired back, furious with this self-important new import from who knew where. The animosity between the two was palpable.

A steely silence descended between the two as nurse battled nurse with Barry's doctors for the upper hand. The "self-important new import" won the battle. Barry would soon be receiving orders. The charge nurse crossed her fingers and prayed Barry would not be sent back to Viet Nam. When the critical day arrived, the charge nurse strode onto the ward with a huge smile on her face as she delivered the good news to Barry.

"Guess where you're going?" she teased, but with such a pleased expression on her face, Barry knew it must be somewhere good. Certainly not reassignment with The Marines. "Puerto Rico!" she nearly yelled with approval. "But there's more even better news," she continued. "Guess who else got orders?" she asked, obviously very pleased about it. "Our busybody new supervisor who got you kicked out of here. And guess where she's going? Iceland!!" she shouted with unbridled joy and vindication.

Barry's six month recovery was at an end. He never heard what became of the other medics who had been blown up in the truck with him. Each had been evacuated to a medical facility somewhere near their home. Barry had only overheard from those staffing the field hospital while he was being evaluated and awaiting transfer that, other than the two Marine drivers, he had been the most fortunate.

Barry Hanley had dodged a second bullet by receiving transfer orders to a Naval Air Squadron instead of a return trip to Marine duty and Viet Nam. He would now be assigned to work with and assist the flight surgeons, caring for those men and women at a small base hospital with a magnificent view of a picture perfect sea. The climate was balmy, the duty light. The only possible cloud on the horizon would be an unexpected deployment of the flight squadron, in which case, he, along with the flight surgeons, would accompany them wherever any future deployment might take them. Barry's luck would hold, and no redeployment would occur during his tour of duty there. It would not be difficult for him to adjust to this new environment, so much more welcoming and pleasant; the only threat, a possible hurricane. That too never occurred while Barry found himself becoming more and more attached to his luck of the draw. This was the kind of place people wanted to escape to and never leave, once there.

The beaches right on the base were some of the most beautiful Barry had ever seen. He didn't even have to go elsewhere to enjoy any down time, relaxing on the sand and soaking up some sun. The enlisted beach was just a short bus ride from the hospital. There was a convenient concession stand for light snacks right on the beach. What could be more perfect?

For Barry, what he came to believe would be more perfect would be for him to be able to enjoy the pastime everyone else seemed to be engaged in, snorkeling. There were many protected coves where the water was calm, crystal clear, and teaming with sea life. There were also a number of very small islands just off the beach, that seemed to be an attraction for dozens of people each time he spent an afternoon relaxing on the shore. It looked like such fun, despite the fact that he didn't know how to swim, he decided to try it. At the PX, without any expertise in the kind of equipment he might need, and not wanting to spend a huge sum of money on this whim, he bought the cheapest things he could find.

He was unaware that he was purchasing mere toy equipment meant for children in a wading pool. The fins were just half fins, fitting over the toes with a strap around the ankles. The snorkel was unlike those he'd seen being used, sticking straight up with a florescent marker around the top to make it very visible, especially to boaters. He chose a model that curved over, pointing back toward the water with a small ball in a basket attached to the end. When the snorkel was submerged the ball was supposed to float up and seal off the end of the snorkel, preventing water from entering. The mask was very flimsy, just a thin piece of plastic with no real tight seal or pressure capacity. Barry didn't know what he was buying and would soon regret it. He was about to almost drown himself once again.

Barry had never gone farther out than waist level, knew nothing about prevailing currents or drop off. Arriving at the beach with his newly acquired, sub-standard equipment, he donned his gear and waded clumsily out to begin having fun. As soon as he got into waist high water, he found he could lay face down and float easily, breathing through the snorkel and surveying the underwater world through the facemask. With the slightest movement of his feet, the fins propelled him forward like magic. The sense of freedom was exhilarating. The view was unbelievable. He was soon much farther from shore than he imagined, captivated by the fish swimming around him, the bright colors of coral and grasses below. They appeared very close. He discovered that if he kicked his fins a little harder and ducked his head, he could submerge to take a closer look. That's when Barry noticed water leaking in around the edges of his faceplate. It was soon collecting under his nose and in his nostrils. The seawater going up his nose caused a sudden panic. He kicked a little too hard trying to resurface and one of his fins dislodged, hanging uselessly on one ankle. Breaking the surface, Barry attempted to take a great gulp of air only to inhale more water. The floating ball at the end of his snorkel had not occluded as it had been designed to, and the entire tube had filled with seawater. He choked and thrashed, dislodging the other fin. Attempting to stand, he discovered the water was way over his head and he went under, dislodging his mask as well, now hanging uselessly around his neck. There was a momentary thought that perhaps this was payback for deceiving his instructors in boot camp! He was now in worse trouble than he'd been in then. He was trying to get anyone's attention to his plight, but they were much to busy enjoying themselves to notice him and his weak croaks for help. Fortunately for him, he was just a few feet beyond the beach shelf drop off that led to deeper water. He was able to thrash his way those last few feet until his toes touched bottom, and he slowly and carefully inched his way back to shore. He kicked himself soundly for having attempted such a dangerous stunt, and vowed he would never do anything so stupid again.

But the attraction of the brief glimpse he'd had of that underwater world and the continued presence of all those others out there enjoying themselves wore on his resolve. They actually were making him angry. He struck up conversations with many of them and learned that what he'd purchased would only have been appropriate for a kiddy pool. With a few pointers and advice, he returned to the PX and equipped himself like a real diver. The price was steep but, he was assured, necessary. This time his mask was thick, sealed and would not leak with increased pressure. His fins fit over his entire foot and would not dislodge when he kicked forcefully. His snorkel jutted straight up, and as long as he remembered to exhale forcibly upon surfacing, he would not inhale any water. The results were amazing. This time, even though he couldn't swim, he snorkeled with the best and was soon a fixture on the water, exploring the small offshore islands, diving down ten to fifteen feet, returning with beautiful specimens; shells and starfish, sand dollars, sea biscuits and fan corals, which he would carry with him and treasure for years. He even earned a reputation in his barracks as the one to see for all the best diving spots. And no one ever knew he didn't know how to swim.

Barry thoroughly enjoyed his tour of duty, becoming so attached to the place and the climate that he was loath to leave once he was notified that his transfer for discharge from the service was immanent. It was a period of downsizing for the military and many job descriptions were being phased out and offered to civilians as civil service positions. Barry inquired as to the possibly that his job might be one of those, giving him the option of keeping his position, while transitioning the authority under which it would be managed. The answer was negative, much to his disappointment.

He would have to either re-enlist, at which point his next duty station would be a crap shoot, quite possibly reassignment to Marine duty, or accept his discharge and move on. He chose the discharge.

Barry had managed to stay in contact with Lewis and Alfred, though the news from them was sporadic and disheartening. He received the worst news in one of Lewis's infrequent letters. Alfred had been killed. He was blown to bits by a mine which he had stepped on and triggered, instituting his own disintegration. Lewis had witnessed it firsthand and was having great difficulty keeping himself together afterward. Barry spent weeks in a deep depression after receiving the news, mourning Alfred's loss, sympathizing with Lewis's burden of coping with the horrendous sight Alfred's demise must have been, and dealing with his own recriminations and guilt that he had been spared the fate of either of his friends. While he had been enjoying a tour of duty in a tropical paradise, they had been living in a steamy hell. Somehow he would have to pull himself out of this self denigrating spiral and go on with life.

Lewis would soon escape his steamy hell, but not before seeing things no one should ever have to see, and picking up some of the devastating pathogens Barry himself had been sure he'd ingested when he was eating all his meals with his hands, due to that sadly substandard mess kit. Lewis sent pictures. He was white as a sheet and thin as a rail. The doctors were having a difficult time treating the resistant bugs Lewis's body was harboring. His emaciated condition and lack of will contributed to the pathogen's successful assault on his failing immune system, but Lewis was not willing to concede defeat. After lengthy and extensive treatment, the foreign bacteria relented and Lewis began to recover both physically and mentally. He too would soon be discharged and face the task of fitting himself back into a civilian world, many of whom were not thrilled with what had happened in Southeast Asia, or enamored of those who'd served there. No rousing welcome was mounted to received Barry or Lewis for their sacrifices or services.

Two of the four friends who had chosen to serve were now gone. One dead. One possibly confined in some mental facility with serious charges against him for his inability to cope with the dreadful ravages of a war half a world away. Barry and Lewis remained alive but forever changed and scarred by their experiences.

They would meet one day after both had received their discharge papers. They would exchange stories and mourn the loss of their two friends, as well as many others who had touched their lives along the way. Lewis would finally open up to Barry by surreptitiously taking him to a gay bar, warning Barry beforehand to keep an open mind, that he might be meeting some individuals whom he could possibly find less than his kind of people. Barry would finally realize what a vacuum he had been living in, and that he was not the only person on earth not driven wild by a huge rack straining to bust out of a top much to small for its occupants. He would learn of his misconception concerning his evening at The Crossroads, and laugh uncontrollably when he learned the truth.

Both men would adjust. Both would forge ahead with life, living it to its fullest, working tirelessly, caring for the sick and dying just as they had been trained to do. These two good friends. These few good men.

CINDER EDDIE AND THE WICKED STEPMOTHER: NOT A FAIRY TALE FOR CHILDREN

We won't begin with "Once Upon A Time" or any of that crap. That's for a totally different kind of tale. And don't be expecting any "Happily Ever After" to happen either. I wouldn't want you to be disappointed, so I'm laying all my cards on the table before I start. All that drivel is perfectly fine, I'm sure, for The Brothers Grimm, but this story is a little grimmer than the Grimm brothers would have liked, so let's plunge ahead with this charming, while alarming, tale.

Eddie Covington was the unfortunate victim of a broken marriage. Divorce is never pleasant and the offspring often bare the brunt of the disappointment and letdown when someone they love, and has always been there, no longer is. Yes, visits are fine but not the same thing. Eddie was coping as best he could when his mother remarried and thrust a stepfather upon him very suddenly.

Mary Flynn Covington Bloom just wasn't able to function on her own. She had a dependant personality and once divorce was a fact of life, she found it imperative to find that someone to depend on once again and quickly. Roger Bloom was that person. He was basically a nice man, but he had a temper and was demanding. Mary found that attractive. She could depend on him to structure her world. She didn't bargain on what might happen if any of that structure should come up wanting. Bruises might happen, and did happen, whenever things didn't go according to Roger. Eddie hid in his room when things got loud and scary. Roger never laid a hand on him. In fact, he was most loving and considerate, considering he was merely a stepfather.

It was an uneasy time for Eddie. He saw little of his dad, George Covington, but was making the best of it. As the years passed Eddie began to feel more comfortable in his new role. Roger was less demanding than he had once been. In fact, he was around less often too. Then Mary began to feel unwell. She languished for days on end, doing nothing. She developed a fascination for her hair and would play with her long red curls for hours, losing all track of time. She had difficulty preparing meals and Eddie tried to assist. Roger was not amused on the occasions when he rewarded them with the pleasure of his company. He refrained from further physical abuse, however, choosing to go elsewhere for sustenance. Eddie didn't know it, but Roger was getting much more than sustenance elsewhere. Mary was oblivious to almost everything by now, spiraling downward into a severe depression requiring hospitalization and ultimately the diagnosis of an inoperable brain tumor, physicians giving her only six months to live. The doctors had miscalculated slightly. In one month she was dead.

Eddie was devastated. Roger was free. He could now move on to marry the little tart he'd been schtupping on the side. Although he liked Eddie well enough, he wasn't his kid after all. He'd simply have to go back to his dad. It was the only logical solution. Therein lies the rub. That's were the canker g-naws. Enter, "The Wicked Stepmother!"

Although Eddie had seen his father once in a while over his years in the Bloom family, he had not seen him often. When he did see him, it was always out somewhere in public; a day's outing, a movie, a ballgame, never wherever it was his dad was then living. Now that he would be moving back with his dad, he was ecstatic with anticipation, sure that life for him was about to get a whole lot better. Unfortunately, that would not be the case.

George Covington had remarried years earlier and now had another son, Pierpont Covington; the name, Pierpont, his wife's idea. George privately thought it ridiculous, but Agnes had been unrelenting in her choice. Agnes thought it made a bold statement about her son's future place in the world. It was "aristocratic," "sophisticated," and she had no doubt he'd go far on that name alone. Pierpont Covington! Eddie Covington was never going to come close.

Agnes was not amused when she learned that Eddie, George's firstborn, was going to be moving in with them. It was inconvenient. She had all she could manage orchestrating Pierpont's life. She didn't have time to spare dealing with an interloper from a previous marriage. George made it clear that Eddie was his son and had nowhere else to go.

"For God's sake, Agnes, his mother has just died and I'm his father and only other relative. He simply has nowhere else to go. We'll not have any problem with him, I assure you. He's a very likeable and obedient child and he's coming to live with us and that's it!" George put his foot down for the second and last time of his life. The first time was when he left Mary. Since marrying Agnes, George had walked on egg shells, there had been no previous putting down of the foot. In time, everyone would rue the day of the second putting down of the foot.

Agnes welcomed Eddie with a saccharine smile and voice, not like her at all.

"Well, you must be Eddie. You're quite the young man," she buttered Eddie up and bolstered his expectations. "We're so very glad to have you come and live with us. I think you'll find life very different here," came a little promise of things to come. "You must meet my son, Pierpont. He's been dying to meet you," she averred, the inflection conveying the direct opposite.

She'd wasted no time informing the "Prince in Residence" that a "Usurper" would soon be threatening "His Kingdom" and that she would see to it that the intruder was thwarted. Such favoritism would not set the stage for any kind of meaningful relationship between the stepbrothers. Of course, that was Agnes's plan from the moment she set eyes on George's little ragamuffin. He could live here, but he'd not be pleased with what he found!

Thus began the "Dark Days of Despair" for Eddie. How could he have been so misguided as to have imagined a new world of love and acceptance with his father at its core, a new mother, and even a brother for company?

His father he rarely saw. George worked for a large chemical company that required long hours and pushed for even longer ones. Some of their mottos were "We Make

Life Worth Living," and "Our Main Concern Is You." Of course, George didn't have much of a life to live. As far as the company was concerned, life was only worth living if they were making tons of money at any cost and their main concern was themselves and how fast they could stuff their pockets with exorbitant profits. George really didn't need to know that. The company would rather those facts remain a secret for the chosen few. George's main function was the promotion of a positive image for the company and singing their praises to the rafters.

His job took most of his time and he was on the road a lot. That was a perfect setup for Agnes. His new step mom was free to handle this new and irritating situation in any manner she thought best.

"Eddie," she'd say sweetly, "be a dear and go down and stoke the furnace. Pierpont says its quite chilly up in his room."

"Sure, Mom, we can do that," Eddie would be anxious to please. Too bad he thought it would be fun for his brother to help him with this or any other chore. Although Pierpont was a good deal younger than Eddie, he was still confident that they were going to be friends and do lots of things together. Agnes had other ideas.

"Oh no, Eddie," Agnes would quickly right his misconception, "Pierpont has a very delicate constitution. He can't be subjected to dust and dirt, especially coal dust. It would cause him to have spasms. You wouldn't want that would you?"

"Well, no," Eddie would concede, although he couldn't quite figure out how anyone could have so many maladies that the simplest of tasks would cause him harm. Down to the basement he would go, add coal to the furnace, stoke the flames, and clean the ashbin. By the time he was through, he'd be covered in coal dust and ashes. "Cinder Eddie" was in the house. When he emerged from the basement Agnes was always waiting.

"I hope you're not tracking dust and dirt across my clean floor young man," she'd pounce the moment one foot hit the kitchen floor. "You just sit right down there on those cellar steps and take off those shoes and socks. Then you very carefully tiptoe up to your room, put those dirty things in the hamper, clean your shoes, and put on some clean clothes. I've got some work for you to do."

She always had more work for him to do. He had no idea there could be so much work to be done. Pierpont never did a thing, but then he did have that delicate constitution, whatever that was. In summer, there was grass to be mowed, weeds to be pulled, the driveway and walks to be washed. In winter, there was snow to be shoveled, and, of course, the gluttonous furnace to be fed, stoked and cleaned. Year-round, his room was never clean enough for his new mom. She'd come in and inspect even nook and cranny. If she found one speck of dust or dirt, he'd have to clean it all again.

"You know you have to earn your keep," she'd say. "You can't expect us to hand everything to you for nothing." It seemed Pierpont got just that, but Eddie somehow got the message that he didn't want to question that. He'd better not go there.

"You do everything your mom tells you Eddie," his dad had advised him every time George was at home. "This isn't easy for her you know. She has twice as much work to do now that you're here. You're the oldest and you have to set a good example and help out all you can. That's my good boy," he'd say. Something was telling Eddie that Agnes had much less work to do now that he was here, but he wasn't in a position to say so.

Eddie would endure the most egregious of slights just to please his father and not cause trouble. Why his dad allowed such slights to occur perplexed him. Perhaps soon he'd get up enough courage to broach the subject.

Christmas was a particularly difficult time for Eddie. The tree was magnificent and the food plentiful, although each time he reached for anything, Agnes would admonish, "Don't forget to save some for Pierpont!" Did she really think he was going to eat everything? How silly!

But under the tree was Disappointment. Pierpont had a shiny new bicycle. Eddie had a pair of sox. Pierpont had a musical instrument with instructions and lesson books. Eddie had some new jeans.

"Wow," his dad would say, "won't you look spiffy in those!"

"Those are the best on the market," Agnes would tell him. "They'll last you for years."

But they never did. The seams came out. They faded quickly.

Soon Agnes would be exasperated with him. "How anyone can go through a pair of jeans so quickly I'll never know!" she'd remonstrate.

Little did Eddie know she'd gotten them for pennies at a seconds shop. That's right! Agnes spared no expense when it came to her stepson. Only the best for Eddie!

Saving things for Pierpont was not always an issue, as many things were made specifically for him. Eddie would not get so much as a crumb of those. Confections were a favorite of Pierpont's and he would have all of them. Cookies and cakes were off limits to Eddie.

"You know, Eddie," Agnes would rationalize, "you are just a tad over weight, and sweets would only exacerbate the problem. Pierpont, on the other hand, has a much higher metabolism and needs the extra calories to maintain himself."

She made "exacerbate" sound like a terrible thing that must be avoided at all costs. But Eddie had a hard time seeing any difference in his weight and Pierpont's. In fact, he thought perhaps his younger brother was a little heavier than he'd been at that age.

There were so many other slights as well. Agnes had a pet. It was as scrawny a little creature as Nature ever cranked out, a mismatch from conception. Dalmatians and Schnauzers should never be allowed to breed! This little Schnaumatian was second only to Pierpont in Agnes's heart. Ugly as it was, she loved and pampered Doodles, lavishing much more attention on her canine than on her stepson. She cooked food for it on a regular basis. Spending extra money on fresh horsemeat for the dog, while skimping on Eddie's diet by loading it with Spam and day old bread, didn't seem to bother her in the slightest. Sometimes she would enlist Eddie's help in the kitchen when baking something special for Pierpont took her attention off Doodles dinner.

"Eddie, come over here and keep stirring this meat mixture while I finish the batter for a new cookie recipe," she'd cajole.

Eddie could never refuse any assistance requested on threat of "banishment," whatever that might mean. It sounded like he never wanted to find out. Obediently, Eddie would stand at the stove and stir the simmering meat stew.

It smelled so good, and the dry Spam sandwich he'd had for lunch was long gone and had not been very satisfying in the first place. While Agnes was otherwise occupied, Eddie would have a taste of Doodles dinner. It was most decidedly more delicious than any lunch Eddie had ever had since coming to live with his father.

Doodles diet, Agnes made certain, was varied and included all sorts of dry and wet food, some prepared, some homemade. She kept bags of dog treats that Doodles favored in the pantry. Eddie sometimes helped himself to a handful, which he snuck up to his bedroom to secrete in the bottom drawer of his nightstand. Saving some for Pierpont often left Eddie hungry at bedtime and no late night milk and cookies were allowed for him. He often helped himself to a handful of dog treats before falling asleep.

He also had trouble sleeping in his new environs. When he had first arrived, settling in had not been a joy. His room was the smallest one Agnes could provide. She was very generous that way. It was on the third floor and just a small finished cubbyhole. The rest of the floor was unfinished storage attic space. The ceilings sloped wildly and steeply down in all directions, making it imperative Eddie watch his head at all times, lest he knock himself out. The only saving grace was that it did have one window with an impressive view all the way to the river several blocks away. He had one single bed, a dresser and a nightstand. There was no closet, just some hooks here and there from which he could hang a few clothes. What bothered him most about his room was the linens on his bed. They were very coarse and scratchy. And there was no pillow.

"Is there a pillow I could have for my bed?" Eddie asked his step mom.

"A pillow! You don't need a pillow. In fact you don't *want* to use a *pillow!* Everyone knows how bad pillows are for your posture! Didn't your mother ever reach you anything?" Agnes was adamant. Eddie got no pillow. Instead, he would wad up some articles of clothing to prop under his head, but they were never as soft and comforting as a pillow.

Now comes the part of the story where the "Fairy Godmother" swoops in with her magic wand and fixes everything. However, Rowena O'Riley was just not going to fit the bill. She wasn't his fairy godmother. She wasn't even a godmother. She'd never had a magic wand, nor ever would. But she was a godsend for Eddie.

Rowena and her husband, now deceased and affectionately referred to as "The Old Boy," had been childless. They had taken in many strays and orphans over the years but never really officially adopted any of them. George Covington had been one of those orphans. Rowena was the only mother George had ever known. He had always kept in close touch with her. Rowena was saddened when George's marriage had failed. She was also saddened when she met Agnes Bach and learned George was going to marry her. Rowena didn't like Agnes from the moment she laid eyes on her. There was something false about her mannerisms. There was something sharp about her voice. It was cutting. There was something sharp about her features, the pointed chin and nose. She entered a room like a ship slicing through the waves, its bow parting the sea, roiling foam outward as it passed. Agnes sliced though the air just as efficiently, throwing off currents which could be felt as she passed. Rowena found it a little disconcerting. She kept her own council. She had no business meddling in George's affairs.

Now George was coming for a visit and he was bringing his son, Eddie, with him. She'd heard of him, but this would be the first time they'd met. Coming up the walk, she could see Eddie was quite a good looking young man, early teens. He'd break some hearts if she could be any judge.

"George," she greeted him, "you look wonderful. And this must be Eddie. I'm so glad your father brought you with him. Come on in the kitchen. I have cookies and milk for you young man, and a little something stronger for you George, if you'd like." Cookies and milk! For Eddie! He was instantly smitten.

"Just a small nip," George accepted. "But only if you're having one."

"I should say I am," and the drinks and cookies were served.

They visited for several hours, Rowena completely taken with Eddie. When they had to go, she was sad they had to leave so soon.

"Tell you what," she said to Eddie, "since your father has so little time to spend with me anymore, why don't you get him to bring you over here and stay a few days with me. I'd really enjoy the company. I bet you'd have a good time. Give you a break from all the work you've been telling me about. What do you think?"

"Sure, I'd like that. Could I dad?" Eddie pleaded. He really liked this lady. He wanted someone to pay attention to him as she'd done all afternoon. "I'll do extra work before I come," he promised.

"Well, we'll have to OK it with your mother, but if she says it's alright, then it's fine by me."

Thus began a period of brief respites from Agnes's control. Agnes was more than happy to have Eddie out of the house. Eddie was extremely happy for the time away from her. Rowena was just like a real grandmother, even if she wasn't related.

"What shall I call you?" Eddie asked.

"You just call me Aunt Ro," Rowena insisted. "Everyone does!"

"How come you're so nice and my mom's so mean?" he surprised her one day.

"Well, I don't know," Rowena answered truthfully. "Maybe it's just the same old thing that you're not really hers and so she feels more protective of her own son, and sometimes that hurts you. What do you think?"

"Maybe, but I think it's more than that. I don't think she likes me one little bit. I don't know why. I do everything she asks without question. My dad says I have to set a good example. I'm the oldest. But I can't ever set a good enough example to please her," he finished with a sigh. "You're so good with children. I can tell. Dad says you took in lots that weren't even yours. How come you and The Old Boy never had any? Oops! None of my beeswax. That's what my real mom always used to say."

"That's perfectly all right. To tell you the truth, I really don't know. Maybe I was just barren. Maybe The Old Boy was shooting blanks! Whatever, it just never happened."

"Why would The Old Boy shoot blanks? What are blanks anyway?" Eddie looked puzzled.

"Now that's something I'm not sure I can, or should, explain. Let's just say it could have been either of our faults, but we never knew for sure whose. Bottom line, we sure did enjoy having your dad with us, as well as a few others we raised over the years."

Agnes would become more and more manipulative with Eddie as he reached puberty and posed what she saw as a threat to her authority. He was getting bigger, stronger. George seemed to have been more than successful in reigning in any untoward teenage rebellion. Others, under similar circumstances, would have blown sky high. Eddie seemed to keep himself in check, although Agnes could now feel the growing resentment building in there, after years of her prodding and abuse. It wouldn't be much longer now before he'd be gone and any threat to Pierpont would cease. That was her hope.

Meanwhile, she intended to get the maximum amount of work out of him before he left her nest. He was now solely responsible for everything in the cellar; the furnace, the coal bin, the tool shelves. She inspected often to ensure the basement was immaculate. When it came to the furnace, the routine was never altered.

"Eddie, be a dear and run down and stoke the furnace," she'd croon. "It's getting a little cool in here." As soon as his foot hit the kitchen floor on the way up, he'd hear, "I hope you're not tracking dirt on my clean floor, young man," and blah, blah, blah. He'd already taken off his shoes and sox, but she didn't even stop to notice.

Finally the day came when Eddie had to get away, not just a visit with Aunt Ro, but away for good. He was going to join The Marines! He enlisted and lied about his age. He was really a year too young but the recruiter had a quota to meet and wasn't into splitting hairs that day. His father was surprised, but not overly so. On some level he knew Eddie had been getting a raw deal, but he hadn't wanted to make waves with Agnes. She really could put the screws to you if she chose. Agnes was thrilled! Eddie was gone! Peirpont's future would not be in jeopardy. She had already cajoled George into signing papers that would protect her son should anything happen to her husband. Eddie was not even mentioned in any of the documents. Everything was a rush. The papers were a blur. George thought perhaps he'd acted to quickly. Maybe he should have protested and had some modifications made. He'd do that soon. Agnes wouldn't even have to know. He wouldn't tell her. She'd be livid when she found out, but he'd be dead. Too late for her to get back at him then. Sadly, George never got around to making those alterations.

Eddie's stint in The Marine Corps was probably the best thing he could have done. He was discharged a man and quite capable of managing for himself. He was also unrelentingly handsome. He was embarrassed with all the attention, but did not hesitate to take advantage of it.

Even other men were looking at him. Some were extremely jealous of his looks and the ease with which he picked up girls. Some looked longingly at him wondering if they stood a chance of a go with him themselves. Eddie sometimes toyed with them like a cat with a mouse, then dropped them cold, taking some pleasure in the disappointment in their eyes and the deflating of their egos.

He knew it wasn't fair. Where had this streak come from? Then it hit him square in the face! This was Agnes's MO. His stepmother was certainly a very self-centered woman. Everything was about her. Then she engendered and encouraged that same egocentrism by proxy in her only progeny, Pierpont. Eddie could see clearly now how he had been the brunt of Agnes's scorn, and ultimately Pierpont's as well, from the moment he'd moved back home with his dad after his mother died. Somehow she'd managed to implant this unhealthy pleasure in other's discomfort deep inside him. He didn't like it. It wasn't a quality he thought should be admired. He'd have to watch himself more closely.

Now that he was a free man, where would he go now? Of course, Aunt Ro! He'd phone her and see what they could arrange.

"Aunt Ro, it's Eddie. How are you?"

"Eddie! I was just thinking about you. Where are you? Come see me. I can't wait."

"I'll be there tomorrow afternoon, Aunt Ro. You sure sound great." He hung up, hoping that she'd be amenable to his staying with her, at least for awhile.

She was more than amenable, she suggested he stay with her for awhile before he even asked. It would make his transition back to civilian life much easier and certainly much more pleasant.

Eddie had no difficulty landing a job. He wasn't sure exactly what he ultimately wanted to do, but had plenty of time to decide. Meanwhile he'd make some money; devise a plan. Aunt Ro would give him all the moral support he needed to get started, and he'd repay her generously for her assistance. Agnes Covington was history, he thought.

As soon as he was on his feet, he realized he needed a place of his own. He was being pursued by scores of female admirers with nowhere to take them besides a hotel, which was expensive and impersonal. It felt cheap. He would never impose on Aunt Ro by bringing someone into her house for the night. He was unaware she knew why he was looking for his own place. It was time. She was not upset by his leaving, but she would miss the company.

"You've got to promise me you'll not forget I'm here," she said when he left. "You come anytime and don't be afraid to bring a friend. I love company."

Eddie hadn't been on his own six months before Aunt Ro had a massive stroke and died very suddenly. Her death prompted a reunion of sorts with the rest of his family. George was not going to miss Aunt Ro's funeral, and Agnes and Pierpont came with him. It was a little awkward at first. George was glad to see his son looking so well. Agnes was extremely aloof. Pierpont was surprisingly chatty. He'd never shared more than a few sentences with Eddie in the past. Now he was ebullient, full of questions, actually seeming to show some interest in his stepbrother for the first time. Agnes was not amused.

Eddie felt he should at least invite them to his apartment after the funeral and they accepted his invitation. George and Agnes expressed the appropriate amount of approval for his new digs. Pierpont drew him aside for a private chat.

"Listen, Eddie," Pierpont began, "I have a little problem that I hope you can help me with. You see, I've been seeing this girl and I can't take her to my house. Agnes doesn't like her. We can't go to her house either. I was wondering if we could maybe use your place once in a while?"

So that's the reason for his sudden feigned interest. He needs a place to have sex with his girlfriend.

It was not surprising, his motives always involved his own interests above anyone else's. Agnes had taught him well.

"I suppose it would be OK. I work a lot. Don't ever let Agnes know what you're doing. She'll be angry with you, but she'll kill me."

Eddie's apartment became a very busy place between Eddie and his girlfriends and Pierpont and his. There were times all four of them were there at once. Surprisingly, there was little friction. The two seemed content with each other, if not bosom buddies.

Pierpont had matured into an even more strikingly handsome man than Eddie, to which he took no exception. He was happy to have such a good looking brother. Together they swept a room full of prospects clean within minutes, throwing all the other men into a panic. Eddie would have to watch himself. He was enjoying this far too much. He had no cause to destroy every man in the room just because he could. Pierpont, on the other hand, did it exactly because he could.

Soon Eddie's list of conquests was becoming alarming. He really needed to slow down. He looked over his list. Alice, Betty, and Candy. Delia, Ellen, and Fay. Gloria, Loren, and Molly. Mary number one, Mary number two, and Mary number three. Paula, Susan, Tess and Veronica. For every letter missing on his list, Pierpont made up for and then some.

Eddie was presently seeing Monique. He was particularly close with her and sharing more information about his past and family than he'd ever shared with any of the other girls. He joked with her about his pain at the hands of his evil stepmother.

"Agnes is a piece of work that's for sure. She's got a sharp tongue and a sharp face. I say you could pick her up by her feet and chop wood with it. I call her "Hatchetface!" And she's got a COLD heart!" And they'd laugh.

Then came the invitation to come for dinner and bring Monique. Monique didn't want to go. She was petrified. Could this woman really be as bad as Eddie portrayed? Eddie insisted she go. I guess she was going to find out.

Agnes inspected Monique through her newly acquired glasses like a bug under a microscope.

"That's a very interesting shade of hair. Is it a new color? I don't believe I've ever seen hair that color. Charming outfit. I hope our furniture isn't too low for you to manage. Perhaps you should come into the kitchen and sit on a barstool to keep me company," Agnes critiqued.

"That's alright mom," Eddie chimed in at Monique's pleading look. "We'll be fine in the den."

"Thank you so much," Monique relaxed. "I thought I was being herded into the dragon's cave," she whispered as they laughed under their breath.

Dinner was no picnic. Conversation was stilted at best. George was unusually laconic. Pierpont and Agnes carried on most of the banter. When Eddie reached for a second helping of anything Agnes was quick to admonish, "Don't forget to save some for Pierpont!"

What is it with this woman? Has she been having nightmares that her only son is starving to death and everyone else is trying to finish every morsel in sight, leaving him to die?

It was almost a reflex action with her! Everyone breathed a sigh of relief when dinner was over. After a very brief stay, post dinner, the visit came to an end.

"Jez! She's even worse than you said," Monique admitted on the trip home. "Don't ever take me there again!"

Christmas came again and Agnes called wanting to visit. She had to come to the city for a shopping spree.

"I really need a place to freshen up and your apartment is so convenient. We haven't seen you for a while. Your dad wants to see you."

"Sure, Agnes. Just give me a call the day before so I can have something in for you. We can have lunch." Eddie hung up and informed Donna that his dad and step mom were going to come for a visit.

"Not Hatchetface!" she trembled. "I don't think I want to meet her. I don't have to be here do I?"

"I'd like you to be. It would give me some comfort to have someone here on my side of things, but you don't have to if you really would rather not. I'll manage."

"You're so pathetic! Alright, I'll be here," Donna agreed with some trepidation. "But if she tries to corner me, I'm out of here!"

George, Agnes, Pierpont and Millicent arrived just before noon. There was a flurry of introductions and lunch was magically served. The sooner Agnes ate, freshened up, and left, the better. After everyone had finished lunch and Agnes had "freshened up," she approached Eddie with a wrapped Christmas gift.

"This is from your dad and me. Open it now. I want to see your reaction," she said as she pressed the package into Eddie's less than anxious hands. "Go on! Open it up!" she insisted.

Eddie tore off the paper and opened the box. It was packed tightly with tissue paper. He pulled away wads of tissue as the top of what appeared to be a lampshade revealed itself. The box was very light. The shade looked like stained glass, perhaps similar to something you might see in a Tiffany's window. By the weight of the box, this was definitely not from a Tiffany's window! Once all the paper was removed, he lifted out the shade which was attached to a swag chain and held it up to the light. It was as light as a feather. Running his fingers around the rim, he could feel the surface give as his fingers brushed over what was supposed to look like soldered glass panels. It was plastic! Where the wrap-around panels met there were several staples.

"It's a good one, too, Eddie," Agnes held forth on her good taste in expensive gifts.

Eddie had to feign surprise and delight. It was almost more than he could muster. He wanted to throw the cheap hunk of crap right at her head. She'd probably gotten it for a few bucks at some roadside farmer's market.

"Thank you, Agnes," Eddie said through his teeth. "I'll hang it somewhere where it'll catch the light." *I'd like to hang it around your neck,* he thought to himself.

"It's from your dad too, Eddie."

"Thanks dad." Eddie knew his dad had absolutely nothing to do with this surprise gift.

Does she really think this is a good lamp? Or did she give me this cheap plastic knockoff just to see if my humiliation would show on my face.

He wasn't going to give her the satisfaction of seeing anything but appreciation on his part.

After they'd left, Donna was very upset.

"Would you look at this cheap piece of shit! What's wrong with that woman? Did she really think you wouldn't notice? I noticed from across the room! Tiffany is turning over in his grave!! If this is a good one, I'd hate to see a bad one! Eddie, you poor thing. How long did you say you lived with that woman?" She was really impressed with Eddie's family.

With the holidays past, the winter set in for real. Temperatures plummeted. Several major snows made travel a nightmare. Thank goodness his apartment was in the city with adequate public transportation to rely on. His car could remain dormant until spring for all he cared. He hadn't planned on going anywhere anyway. Eddie occupied almost all his time working. He had a date now and then. Iris had come along just when he'd needed a pick-me-up. Now she was history as well.

Several weeks after the last snowfall, with daffodils and azaleas beginning their yearly show, Eddie got the phone call from his stepmother.

"Hi, Eddie," Agnes began, as if she were calling for a little chat and a catch up, "I thought I should call you and let you know that we buried your father yesterday."

Silence.

"Eddie? Are you there?"

Silence

"Hello, is anyone there?"

"You did what!!" Eddie roared into the phone. "You did fucking what!!"

"We buried your dad," Agnes repeated, like she informed people every day that they'd just buried their dad. "We thought you ought to know," she finished weakly.

Eddie hung up. Then he picked up the phone and hung up again. Then he pick up the phone and banged it up against the wall until the plastic cracked and the wall board began to pulverize.

"That bitch!" Eddie screamed. "Who the hell does she think she is? That BITCH!!" He couldn't see where he was going for the tears in his eyes and tripped over a chair leg, hitting his head on the corner of the dining table, knocking him almost unconscious. Almost an hour later when his head had cleared and he remembered what had happened, he broke down and sobbed until there were no more tears left to shed. Then he got up and went on with his day, and his life, and his plans.

Pierpont appeared at his door three weeks later as if nothing had happened with a new conquest. It was hard to remain even remotely civil. Even if Agnes hadn't thought enough to call and let him know his dad was ill, or dying, or dead, at least Pierpont should have. He wasn't about to breach the subject because he didn't trust himself right now. If the answer to any questions Pierpont might pose turned out to have the same self-centered, only events that effect me are important, why should I have been concerned about you, kind of content, he wasn't sure what he might do. He would wait.

He had a very busy summer ahead and he hadn't the time right now to deal with any of this. That would come later. He'd agreed to help with a local dramatic production which was slated to run through the end of the summer, if the response was adequate. He had much to do at work as well. He'd have no time to think; perhaps three months of blessed non-thinking.

The drama company desperately wanted him to assume one of the lead roles. They were mounting a stage production of the B-rated super thriller, *Psycho II*. They wanted him to play Norman Bates.

"We really need you to do this for us," everyone begged. "We don't have anyone half as good looking as you and that's very important for the part. This creep has to be absolutely adorable or it won't work. The audience has to be completely in love with you, so they can really be shocked and hate you at the end. We know you'd be perfect. You're already more adorable than anyone has a right to be. We might really have to work on the creepy part. Please say you'll do it!"

He relented. It might be fun at that. He'd only imagined doing scenery, costumes, make-up, lighting, anything behind the scenes, not on stage.

So, Norman Bates, here I come! he thought.

The play was a huge success, playing to a sold out house and enthralled audiences the entire summer. When the play closed, it was actually a letdown for Eddie.

The summer was over. A chilly fall had set in. He hadn't seen Pierpont the entire summer. Perhaps he and his charming and thoughtful mother had taken a long vacation on his father's money.

Eddie really didn't care. It was time to move on. Time to finish things. It wouldn't do to let things fester much longer.

He called Agnes but got only the answering machine. He didn't leave a message. No point. Perhaps they were out of the country. Until she picked up in person, he'd wait.

A week later his call was answered.

"Oh, Eddie. How are you hon? We haven't heard from you in so long we thought you were mad at us."

Mad at them! I'm furious!!

"I just thought it was time I came for a visit. I've finished a long summer of work and did a play three nights a week with a matinee on Saturdays. So, I have a little free time."

"Oh Eddie we heard about the play. Everyone was saying it was fantastic and that you were soooo goood!"

"Yes. As a matter of fact I think I was. Maybe you'll get to see it sometime. Are you going to be home this weekend?"

"Sure Eddie. Are you bringing someone with you?"

"No, Agnes. I think for this visit it should be just family. See you on Saturday."

Friday night brought heavy rains across much of the city and even heavier downpours to the north. Flash flood warnings were in effect. Saturday dawned cold with a light drizzle turning to sleet. It was going to be one hell of a drive to the Covington's Castle where Her Queen Majesty and the Crown Prince awaited his pleasure. It took longer than he'd planned to get there, but, no matter. There really wasn't any great rush. He had the weekend off and nothing better to do.

Agnes met him at the door. "Eddie, you look wonderful! I think the stage must agree with you."

"So I've been told, MOM," he exaggerated. "I may do another soon. It's really quite liberating. Where's Pierpont?"

"Well, I told him you were coming, but he had this previous engagement that he said he just couldn't break. He might make it for dinner. Maybe not. You know how young people are."

"Yes, Agnes, I certainly do. But Pierpont can just do whatever he likes. It won't upset me. We'll have a nice visit even if he's occupied elsewhere."

"Well, aren't you sweet," Agnes cooed. "Come sit down. We'll have a sandwich, then I'll start to prepare dinner."

They sat at the kitchen table across from each other as they had when Eddie had been small and was trying with all his might to get this cold, unfeeling woman to like him just a little. Agnes had made chicken salad. She was a good cook if nothing else. He'd never gone hungry, physically. He'd only starved emotionally. The sandwich was very good. As he reached for another, his hand paused above the plate waiting for the expected response, "Don't forget to save some for Pierpont!" This time it didn't come.

Is she falling down on the job? What if Pierpont comes home hungry and all the chicken salad sandwiches are gone? Whatever will she do then?

But as he wrapped his hand around the remaining sandwich and brought it to his lips, the old Agnes broke through, a little less adamant than usual.

"Maybe we ought to save one for Pierpont?" questioning. Then, "Oh, go ahead and eat that sandwich. If he's hungry when he comes home, it's his own fault. He'll just have to wait for dinner!"

Eddie finished the sandwich. Agnes cleared the table and started laying out the fixings for their dinner.

"We haven't seen you for so long I thought I'd fix something special," she said, as she busied herself at the counter. "Oh, Eddie, would you be a dear and go down and stoke the furnace. I think it's getting even colder outside. I'm feeling a little chilly," she asked, with the same old poor, helpless me sound in her voice.

"Sure thing, MOM," Eddie acquiesced with filial deference.

The same old cellar greeted him with its familiar acrid smells but more cobwebs and dirt than he'd ever have been able to get away with when he had been responsible for its cleanliness. He shoveled additional coal into the furnace, stoked the flames and quickly emptied the ash box.

When he emerged from the basement, Agnes was at the kitchen sink already well into preparations for dinner. As his first footfall hit the kitchen floor, the almost forgotten litany began.

"I hope you're not tracking dirt and dust on my clean floor young man," Agnes spouted as if a recorded message had just kicked in. Eddie glanced down and saw that he had not remembered to remove his shoes and sox. It had been so long since this scene had played out, he had completely forgotten how this was supposed to go. But it was coming back to him now.

Agnes continued, "You just sit down on those steps and blah, blah, blah, then you just blah, blah, blah, and put on some blah, blah, because I blah, blah, blah." Eddie heard the words but they were all muddled up and incoherent. He knew what he had to do.

He went back to the steps. The ritual had to continue. Nothing would be right until it was done. He should have known that when he went down to the basement in the first place. He'd have to finish it now.

He was right behind Agnes as she labored over her preparations. Eddie had removed his shoes and sox, as required. He'd tip-toed quietly, as he'd been instructed hundreds of times before. Only now he held the coal shovel firmly in his grip. It swung in a wide, powerful arc, as it smashed into the back of Agnes's head with a sickening crack.

The pairing knife Agnes had in her hand flew, embedding itself nicely in a ripe pineapple sitting on the counter. She wouldn't be needing the knife anymore. Fresh pineapple was one of Pierpont's favorite things. She'd planned on slicing the pineapple for dinner. She wouldn't be doing that now.

Blood splattered liberally across the kitchen window and the upper cupboards. Agnes dropped like a sack of potatoes, which she'd been peeling for dinner. Some ruby droplets dripped from the cupboards and glistened on a number of the white orbs, finished potatoes, heaped in a serving dish on the counter. She had been planning on making mashed potatoes from scratch. She wouldn't be making them now. Agnes seemed to have been scratched herself. Her head lolled at an impossible angle atop her shoulders. The whack to the back of her head had definitely broken her neck; snapped it like a twig. Her head was caved in like an over-ripe pumpkin. "All the King's Horses and All the King's Men" wouldn't be putting this eggshell back together again.

Eddie calmly left the kitchen and walked three blocks to the river, carrying the coal shovel over his shoulder like a rifle. The water was very high and churning from the deluge of overnight rains to the north. He threw the shovel as far as he could into the raging torrent, now rushing high along the banks. It quickly disappeared, swept away downstream in an instant.

He returned to the warm and cozy kitchen, feeling a little hungry after his exertion.

Too bad there isn't another chicken salad sandwich, he thought, but he'd already eaten Pierpont's sandwich. *I hope he isn't hungry when he gets home because there isn't going to be any dinner tonight. I don't think Agnes is up to that. She always did make great mashed potatoes though.*

Eddie suddenly realized his feet were really cold. He looked down to see he was barefoot.

How come I'm barefoot? he thought. Then he remembered. *Of course I'm barefoot. I'm always barefoot when I come up from the cellar. Can't track dirt on Agnes's clean floor.*

Cinder Eddie had stoked the furnace well and the kitchen, along with the clean linoleum floor, was warming up considerably. He could now feel the warmth coming up from below on the soles of his feet and his toes. He noticed Agnes lying on the floor in front of the sink, apparently taking a break from her dinner preparations. She looked smaller than he'd ever remembered; deflated, somehow less threatening.

No use disturbing Agnes now, Eddie thought. *Let sleeping dogs lie, and all that. Guess there's nothing left to do but wait. Maybe Norman will keep me company. We'll wait together. Whoever said there wasn't any Happily Ever After?*

THE MIRROR

JEFFREY Holmes was an avid antiques collector. He was also an incurable pack rat and addicted to visiting every flea market and junk store he could possibly find. He had, within the walls of his considerable monster of a house, many dozens of pieces any art and collectables dealer would have paid a small fortune to purchase from him. They would have recouped a nice profit from the resale with ease, but Jeffery was not in the habit of parting with any object d'art once he had it in his possession. Unfortunately, the vast majority of his "treasures," which adorned every room, wall, shelf, table, nook and cranny of his inherited house, were worthless tchotchke, having value to him alone, and he, himself, was not always able to explain the attraction that had prompted the purchase in the first place.

He lived quite comfortably among his treasures in the fifteen room mansion that was left to him when his invalid Mother passed away some two decades past. She had kept the family home as cozy as if it had been a three room cottage, devoid of clutter and as clean as two full time house servants could keep it. Jeffery was permitted to pack his own quarters with as much "junk," as his Mother referred to his odd collection of "weird things," as he liked, as long as they did not spill out into the rest of her perfectly organized home. Once she died, all restraints were removed, and Jeffery was free to indulge his every whim when it came to filling the entire place with anything and everything that caught his eye. There were no financial restrictions to hamper his headlong, hog-wild hurry to acquire whatever his heart desired. His Mother had left him a fortune along with the house, a house not unlike Hitchcock's foreboding mansion on the hill in *Psycho*.

He abruptly dispensed with the housekeeping staff. They had been well compensated upon his Mother's death, and he felt no obligation to keep them on. They were not particularly enamored of his collecting habits anyway, and had always refrained from entering his quarters even while his Mother was still living. Jeffrey didn't mind a bit if some of his precious finds were somewhat dusty. He was never comfortable with anyone touching his things, ever.

In no time at all, the place began to resemble one of the many flea markets from which the plethora of collectibles had come in the first place. Jeffrey never saw the rooms as cluttered, no matter how crowded they became. The top of a coffee table might be completely obliterated by the number of objects displayed upon it; he could always push things a little closer together to make room for yet one more trinket he had been unable to pass up.

Jeffrey found an eerie sense of calm and serenity when surrounded by all the things he'd purchased. He would sit for hours in one room or another admiring each and every individual object, one at a time, recalling where he'd found it and the joy it had given him upon its inclusion into the whole that was his domain. Needless to say, he was considered extremely odd by everyone who knew him, and those who met him for the first time were soon struck by his unusual affect; the label, "ODD," pinned securely above the mental picture they formed of him in their minds.

He had no close friends or companions. He had dated off and on when he was younger, but the girls he went out with were soon put off, if not frightened, by his strange behavior. Not many young girls found a date consisting of a visit to a local flea market much fun. Understandably, parties were not his forte either, and the few to which he'd been invited and attended were a disaster. He was inept at conversation, other than that dealing with some rare find that might be the only thing about which he could converse. None of the young people he knew were the slightest bit interested in antiques, let alone junk!

By the time his Mother passed away, he had become a total recluse, happy with nothing more than the material flotsam and jetsam with which he had surrounded himself. And yet he was never completely satisfied, for he continued to search for yet more and more pieces to cram into the already overloaded, dusty maze that had once been his Mother's refuge of order and cleanliness.

There wasn't an antique dealer or flea market seller in the area who was not well acquainted with Jeffrey or his obsessions. Each and everyone of them had made a huge amount of money from his sometimes frantic purchases. They were hard pressed to keep new stock on their shelves and in their bins to satiate his passion for ever more acquisitions. So, they were not entirely thrilled to see a new establishment open its doors to water down the income they had come to depend upon. They all knew the minute the shop opened for business, Jeffrey would, in all probability, be its first customer. And in that they were entirely correct.

Jeffery did not miss the sign in the window of a vacant storefront announcing: Opening Soon / Lost & Found. He watched with great interest and anticipation as the interior of the shop took shape; fresh paint, display cases and shelves being installed by a bevy of workmen in white coveralls. The work was completed in record time; the new owner obviously anxious to open for business quickly. The new proprietor appeared early each morning to take charge of his crew of workman, seeming to urge them to work even faster, pointing and gesticulating, letting loose with a string of oaths when he saw something that did not meet with his approval. Horace Finnegan was an extremely tall and beanpole-thin man. He had a huge hooked nose, a most noticeable Adam's apple and glaring beady eyes that gave him the look of a carrion-feeding buzzard. Just at a glance he looked shady, nefarious, a resurrectionist personified. He dressed entirely in black, gave no one the time of day, and Jeffrey thought he was going to like this new merchant a lot. Jeffery could hardly wait to see with what this most unusual man was going to stock the new hunting grounds.

Once the interior of the shop was completed, Mr. Finnegan covered all the windows with paper so that no one could see into the store. In the middle of the night, while the town slept, vanloads of merchandise unloaded their cargo through a rear delivery entrance, and Horace

Finnegan labored into the wee hours, lovingly arranging his offerings in the most pleasing of arrays throughout his newest endeavor. Horace was a well-seasoned entrepreneur, having set up similar shops across most of the country. He much preferred operations in a small bedroom community, adjacent to a bustling city, to one in the thick of an urban business setting. He didn't like being sandwiched and squeezed in between rows and rows of storefronts. He abhorred the throngs of harried people who threaded their way along such crowded sidewalks, rushing to and from their pathetically empty life pursuits. He wanted people to come to him specifically. He needed them to have to take the time to find him and go out of their way to peruse his unique wares. Once open and advertisements had been posted, they would come. They always did. Little did he know one of his best customers was already scoping out this, his most recent shop.

Once Horace had almost everything just where he wanted it, he put up the Grand Opening sign with the day and time of his unveiling. Jeffrey made a note on his calendar with a red marker and actually had trouble sleeping the night before, this grand opening filled him with such excitement. He had the uncanny premonition that he was going to find something very special waiting for him in this new haunt. He had already put up a business card on his refrigerator with one of dozens of refrigerator magnets he'd collected. Horace had been passing out his cards on the street for days before his official opening; one at a time to anyone he passed, as well as a goodly handful to other local business establishments all over town.

These cream-colored, handsomely embossed cards, along with large advertisements in both major city papers and all the smaller suburban publications, would assuredly insure his usual spectacular initial showing of some particularly interesting things garnered from every corner of the world.

Jeffrey read and re-read his card each time he passed through the kitchen, feeling a tingle of renewed excitement each time.

LOST & FOUND
ANTIQUES & COLLECTIBLES
OF UNUSUAL QUALITY

Horace Finnegan <><> Proprietor

Jeffrey set his alarm to awaken him early on the big day. He wanted to be up and dressed, partake of a particularly hardy breakfast, and be the first patron in line to enter Mr. Finnegan's emporium of the rare and hypnotizing. Jeffrey often found himself standing in a trance-like haze in front of some bauble others might find insignificant or even repugnant. He would inevitably leave that shop with the mesmerizing object firmly in his grasp, already knowing the perfect spot to showcase it once home.

He arrived at Lost & Found an hour before it was due to open for the first time and was thrilled to see he was indeed going to be its first customer. As the hour drew nearer to nine, a few more enthusiasts began to gather in front of the store. The paper had not been removed as yet from the display windows, so no one had an inkling just what kind of merchandise might be awaiting them inside, but there was a definite sense of anticipation. At five minutes to nine, several white coverall-clad workman hurriedly removed the obscuring butcher block paper from the windows to reveal just a meager sampling of what lay in store inside.

Several large paintings in ornately carved gold frames were artfully displayed and lighted on easels, one in each window. Some fantastic pieces of leaded crystal sparkled with irradiant brilliance on pedestals, the morning sun throwing tiny arced rainbows around the display area. Several large silver offerings sat on the deep green velvet flooring. A few strategically placed potted plants completed the display's beckoning call. Immediate "ews" and "ahs" were elicited from the onlookers as the workman crumpled up the paper and spirited it away, leaving the windows to work their magic.

At precisely nine a.m. the front door was unlocked with an inviting click and Jeffrey was the first to enter the cavernous space within. He was immediately transported to another realm. This was the purview of fantasy he'd been expecting and beyond any other Jeffrey had experienced. He stood immobilized several steps inside the entrance, other patrons having to wend their way around his inert statue-like stance. This was no ordinary junk store! No jumble of cast off items, long since having lost their luster or appeal, could be seen anywhere in the displays that abounded throughout the vastness of the space before him.

After spending an inordinately long time rooted to his spot just inside the front door, he was able to find his legs once more and move slowly into the depths of this new treasure trove of fascinating finds. Dark, rich mahogany furnishings stood in regal rows along the walls. Buffets, breakfronts, bookcases, head and foot boards, attested to Mr. Finnegan's good taste in exquisite, hand-carved masterpieces. Ornately embellished dining tables with matching chairs were interspersed meticulously in the open spaces in the center of the room, each table stunningly appointed with a different set of china, silver and stemware. Gleaming silver candlesticks rose above each setting. Nothing was missed in the proprietor's efforts to draw prospective customer's eyes to the grandeur of each dining tableau. Nothing was missed in the proprietor's efforts to draw the wallets, checkbooks and credit cards out of prospective customer's pockets. Mr. Finnegan wasn't particularly concerned that what he'd created here in his emporium would not have the same grand effect once transposed to some of the modest settings of those who now gazed with longing at his wares. His only objective was to make money. And he had done so with aplomb many times before. He had no doubts about repeating his success here in this off- the-main-road, bedroom community. These people were his bread and butter.

Horace Finnegan took note immediately of Jeffrey Holmes. He recognized his type. The glazed look in his eyes the moment he set foot inside the door. This was someone who recognized quality when he saw it, and would not hesitate to pay for it, even at Horace's inflated prices. Horace had already heard rumors about this man and rubbed his hands in anticipation.

Jeffrey was oblivious of Horace's presence. He wandered in amazement among all the mesmerizing merchandise arrayed before him. His gaze finally settled upon a particular piece from which he could not take his eyes. Setting in the middle of an ornate breakfront with a mirrored back was a large crystal bowl. It was intricately cut with a pleasing design. The heavy leaded glass shimmered and gleamed from within. The bowl rested upon a rotating light source that lit up every facet from below and showered the surrounding surfaces with dancing patterns in rainbow colors. Those patterns were re-projected yet again from the mirrored back of the breakfront. The effect was indeed hypnotizing. Jeffrey stood transfixed before the dancing patterns that now played across his face and reflected one more time from his glasses. He had found his next acquisition. He would not leave this shop without it. He was well aware of the workmanship of this rare piece and knew instinctively acquiring it was not going to be cheap. Of course, he had no qualms about paying whatever it might take to possess this glittering piece of glass.

Once he was able to break his trance, he sought out Mr. Finnegan to finalize just such a transaction. He found the proprietor deep in conversation with a buxom woman who had her eye on a large hand-painted piece of porcelain. Jeffrey thought the representation of the Reubanesque, large-breasted woman holding an apple in her outstretched hand a bit gauche, but then there was no second guessing some people's taste. The apple wielding woman, obviously representing Eve, reclined against a tree around which was entwined a particularly ugly serpent, from which Jeffrey could almost hear the voice of Satan taunt, "Go ahead. Take a bite!" The hair on his arms stood up. Wouldn't Mother approve. She always did like to regale him with the most frightening and repugnant Bible tales just before he drifted off to sleep. He still had nightmares from many of the grosser stories, each of which Mother had embellished just for his edification. Jeffrey knew she'd meant well. She wasn't trying to scare the bejesus out of him, but she had. Jeffrey kept his own council about the after effects of her nightly readings.

The woman had finished her conversation with Mr. Finnegan and was writing him a check with a flourish just as Jeffrey returned from his reverie. The buxom Eve was going home with this buxom, satisfied customer and Jeffrey was relieved to see both of them depart.

"I am most interested in that illuminated crystal bowl there on the mirrored breakfront," he wasted no time in claiming his prize lest someone else beat him to it.

"Ah, yes," Horace Finnegan crooned in his most authoritative tone. "That is, indeed, an exquisite piece. It is an extremely rare example of that particular pattern and an antique from a large collection once owned by Austrian royalty. I had quite a time trying to talk the former owner out of it. That kind and quality in Austrian leaded crystal is seldom seen anymore."

"Yes, yes," Jeffrey interrupted impatiently. "How much is it? I must have that piece!"

"Well …," and Horace deliberately drew out the pregnant pause for full effect as he had rehearsed so many times in the past to customer's consternation. They could imagine all sorts of scenarios in that pause. *That bowl is not for sale! The bowl is already spoken for!* It only enhanced the prospective customer's desire to have whatever they had their eye on at any cost.

"How much!" Jeffrey prodded, imaging exactly what Horace had intended.

"It's really a very rare find for me. The price will have to be commensurate with the time and effort I expended, as well as the outrageous price I agreed to pay for it."

"The price is no problem for me," Jeffrey hastened to inform this infuriating man. "Just name your figure and I will gladly purchase it on the spot!" Always music to Horace's ears.

"$2600 ought to cover my trouble and put a few pennies in my pocket," the merchant announced, more than tripling what he had paid for a very nice cut glass bowl, but no priceless former possession of royalty by any means. He was routinely able to get away with such tactics because he had a little of the con-man in him. His merchandise was prime, if not priceless, and expertly displayed.

"I must also have the light source the bowl is turning upon," Jeffrey added. "I will pay extra to have it."

"Hmmm ...," another pause. Horace would not hesitate to sell anything but he didn't wish his customers to know that. "I don't usually sell my display equipment," he let Jeffrey know, knowing he was going to be able to sell the light pedestal the bowl was displayed on for much more than it was worth as well. He had several other pieces in the shop which could immediately take the bowl's place and become just as enticing, but he could also easily replace the rather cheap, lighted, rotating device to showcase another piece. Horace was well aware the effect light had on even cheap pieces of plain glass when seemingly illuminated from within. After an appropriate amount of deliberation Horace "relented."

"Very well. You will rob me blind and remove all my tricks of the trade, but for $200 you may also have the lighted pedestal," the spider informed the fly. Could he have sucked him any drier? Perhaps. Best not to push his luck too far.

Jeffrey felt faint with relief. The moment he'd seen that bowl, he'd had a premonition that someone else was going to beat him to it. He hurriedly wrote Mr. Finnegan a check for $2800. Mr. Finnegan, already aware of Jeffrey and his penchant for trinkets, was just as aware that Jeffrey could more than afford his new toy, and hesitated not one second to accept the proffered check. He knew full well the check was solid; as solid as Jeffrey was flakey. It had taken Horace little time, or effort, to ferret out this potential gold mine, and he intended to take full advantage of that knowledge. That's why he'd given Jeffrey such a "fair" price on that simply nice bowl. No sense breaking the bank on the first transaction.

Jeffrey hastened home with his treasure and decided he had to place it somewhere where he could most admire it for the near future. He placed it in his bedroom atop the dresser at the foot of his bed, so that he could lie in bed and gaze at the spinning rainbows as they danced around the room; catch the glint of embedded light as it flickered from each cut and facet of the bowl's surface. He would go to sleep by its light. He would see it if he awoke at any time during the night. It would be there, turning, to greet him as he awakened in the morning, catching the early morning rays of the rising sun spilling in the window across the room; caught and refracted as they bounced off in prismatic splendor from patterns etched deeply into the bowl's convex sides. It had been some time since he'd been so enthralled by anything quite this perfect.

The very first night he stared for as long as he could keep his eyes open at the bowl and the living, dancing wall paper it produced. He slept deeply and dreamt darkly that night. He found himself in a royal court. The King and Queen were resplendent with glittering, jeweled crowns; lush, velvet, fur-trimmed capes, as they sat imperially on their thrones. A ball was in progress and dozens of whirling couples, just as finely attired, spun around the polished floor of the ballroom. A small orchestra was playing lilting, waltz music from an alcove directly across from the royal couple. It was indeed a thrilling site. But wait! Something was not right.

Off to one side, along one wall, a feast was being set up by serving wenches. Great platters of meats and cheeses were being delivered to the serving buffet table. At the far end sat Jeffrey's crystal bowl. It was filled to the brim with a dark red liquid that Jeffrey was afraid might just be blood. But that was crazy. This was a fine affair. It was probably a rich dark red wine or punch of some kind. The bowl turned slowly on its base, but no dancing prisms jumped from its surface to dance across the ceiling and walls. Instead black smudges swirled around the room like little oil droplets, leaving greasy trails behind them as they passed. The effect was ugly and frightening. *How could refracted light look like dark black oil smudges?*

As Jeffery watched, the dance ended and people began to fill plates with mounds of the succulent looking meats and delicious cheeses. Goblets were filled from a large ladle that rested in his liquid-filled bowl at the end of the buffet table. Toasts were made and drained. Everyone seemed happy, but still Jeffrey had a premonition of doom just about to descend upon the entire company. As he watched with trepidation, his fears were fulfilled as one after another of those assembled for the evening's festivities lurched and stumbled, grabbed their stomachs with grimaces of pain. Their eyes bugged out in terror as they had trouble finding their breath. They fell, writhing in agony on the floor of the ballroom as the King and Queen looked on impassively. Then the King also slumped on his throne, seizing as he slid to the floor. Jeffrey heard laughter. It sounded familiar. He didn't want to hear anymore of that laughter, but he was unable to turn it off. Then the Queen turned to face him from across the ballroom and he realized why the laughter sounded so familiar. The Queen was his dead Mother, laughing with great glee as her eyes bored into him like lasers.

"Have a glass of punch, Jeffrey," she invited him. "It'll settle your stomach, you horrid little toad! Look how it's settled your father," she pointed out with one bejeweled, red-tipped finger. Then she began to laugh uncontrollably once more.

Jeffrey awoke with a start. The sun was streaming into his window, its beams hitting the bowl atop his dresser. The bowl was now empty and throwing the expected prisms around Jeffrey's room, just as he had imagined it would. However, somehow he was not as enthralled by his purchase now. Of course, it was just the dream. But what a bizarre dream it had been. He was now anxious to dress and get out of the room, leaving the bowl behind, and the dream as well.

He would spend the day in other pursuits. The bowl could have the room to itself for now. He switched off the light under the bowl. It abruptly stopped turning. Jeffrey dressed and descended to the kitchen for breakfast.

Did he hear a slight tinkle of the laughter from his nightmare as he hastily scrambled himself some eggs? He stopped and listened more closely. Silence. He had never liked his Mother's laugh. It was somehow not a contagious outburst of mirth, rather a mischievous knowing giggle over something she knew and he didn't. He'd always found it disconcerting rather than endearing.

Jeffrey spent the day driving through the country with his binoculars, stopping to watch for birds and wildlife, actively pushing the night before from his mind. The fresh air and abundance of birds he found to observe during his afternoon drive helped to considerably blur the memory of the ballroom full of dead dancers, along with their King and the wickedly leering face and haunting laughter of it's surviving Queen, in his mind.

By the time he was ready to go to bed that night, the dread with which he'd awakened that morning had faded, and the details of why he'd been so rudely propelled from his sleep were very fuzzy, as most dreams become just moments after their departure. The sight of his precious crystal bowl did not disturb him. Instead, he remembered the joy with which he'd carried it home the day before, and how he'd chosen its particular resting place. Switching on the light below the bowl, he prepared for bed. Soon he was once more rapturously entranced by the swirling patterns of light as they danced across his bedroom walls and ceiling. He drifted off to sleep.

He slept soundly for some time before something roused him from his slumber. A sound. Weak at first. Then becoming more insistent and demanding his attention. It sounded like fluttering. Bird's wings, feathers rustling one against another. Perhaps a bird had somehow gained entrance into his bedroom. He opened his eyes cautiously, peering around the room to pinpoint the source of the sound, ever increasing in intensity.

His bowl threw its usual patterns of light, but did not reveal any frightened, trapped bird anywhere in the room. He reached for his glasses, the better to see into the far corners, sure that would solve the mystery. Instead it brought the dancing patterns of light into sharper focus, and they were not as they had been. They seemed larger. They were less sharply defined. They had weakened in intensity to a milky, ethereal quality. As his brain continued to tell him that a bird was trapped somewhere in his room, the sound of its beating wings multiplied tenfold, making him start. Instead of looking for the illusive bird, he now saw numerous birds. They were not flesh and feather birds, but began to become evident in the fleeting swaths of reflected light being thrown around the room from deep with in the crystal bowl. They grew larger still. A flock of ectoplasmic doves were encircling him.

♈ ♈   ♈   ♈
  ♈   ♈   ♈   ♈
♈ ♈   ♈ ♈   ♈
  ♈ ♈ ♈   ♈
    ♈   ♈   ♈

Around and around they flew, the sound of their wings now filling the entire room with their frantic beating. Then as each bird turned its head to look squarely at Jeffrey as it passed directly in front of him, their beady eyes rebuked him, their beaks gave voice to their disapproval.

"Tweet-tweet. Twitter-twit. Twit-twit!" they called louder and louder.

Then he was aghast to see the tiny face of his Mother on each one, a cold hard stare trained upon him. The bird's beaks were moving, becoming his Mother's mouth, at first just the twittering of the doves, but then it became a cry from his Mother as they flew in front of him.

"Help me, you ungrateful twit!" her unmistakable voice reached his ears, over and over as each bird passed. Then, "Let me out of here!" revolved around the room several times. "You'll regret it, you wasteful lout!" followed. A return to the intial plea, "Help me, you ungrateful twit!" completed the cycle.

Jeffrey sprang from his bed and pulled the plug on the spectral spectacle, abruptly banishing the accusatory Mother-headed flock. He switched on his bedroom light. He removed the bowl from the pedestal and sat it on the dresser. Opening a bottom drawer, he shoved the offending illuminating device into the back and covered it with seldom worn clothing, closing the drawer with a thump. He picked up the bowl and took it downstairs to the study where he made a niche for it on a shelf, out of the way and unlikely to receive any kind of bright, direct light. Whatever might be in that bowl would not be coming out again! Jeffrey returned to bed and slept fitfully till morning.

Upon rising, he fixed himself a hearty breakfast, then proceeded to the study to take a look at his newly acquired and hastily repositioned treasure. The bowl was as innocuous as it could be, setting wedged between a marble bust of Voltaire and an ivory rendering of some Indian Goddess. Not a sparkle of light reflected from it. There was nothing menacing in its demeanor. It was, for all rights and purposes, a very nice glass bowl. Jeffrey would leave it there. He would, from time to time, look at it and wonder, as he did about many items with which he was surrounded, why he had gotten the thing in the first place.

As with every one of Jeffrey's treasures, it would not be long before he felt the urge to look for something more, something new to cram into his already crowded quarters. His next foray would come just a bit sooner than normal, due to the unexpected and disturbing consequences of his last purchase. When he had time to consider the incident in retrospect, he realized he had not really seen much of Mr. Finnegan's wares, so quickly had he been taken by that unfortunate crystal bowl. He owed it to himself, as well as Mr. Finnegan, to give Lost & Found another more deliberate look.

Entering the shop just after a solitary lunch at a popular café just blocks from Lost & Found, he was once again struck by the overall grandeur of the place. There were many customers admiring the eclectic, elegant, unusual and even bizarre offerings, tastefully displayed for their consideration. Jeffrey saw that Mr. Finnegan was extremely busy with his prospective buyers, and now chided himself for his rush to snap up the first item that had caught his eye on his first visit. This time he would take his time. He would explore every nook and cranny with deliberation before settling upon his next purchase. He would not be urged to rush into anything because of some silly premonition that the very thing he wanted would be spirited away from him by one of these other shoppers.

He attacked the job before him with the planned discipline of a marine search effort, plying a grid so as not to miss what he was searching for, even though at present he had no idea what that might be. Horace Finnegan had not missed Jeffrey's entrance, even though he was quite busy today with many more customers than usual. He noted Jeffrey's deliberate military like precision as he examined everything closely, going from the front of the store to the back, then reversing, not missing a shelf, a table, a vase, a fork. Horace was certain Jeffrey would find something that he would not be able to leave the shop without, and Horace would be most pleased to fleece him for that privilege. More customers were arriving and Horace forgot about Jeffrey, leaving him to make his choice at leisure.

Jeffrey was enjoying his search immensely. He had covered more than three quarters of the shop when he felt the need to use the restroom. Conveniently, at the rear of the shop, directly in line with the path he was now on, was a sign: RESTROOM. Upon using and leaving the facilities, he noted a second door, this one unmarked, slightly ajar, next to the restroom. His curiosity was piqued, and glancing around to ascertain he was not being observed, he quickly opened the beckoning door, slipped in, and returned the door to its previous slightly ajar position.

Sure he had not been seen, he turned his attention to what was evidently a storeroom/workshop. At the rear was a large delivery entrance with an overhead track where trucks could back in and unload bigger items such as furniture. The room was filled with crates and cartons yet to be unpacked, some piled two and three deep on pallets. Others sat around open and in the process of being emptied. Along one wall was a long table filled with a jumble of items in great disarray, unlike that of the main shop. Many of the items seemed in poor shape, very used looking and tarnished. At the far end were a few pieces that were obviously being restored, probably by Mr. Finnegan himself. A large silver serving tray was propped against the wall, one half dull and ugly, the other shining and new. A small foot ottoman sat in front of it. The footstool's discarded and frayed cover lying in a heap on the floor, and a new and resplendent upholstery almost completely attached. One corner had not yet been affixed, the decorative tacks for that job lying nearby. Jeffrey thought it refreshing to see that Horace Finnegan actually put some work into his business, rather than merely buying items and reselling them, putting no effort into the process, simply passing items along from his seller to his buyer as so many merchants did.

He was about to return to the main shop when something in the far corner caught his eye. At first it gave him quite a start. Partially in shadow from surrounding stacks of boxes, it initially looked like a seven foot ghost. The featureless head protruded just above the shadows. Halfway to the floor, and in shadow, protruded the nubby arms of the apparition. Once Jeffrey looked more closely, he realized it was a tall, sheet-draped object, and he was not about to leave the workroom before finding out what is was.

Advancing to the corner of the room, he carefully pulled the obscuring cover from what was one of the most beautiful things he'd ever seen. A superbly framed oval mirror in an ornately carved mahogany frame stood more than seven feet tall on a castored base with equally impressive carved footings. Two gracefully curved and carved armatures held the mirror suspended by a rod on each side, allowing the frame to be tilted to whatever angle the observer might choose.

Jeffrey was so taken by this accidental discovery that he failed to note his own reflection staring back at him in awe. When he finally became aware of his double standing there in front of him, his entire person, from the top of his slightly balding head to the tip of his overly worn shoes, he was not impressed with the reflection. The image he saw in the mirror was sharp and clear. Every flaw and shortcoming was there to behold. The surface of this mirror was flawless and what Jeffrey observed in its depth seemed larger and more real than the reality around him. He backed away in defense.

Strangely, the farther he retreated from the mirror, the better he liked what he saw. The room reflected in the mirror still appeared larger than that in which he now stood, but he was now somewhat smaller, his rough edges smoothed out a bit and he thought a little more attractive. He could not recall a time when he had seen himself so portrayed, full length. Normally he saw only what was reflected in the medicine chest mirror when he shaved. He had never liked very much what he saw there.

Now he took several more steps back and re-examined himself. Brad Pitt, he was not, but neither was he Dorian Grey. He thought he had some inkling why no one ever took a second look at him, but then he'd never cared that they hadn't. This mirror was a most fascinating phenomenon. He must have it!

Over his shoulder, he saw Horace Finnegan hurriedly approaching. Horace had indeed seen Jeffrey slip into his workroom, but had been busy with several sales and had only just now the opportunity to follow him into this private space. He had every intention of ejecting him from the storeroom and locking the door as he had evidently forgotten to do earlier.

"Mr. Holmes, this is my private work area and it is not open to the public. I think I may have inadvertently left it open, but you must return to the showroom immediately!" Horace firmly announced as he tried to shepherd Jeffrey out of the room.

"Wait! Wait! I'm very sorry if I'm not supposed to be in here, but, Mr. Finnegan, I must have that mirror!" Jeffrey almost begged.

THE MIRROR. The mirror. What is it about this mirror, Horace thought to himself. He'd never had this garish mirror in his possession more than one day before it was sold. He'd had every intention of making some revisions in the piece. It was impressive in a strange sort of way, while at the same time foreboding and repellant. He didn't know why he'd bought it in the first place, but he had to admit it had made him a great deal of money without any revisions and with no effort whatsoever. Since the mirror resold the moment it was back in his possession, there it stood, now divested of the dust cover he'd thrown over it, in its original "glory." He had hoped this time to perhaps rework the damn thing and even keep it for himself. Now here was yet another buyer, obviously bewitched by this infernal object.

Horace had first purchased the mirror at an estate sale for a ridiculously small price. No one seemed interested in many of the pieces being offered that day. He'd snapped up most of them for himself and made a large profit from the resale of each and every item he'd bought. None of the other sales had returned for a repeat performance except this mirror.

The story of why everything was being sold that day was a sad one, to be sure, but Horace had never been the maudlin type, allowing sentiment to cloud business decisions or superstition to overwhelm logic. The house and everything in it had belonged to a wealthy old socialite who had mysteriously disappeared. After a missing persons report had been filed by the distraught husband, the police suspected the disappearance might have been the result of foul play. And, of course, they zeroed in on the husband as their prime suspect. Unfortunately, there was no evidence of foul play, and they had combed the house and grounds with a fine toothcomb. There never was a body or any explanation as to where or why the woman had vanished. Once all avenues of investigation had been thoroughly followed, the case went stone cold. Then the husband retreated into the huge old mansion to live hermit-like and people seldom saw him out of doors. He had food and necessities delivered. When a food deliveryman received no answer one morning, he notified the police. The husband was found hanging by one of his favorite neckties from the rafters, and just in front of this selfsame full length mirror. The police speculated the he had indeed somehow managed to kill his wife and dispose of her body, leaving no evidence for them to nail him with, then eventually, riddled with guilt, had hung himself. They morbidly supposed that he had done the deed in front of the mirror so that he could see himself as he took his life as some sort of self exculpatory ritual. *Bad man, bad man! You killed your wife, now you must pay by killing yourself, and you have to see yourself do it.* It was all just supposition. Never a shred of proof that any such thing had occurred. The facts remained, the husband was dead, the wife was still missing and presumed dead, and everything was up for grabs at the estate sale. Horace had made a killing.

The mirror had just been delivered to his shop when a young couple came in and saw it. They immediately had to have it. They were to be married and the groom-to-be wanted to purchase it as a wedding present for his bride. She had ignored everything else in the shop to insist that all she wanted was that mirror. Horace had quickly recognized his chance to fleece the young couple and unload the mirror for a handsome profit. Since he'd paid so little for it in the first place, he didn't feel unjustified in raising the sum he wanted for resale considerably. It really had been worth a great deal more than he'd paid. But still, a 400% profit was pushing it, even for him. However, the price was paid and the mirror was delivered. He never expected to see it again.

In that he had been mistaken. The wedding never took place. The bride stood the groom up at the alter. She had been seen in her wedding gown shortly before the ceremony by several of her best friends. They reported later that at the time she had seemed inordinately nervous. She had even voiced second thoughts about her wedding. Her friends had simply chalked it up to "cold feet," or "pre-wedding jitters." But *The Wedding March* never played, and the bride was nowhere to be seen. It hadn't been so very long since Julia Roberts had done the same thing, and more than once, in *The Runaway Bride.* But she had not just vanished. She was still there working on yet another relationship that was anyone's guess would end up in matrimony. This bride was just gone. The groom was beside himself. The wedding presents had to be returned. The mirror found its way back to Horace's shop for pennies on the dollars that were paid for it. Horace was not particularly overjoyed to see it return, but since it had come back, he thought perhaps he was meant to have it for himself. This time he would work on it and soften its aspect somewhat, modernize it a little, make it less foreboding. He never got the opportunity.

A film production company was in town making a movie on location, using lots of local landmarks as backdrops for their story, and a number of local people as extras. One of the producers strolled into Horace's shop the morning he'd repurchased the mirror. The producer was ecstatic over the piece and insisted he must have it.

"It will be perfect for several scenes in my movie," he had told Horace. "And once we wrap, I definitely want it as a memento from this film. I just have a feeling that this time I'm going to hit Oscar gold. This mirror will be worth a fortune!" His enthusiasm was contagious and it was also going to make Horace a great deal of money. Again! Horace sold the mirror for the second time at an 800% profit.

Much to the enthusiastic producer's dismay, his film was a monumental flop. He had had several before and now he was *persona non gratis*. No one wanted to work with him. His reputation for flops preceded him. He became despondent and spiraled downward into depression fueled by overindulgence in alcohol. His frantic wife said he spent hours sitting in front of his precious mirror talking to himself, and staring into its depths as if he'd find the answer to his failures within its mirrored surface. Then one day he simply sat down in front of it and blew his brains out. There was blood spatter everywhere except the surface of his silly mirror. His wife had tracked Horace down to his new shop and immediately shipped the mirror back to him, paying for the shipping and asking only that he take it back. She never wanted to lay eyes on it again. Horace hadn't expected to lay eyes on it again either.

And now here was this Jeffrey Holmes person in his workroom demanding to purchase the mirror, having discovered it by accident, snooping where he didn't belong anyway.

What is it about this old mirror that these people find so enthralling? Horace thought to himself. *It's like the mirror is drawing them in. They arrive at almost the same time that the mirror does. Next thing you know people will be waiting in my shop asking when that mirror is going to be available!*

Whatever the attraction, Horace was not about to question his good fortune for the third time. He would up the ante considerably also. He would more than double the last already inflated purchase price, and see just how anxious Jeffrey was to actually buy his latest obsession. After all he was a businessman. Perhaps if the price were high enough, Jeffrey would not be so interested, and Horace, himself, would hide the mirror away somewhere and attempt to find out just what the attraction was that drew people so quickly to its lustrous reflections.

"You realize this is an extremely rare find?" he asked. "In fact, it may very well be a one of a kind. I, myself, have never come across another like it in all my travels," Horace set the hook.

"I'm sure it must be very expensive," Jeffrey agreed, "but, the price is not a factor. Something drew me into this room and I was just about to leave when I noticed it. I couldn't leave until I'd seen what was under the dustcover. I knew as soon as the cover fell to the floor that this was why I'd come to your shop today, of all days," Jeffrey finished, as he fished his checkbook out of his jacket pocket.

"Very well, Mr. Holmes. My price for this magnificent mirror is $30,000. I cannot possibly take a cent less." Horace was surprised to see that Jeffrey did not flinch. Not a moment of hesitation as he hurriedly wrote the check for the exorbitantly inflated price Horace had just quoted him.

Jeffrey's hands were actually shaking with excitement as he finished the check with a flourish and handed it to Mr. Finnegan. He wanted to grab the mirror and wheel it out of the store immediately. He looked suspiciously to the right and left, as if daring anyone else to come between him and his latest possession. He had the overwhelming premonition that if he didn't get the mirror out of the store now, something would happen to it before it was delivered to his house.

"I'd like this delivered immediately, please," Jeffrey informed the more than pleased businessman, as the check disappeared into Horace's pocket.

"I'm afraid I'll have to charge you a small delivery fee for such a fast delivery. I'll have to call someone for that purpose," Horace informed him, pushing his luck to the limit.

He needn't have worried, as Jeffrey pulled a wad of bills out of his wallet and peeled off three twenties without even asking how much. Horace smiled appreciatively as he stuffed the cash in along with the check, knowing two of those twenties were his. The deliverymen would gladly transport the mirror for twenty. The two of them could do the job in twenty minutes. Ten bucks apiece for twenty minutes work wasn't an offer they received often.

JEFFREY was beside himself until the delivery truck rolled up his driveway a little more than ten minutes after he'd arrived home. He had visions of a devastating fire at Lost & Found, decimating everything within it, including his mirror. He saw the delivery truck forced off the road and overturning, destroying his purchase before it had reached his house. He watched the two men as they unloaded the heavily shrouded bundle from the back of the truck, sure they were going to drop it and smash it to bits.

They did not. This was not the largest or heaviest item they'd delivered by any means, and they were quite adept at maneuvering this item, whatever it was, adroitly out of the truck, into the house. After all it was on wheels, which made their job even easier. Once the bundle was positioned where the customer had designated, they removed the heavy wrapping material and saw that it was a very ugly mirror. A very large ugly mirror. At least they both agreed between them that such a thing would never end up in their homes. There was no second guessing some people's taste.

Jeffrey was so relieved to see that the mirror had been unharmed, not even a scratch on any of the wood, that he gave each of the men an extra ten dollars for their trouble. Both men were very surprised but accepted the extra money without question. They had each just made a dollar a minute for this delivery. If only they had more jobs like this one!

Once the men had departed, Jeffrey had time to admire his newest acquisition. He positioned the angle just right to reflect the room to its fullest advantage, as well as himself, head to toe, as he'd first seen himself at Finnegan's shop. He was not wrong about what he'd noticed there. He did look younger and more attractive. True, he was still overweight, somewhat; balding, more than somewhat; a little round shouldered, and the glasses were not becoming at all. But still, he looked better than he'd imagined he could. Even the room behind him looked better. Bigger. Brighter somehow. He was extremely pleased with this new purchase.

He approached the mirror for a closer look. The surface seemed unusually luminous and reflected every detail with a crisp clarity he had never seen in any other mirror. He reached out to touch the surface and felt a strange vibration that startled him, and he reflexively withdrew his hand as if he'd touched a hot stove. But the surface was certainly not hot. Tentatively, he reached out a second time, feeling the same slight vibration, this time prepared for the sensation. He pushed his fingers slightly against the surface and was unnerved to see a slight pucker in the reflection, as if his fingers had indented the surface that they had touched. Withdrawing his fingers, the image reverted to its normal appearance, no distortions visible.

What an odd turn of events. What kind of merchandise is Mr. Finnegan selling anyway? Jeffrey thought. He certainly hoped this was not going to be a repeat performance of his first purchase from Lost & Found.A second push against the glass yielded no distortion. The glass was as solid as a rock. Perhaps it had just been his imagination, so expectant he'd been to place and admire his latest find within his already crowded house of finds. He was sure he was going to get a great deal of pleasure out of this mirror.

Jeffrey went about his day as usual, admiring all the things crammed one against another as he made his way around the house, making sure to pass the mirror frequently to see if he was any better looking as the day wore on. He was not, but still remained just as good looking as he'd appeared as he'd backed away after the dust cover fell to the floor in Horace Finnegan's shop.

He noted the crystal bowl on his rounds, still wedged between Voltaire's bust and the Indian Goddess. It now revealed itself as just the nice crystal bowl that it was, no glittering reflections came from its depths. No direct light lit its surfaces, calling forth dark, oily blotches or milky, flocking birds. It was, after all, a decent addition to his collection. He had been silly to let his imagination run away with him. But, just in case, he would keep it were it now resided, safely out of any rays that might rekindle whatever it was that had so spooked him just days ago.

Jeffrey stopped for one last time to admire himself full length in the mirror before he went to bed. He fell asleep quickly and slept dreamlessly for awhile. Then something awakened him. He listened to the usual sounds of the old house as it creaked and settled. Just as he was about to drift off again, he heard it. A soft humming coming from outside his door. He glanced in the direction of the now louder humming and noticed a faint light creeping in under the bedroom door. He got up and approached the door slowly, quietly, still hearing the humming. It sounded like a woman's. When he opened his door he saw the light was coming from the mirror, but as soon as he took a step toward the source of the humming, it stopped and the light went out. He crossed the room anyway and turned on a light. Everything in the mirror was just as one would have expected. He saw himself standing there in the wane light of a single lamp peering into his own eyes. No humming. No light from the mirror except that being reflected from the lamp he'd switched on. He turned off the lamp and went back to bed. The night passed uneventfully. He arose in the morning convinced once more that he had been the victim of his own imagination. His Mother had always said he had an overactive imagination. She had probably been right.

The next day was warm and breezy and Jeffrey spent it outdoors, as he seldom did, cleaning out all the winter deadheads and few surviving weeds from the winter. The few beds around the old house would soon be full of all the blooms from a myriad of roots and tubers and bulbs that his Mother had planted and tended to until she no longer could. She had enlisted his reluctant assistance once bending and stooping became to difficult for her. Jeffrey had done very little in the way of tending the beds since she died and he'd let all the servants go, so what survived was pretty much up to the beds themselves. It looked like there would be quite a few survivors despite his lack of care or interest.

He made it a point to pass his mirror as many times as he could throughout the day. It fit perfectly there in his sitting room. He could not believe what a difference just that one mirrored surface had made in the complexion of that room. He had always avoided mirrors in the past. He'd never much liked what he saw in them. They'd only reinforced his Mother's pronouncements that he had a weak chin, poor posture and an ungainly gate. He didn't see that in this mirror.

He retired to bed exhausted, as he seldom was, after a day of rare exercise putting the yard in order for the coming spring. He had stopped for one last look at himself before turning in for the night. After all that exercise, he fell asleep immediately and slept soundly for hours before something awakened him once again. The humming was back. Distinct this time. It was definitely a tune, but he didn't recognize it. It was a woman's timbre. The light was once again coming under his door, perhaps a bit brighter than the previous night. He crept quietly to the door and opened it ever so slowly. The light remained on and the humming was louder, both emanating from the mirror. He inched his way softly toward a vantage point where he could see into the mirror's depth and the reflection of his sitting room around him.

There in the center of the room was an old woman who was at present oblivious of his presence. She had grey hair, platted and wound around her head many times. She was quite a frightening sight in her black dress and austere and pointed countenance. She could have been The Wicked Witch of the West but for the absence of green skin and a pointed black hat. But the dress could easily have come directly from Wardrobe. She was swaying side to side as she hummed the tune Jeffrey still could not place.

Then Jeffrey jumped back. The room he was looking into was not his sitting room at all. It was similar. It was furnished with many antique pieces, but they were all tastefully arranged and definitely not his. And nothing was out of place. No familiar clutter could be seen anywhere in that foreign room. No jumble of paintings one upon another, frame to frame, covering every inch of wall space. There the paintings were showcased with lights above, bringing out the subtle colors of each work of art, original oils and of great value, Jeffery had no doubt. However, his sudden movement had attracted the woman's attention.

"You there! Who are you? What are you doing in my house? What are you doing in my room?" she asked in quick succession as she made her way toward the mirror. "I shall summon the authorities! Answer me! Why are you in my room?"

"But I'm not in your room!" Jeffrey stammered. "This is my room! You're in my room!"

"How absurd! This is most definitely not your room, it's mine. And I should know, I've lived in it for more than half a century. Who are you? Did my husband send you? Did he tell someone after all? Is that what this is all about? Are you from the police, because if you are I shan't come out. You'll have to come and drag me out I assure you. I know I've been horrid but still…," she tapered off into a fearful silence.

"I haven't a clue what you're talking about," Jeffrey tried to convince her. "I'm not from the police and I have no idea who your husband is. I was awakened from sleep in my bedroom by the lights and your humming."

"Who are you?" she asked again a little more at ease.

"Jeffrey Holmes," he identified himself, feeling most ridiculous standing there in the middle of the night talking to this strange woman in the mirror.

"I don't know any Jeffrey Holmes, never have. I don't recall my husband ever knowing one either. You don't by any chance know that crazy film person who almost drove me to distraction not long ago. Perhaps you're a friend of his?"

"Sorry, I don't know any film people," Jeffrey assured her.

"Thank goodness for that! I thought my husband had sent him at first, until I realized he was just loony tunes and soused to the gills on hard liquor. He was such a whiner. 'Poor me! Poor me! My career is in the toilet! No one wants to work with me. All my films are flops. My wife is going to leave me.' And he had the temerity to blame his latest box office failure on me and my mirror. Can you imagine? My mirror caused his film to flop! Have you ever heard anything so ludicrous? He was a certified nut job! I was so relieved when he stopped coming. I thought I heard him talking, no, make that whining, to someone else several times, but when I came out, no one was there. Then there was that one time I thought I heard a gunshot, but no one was there then either. So, my husband didn't send you?" she asked again.

"Really, I don't know your husband, and I'm not from the police," Jeffrey assured her a second time.

"Well, I can't tell you what a relief that is," the old woman said as she turned to walk away. Then she paused and turned back again. "You must come and visit with me again. I don't get many visitors, and you seem a nice enough person. Good night." And she left the room, turning off the lights as she went through the door, most probably to her bedroom.

Jeffrey was left standing in the dark, staring into his barely discernable reflection. He switched on a lamp. There was his room just as always, and its reflection. There he stood in his pajamas. Had he actually been standing there in his pajamas, having a conversation with a strange woman in his mirror? He turned off the lamp and went back to bed, to lay there awake for some time trying to remember what had happened. It all began to fade and seem very unreal when he finally dropped off to sleep and slept until morning.

The next day he spent a number of sessions sitting in front of the mirror willing the old woman to appear. She did not. All he saw was himself, staring at himself like an idiot. Perhaps he was losing his mind. His Mother had always said he was high strung and that it would come to no good end one day. Maybe she had been right. It was beginning to look like she had been right about a lot of things that Jeffrey had taken umbrage to growing up.

Before going to bed, Jeffrey sat for one more session in front of his mirror, hoping the woman in black would enter his room, or her room, or whatever was happening. She did not. He retired to bed and had no difficulty falling asleep. Sometime in the wee hours he heard a piano playing. The light was coming under his door. He got up and went into his sitting room to find the lights on in the other sitting room, not his sitting room. The door to the woman's bedroom was open and the music was coming from there. He closed his bedroom door with a bang, and the music stopped abruptly.

"Who's there?" the old woman called out.

"It's me, Jeffrey. Remember you said I should come back and visit again?"

"Ah, Jeffrey," she said as she entered from her bedroom, this time in a flowing apricot dressing gown trimmed with white angora. The beautiful attire did nothing to soften the still angular features of her face. "Did my playing disturb you?"

"Well, not really. It was very nice, but, I was asleep," he admitted.

"I should have know as much. I knew there must have been a reason you were in your pajamas the other night. I must have asked a lot of silly questions. How silly of me to think you'd been sent by the police in your pajamas! Although you did give me quite a start."

"I have to admit, you gave me one as well," Jeffrey returned, pulling up a chair and making himself comfortable. He also had to admit to himself that he was intrigued by what was happening. "I don't understand why you're so afraid of the police. What have you done?"

"Since you didn't know my husband and are obviously not with law enforcement, I guess it's safe for me to confess that I may have treated my husband a bit shabbily at times. Well to be completely honest, I treated him very badly, very often. In fact, I'm positive I was the cause of his demise. I think I could be arrested and face a trial, even jail time. He did push me into it though."

"I find that hard to believe," Jeffrey took to calming the woman, who now seemed upset and nervous. "Why would you think such things?"

"My husband was a piece of work, let me tell you," she began, obviously wanting to tell all. "I should never have married him. He was no first prize believe me. He wasn't even a fifth runner up. But beggars can't be choosers. Mother always stressed that. And I was no prize myself. You see me as I am? Well just imagine that, only fifty years younger. When you're my age you can get away with it. The face with character. I'm old. I've earned it. But this face fifty years younger! Not pretty. He was no looker either. We complemented each other in our unattractiveness. 'Remember, beauty is only skin deep,' my mother always counseled. Well, there wasn't any beauty under my husband's skin. He was unattractive through and through. Now you seem different. I can tell right off. You certainly weren't showered with looks yourself, beg your pardon, but that's only the surface. Though you seem to have reached the limit of the expiration date of middle age and aren't likely to flower any further, just as I never have, there's a kindness in your eyes and manner my husband lacked totally. When my parents died and I inherited all those millions, it was even worse. I blame myself. It was my fault and my decision. Let me give you a piece of advice. Never buy a pig in a poke! Throw open that poke and get a good look at the pig before it's too late."

Jeffrey frowned. He hadn't a clue what she was talking about.

"You look confused. Well of course you are. Excuse me if I'm blunt, but what I mean is, don't wait until after you've tied the knot to test the equipment. If the equipment is inferior, the results are going to be inferior. My husband's equipment was grossly inadequate. I hadn't a clue. No one ever told me a thing about sex. I was appalled on my wedding night. Now you're blushing. You have to remember I come from a very different time, a different generation. Things like that weren't ever discussed in polite and decent society. My initiation was very painful and continued to be so my entire marriage. It was like being poked with a short, sharp stick. Not only had my husband gotten the short end of the stick on looks, he'd gotten the short stick as well. Ah, well. It's over now, thank goodness. Anyway, I did want children, so I had to submit to being rudely prodded in order to fulfill my motherly instincts. We did manage to have two children with his little nubbin. And knowing what I know now, I think I'd even take that back. A boy and a girl, two of the most self-centered, ungrateful, money-grubbing progeny one could ever wish for. Oh, they were fine as infants and toddlers. Then my parents died and all that money was ours. My husband went wild with overindulgence, giving them everything, spoiling them absolutely rotten. They became an ugly little pair of "gimme" artists. They developed the most unattractive overactive egos you can imagine. No one liked them. Not even me. I don't speak to them to this day. My husband fostered all that greed and avarice. I tried to put the brakes on at every opportunity, but he wouldn't hear of it. I was so angry with him. Once we'd had our family, I'd had it with his little pecker as well. No more pig in a poke for me. No more poking at all for him. He didn't like it. We fought a lot. I wouldn't relent. I think he must have found other pastures, bless his short changed little … . But that isn't the worst part. That's not why I'm afraid of the police. He tried to kill me! Yes he did. He put his hands around my throat and I thought my time was up. I managed to break free and ran in here to hide. I was sure he'd come in after me, but he couldn't. He didn't know how. Can you believe it? I was safe. After awhile the police came. They thought he'd killed me. He almost did. They almost had it right. I was afraid he'd try to tell someone where I was. I guess he never did. He must have known people would have thought him crazy if he had. I bided my time until everything had quieted down and then I began to wear him down. I thought I had a right to get back at him for all those years of pain and poking, all those years of ruining our two beautiful children. And then there was the attempted murder thing. 'You've been sinful,' I'd tell him. He was always big on *The*

Bible as long as it didn't interfere with what he wanted to do. "You tried to murder me in cold blood. You have to pay for that!" I'd repeat over and over in a wispy voice like from the beyond. He never could figure out where I was, how I could be there looking at him, taunting him, accusing him, and he not be able to get to me. I think he thought he was losing his mind. Eventually, I talked him into hanging himself as punishment for his ill deeds, right there in front of me. I guess I was worse than he was. That's why I still think the police might figure it all out and come after me. But I shan't come out on my own. Never! They'll have to come in after me and drag me out kicking and screaming."

Jeffrey sat in stunned silence. He had some difficulty dealing with everything he'd just heard. That this total stranger should pour her heart out to him was endearing, and at the same time disturbing. He didn't know what to say.

"Well, that's the whole ugly story, so you can see why I'm so jumpy and afraid," she finished, as she looked at him for some kind of response.

"I'm so sorry for you that you've had to endure such pain. Your husband sounds like he was a most insensitive sort. I can't say I really blame you for your actions, if all you say is true. Perhaps you needn't worry about hiding anymore. When did all this take place?" Jeffrey asked her. He was relating to her pain in a very personal way. He'd suffered his own abuse in silence for years.

"I'm not exactly sure how long it's been. You see time isn't what you might expect here on the inside. Sometimes it seems interminable. Other times I fear weeks may have gone by in the blink of an eye. It's very confusing. Perhaps you should try it for yourself and see what you think. You impress me as just the type of person who would know how to gain entrance. I discovered it years ago. I used to come here sometimes just to get away from everything. I never stayed very long. My husband never knew anything about it until I ran screaming for my life the day he tried to kill me. Now I've been here who knows how long. Do come in for awhile. I'd adore a little company," the woman pleaded. "You won't have to stay if you wish not to. I'm sure you have other things to do more pressing, but do come in and sit with me briefly. I would take great comfort just to have someone hold my hand and tell me everything will be alright."

Jeffrey was suddenly on his feet and standing directly in front of the mirror. He should have been nose to nose with himself, and yet all he could see was this distraught old woman begging him to come to her and offer her a little solace. He put his hands on the surface of the mirror and felt that familiar vibration he'd felt the first time he'd touched it. A slight push brought about a feeling of sponginess and a puckering of the surface causing the reflections of the room, her room, to distort and blur. He pushed a little harder and his hands went through the now permeable material and now he could see his hands on the other side. They were a little blurry but intact and he had normal sensation in both hands. He flexed his fingers. They seemed absolutely normal. He moved forward, and as he did so, the rest of his body slipped through the membrane, or whatever it was, that now was the mirror's surface. He looked down at his hands and feet and they were once again solid and distinct. The woman came toward him and took both his hands in hers. He glanced over his shoulder to see that the mirror now reflected both of them and her inviting room. His sitting room was nowhere to be seen.

"How lovely. I just knew you'd be able to do it. My husband was a total ninny about the whole thing. Sometimes he'd come up to the mirror and pound on the surface with his hands and scream, 'You come out of there you BITCH!' and I'd just laugh and dance around in a circle. He would get livid and his face would get so red I thought he might have a stroke. In fact I had hoped he might have a stroke, then I wouldn't have had to have him hang himself, would I? Come. Sit down. We'll have a nice chat, you and I. I've spilled the beans about me and my life, now I want to hear all about you. You definitely have a tale to tell or you'd never have gotten in here. So, now, tell me about Jeffrey Homes."

They must have talked for hours, or perhaps days. Jeffrey saw what she had meant when she said time wasn't exactly what one might expect on this side of the glass. She was indeed a most fascinating person. How Jeffrey would have loved to have had a mother like this one. He told her everything about himself. She was an avid listener and a wise counselor. Jeffrey couldn't remember when he had enjoyed someone's company so much. He had learned to be a loner. His Mother had always insisted on that and he had complied. Now he felt lighter than he'd ever felt in his life, like a huge weight had been lifted from his rounded shoulders. He even sat up taller in front of her as he unburdened himself.

At some point, when their visit was at its end, and she was ready to retire, he exited the same way he had entered. The light in her sitting room went out and he found himself back in his own sitting room. Everything was just as it had been except for himself. And he would never be the same.

JEFFREY could hardly wait for the next night, hoping for another visit with his new friend. He had awakened that morning with such purpose and, until now, unknown sense of joy. Somehow all the things around him seemed to pale in comparison to this wonderful mirror and its strange inhabitant. He felt suddenly cramped by all the clutter. Why had he stuffed all these things in here?

Perhaps I'll have a yard sale, he thought. *Wouldn't that be a turn of events. Jeffrey Holmes conducting a yard sale?* He'd never parted with anything in his life! It was certainly something to consider.

He was anxious to get to bed that night. He would have another long conversation with his woman of the mirror. He felt she'd been a great addition to his otherwise bleak and lonely existence. He had trouble getting to sleep, so anxious was he to have her make her appearance. Finally he drifted off. As he expected something awakened him during the night, but it was not the familiar humming or the soft tinkling of a piano that had done it. It was an alarming and pitiful sobbing that had jarred him from his slumber. The light was coming in under his door as usual. He arose and went quietly into the sitting room.

There in the mirror was another completely different room and yet another strange person. The room was brightly lit and clothing of different types and sizes was strewn haphazardly about, some on the floor, others spread across an ample sofa against one wall. Directly opposite the mirror's vantage point was a dressing table with another much smaller, much plainer mirror. Seated at the dressing table with her back to Jeffrey and her head in her arms was the source of the sobbing; a young woman in a wedding gown.

Jeffrey watched in silence for awhile before deciding he should probably get the young woman's attention. He cleared his throat.

The young woman's head flew up as she searched for the source of the noise. She must have seen Jeffrey in her dressing mirror, although he saw only the woman's tear and makeup stained face and the reflection of the full length mirror, devoid of him, through which he was peering in at her.

"Who are you? Did my fiancé send you? Maybe one of my friends, my bridesmaids?" she asked, wiping a hand across one cheek, smearing a long swath of mascara under that eye as she did so. The other eye already had a matching smear. She appeared rather raccoon-like and Jeffrey had to bite his tongue to stifle a giggle. Was he now to have a conversation with a cartoon-like raccoon bride? It wasn't what he had been expecting at all.

"No," Jeffrey began. "I wasn't sent by your fiancé or any of your bridesmaids. I don't know who any of them are. I don't even know who you are," he had to admit.

"Then why are you in my room?" she asked.

Déjà vu! "I'm sorry, but I thought this was my room."

"How could it be your room? It's always been my room. And why are you in pajamas? We're supposed to be having a wedding. No one comes to a wedding in pajamas. Do they?" she finished, as if perhaps they might under some bizarre circumstances. Jeffrey had to admit this was becoming a bizarre circumstance, and pondered how he should proceed. Before he could make that decision, the young woman broke out into fresh bursts of sobbing.

"What shall I do? What on earth shall I do?" she asked herself, since Jeffrey hadn't a clue what this was all about yet. "Everyone will be so angry with me. I've probably ruined everything already. And now my dress is ruined on top of everything else. I can't let anyone see me like this. I'm a total mess. What an idiot I am!" she finished as she ripped the veil off her head and threw it in a heap on the floor. She once again noticed Jeffrey and stopped her tears long enough to pose yet another question. "You aren't a friend of that horrid Hollywood producer are you?"

Jeffrey's breath caught in his throat. This was now out of control and he was seeing spots before his eyes. *Could this woman be talking about the same producer I just heard about the past several nights from my new friend, the producer who suddenly stopped coming?* He blinked his eyes to clear the spots. He felt light headed, as if he might faint. The spots would not go away. Instead they solidified and turned a dark maroon. They were still in front of him. They were all over the front of the wedding dress. The bride-to-be now stood directly in front of him and her dress was covered with dark maroon spots, some smeared as if she'd tried to brush them off. Jeffrey thought he might throw up. He had a terrible suspicion about what those maroon stains were, and was afraid to ask, but was compelled to anyway.

"What happened?" the question came tumbling out of his mouth. And the answer came back just as quickly and just as macabre as he had expected.

"It's that horrible Hollywood producer's blood. He blew his brains out right in front of me!"

Once Jeffrey had overcome his urge to hurl, and regained some sense of composure, he thought he could see some inkling of where this was going. At least he thought so.

"Miss, I don't know the producer you're referring to, but I know *of* him. A friend of mine knew him in a sense. She had a number of conversations with him and I gathered they were very disturbing and distressing for her."

"Disturbing and distressing? That's an understatement. The man was a complete ass. He barged in here and began bellyaching about his awful life and all his box office flops. I'm beside myself trying to decide what to do about this wedding and my boyfriend and all the guests sitting, waiting for me to come down the aisle, and here comes this idiot, drunk as a skunk and blaming me and this mirror for all his misfortunes. What a load of crap! Then he has the nerve to blow his brains out all over my wedding dress!" She burst into another fit of sobbing. "What am I going to do?" she pleaded, looking to Jeffrey, standing there in his pajamas, to furnish her with the answer.

Jeffrey thought he just might be able to help, but he needed a little more information first. He would have to precede with caution so as not to further confuse or disorient this poor young woman, who had no idea that her wedding day had long since passed and the mirror into which she had run for refuge was no longer where she thought it was.

"Miss, my name is Jeffrey and I got here quite by accident, but I think I might be able to help you. I'd like to ask you to grab that box of tissues off your dressing table and the chair and come sit here at the mirror while we try to figure things out. Can you do that for me? You'll just have to trust me, even though you haven't a clue who I am. I hope you can do that too," Jeffrey gave her instructions in as calming and supportive tone as he could manage. This was, after all, brand new territory for him.

The blood-splattered bride did as she was bid, and once she'd settled herself in front of the mirror and dried her face sufficiently with handfuls of tissues, Jeffrey began to help her as if he were a licensed therapist. Somehow the right questions came to him.

"Tell me about when you first discovered the secret of this mirror," he began.

"It was on the day my fiancé bought it for me as a wedding present. We'd gone into this really neat antique shop as a lark. I hate antiques. And there was this creepy man who ran the place. He sort of scared me. He had a real creepy look. It made me think of some old movies. You know. Grave robbers. Body snatchers. Vampires. All that stuff. He was dressed in black and looked at the very least like a funeral director. If he'd asked us, 'May I show you our selection of caskets?' I wouldn't have been the least bit surprised. I was just about to suggest we get out of there, when I noticed this tall oval mirror in a dark carved frame and I just had to go look at it. It was the most beautiful thing I'd ever seen. There was just something special about it and it's all I wanted my boyfriend to buy me for a wedding present."

"I know the feeling," Jeffrey interjected. "Go on."

"Once I had it here in my room, I discovered how it vibrated when I touched it. And if I pushed into the glass I could slip into it, you know, sorta like *Alice in Wonderland*, only without all the crazy animals and that demented Queen."

"And what were you feeling at the time you were going into this mirror?" Jeffrey asked next.

"Oh, I was so confused and upset. I was getting married and I didn't know if it was the right thing to do. My parents were so enthusiastic. 'It's high time you settled down young lady,' they said. They thought I'd waited long enough. Lord knows they kept pushing me to wait long enough, then suddenly it was time. But who's time? I wasn't sure I was ready. I didn't know if I was marrying the right person. I was so torn I just pushed my way into this mirror several times just to sit and think, away from everyone. It was so peaceful and quiet. But today, my wedding day, has been the worst. I've been here ever since I came in. I've been trying to decide whether I should go back out now or what, and then this jerk from Hollywood shows up and he's no help whatsoever. He didn't even want to hear me speak. He kept saying, 'Shut up you bimbo bride!' He called me a bimbo bride! 'You ruined my film, you and this stupid mirror. You've ruined my life. My wife is going to leave me and it's all your fault!' he screamed at me. He was so drunk he couldn't even stand up. He sat on the floor and drank even more, right from the bottle. Then he pulled a gun out of his pocket and shot himself in the head! I screamed and screamed and no one came. My dress was red with his blood. And then everything was gone and there I was alone until you showed up. What shall I do? All those people are sitting down there waiting on me and my fiancé must be beside himself by now. I still don't know if I want to marry my boyfriend," she finished with a despondent sigh.

"Let me start by saying this, and don't ask me exactly how I know. It would be very complicated right now to go into detail. You can stop worrying about your wedding guests. They went home a long, long time ago. Wait! Wait! Just let me finish. I'm sure your boyfriend was very upset, but he's also had time to deal with your not showing up by now. You see basically, time in there were you are isn't exactly as you might expect. Sometimes it goes faster, much faster. Sometimes it drags. While you've been thinking that it's been dragging, it flew by. This mirror isn't even any longer where you think it is. Believe me, this mirror is now in my sitting room, which you, unfortunately, can't see. You still see the reflection of your room on your wedding day, but I bought this mirror days ago and nowhere near the place where you were going to be married, and put it in my sitting room. Your sobbing woke me up. Somehow we both know the secret of this mirror, while most people do not. What might be helpful for you is to figure out why you know the secret, when no one else you know does. Maybe we can find out together," Jeffrey suggested.

"You mean my wedding's over?"

"Your wedding never happened. All the guests went home. Your boyfriend took the mirror back to the antique dealer. And I have a very good idea who purchased it next. The Hollywood producer! And after he killed himself, somehow the mirror found it's way back to the same antique dealer, whose name, by the way, is Horace Finnegan, and then I bought it." Jeffrey had pieced the mirror's journey together rather well.

"How very weird and confusing. You mean I've been being shipped around like a piece of freight? And I didn't even know it?" The girl was freaking out.

"Just try to relax. You are just fine and everything will be alright. I think we might be able to fix things up. I have to tell you, and don't let this scare you, but you're not the only one in there being shipped around, even though you've never seen anyone else except me and the producer. There's another woman, a very elderly woman, who also ran in there just as you did in a crisis, and has not come out yet. Only she's been in there longer than you have, I'm sure. She has her own room as you have yours. We've had several long conversations and I think she can help you as well, at least indirectly. I may have to ask some very personal questions of you. I have to say the conversation I had with the other woman in your mirror were most embarrassing, but extremely productive. What do you think?"

"Well, if what you say is true, and my wedding day's long gone, and I'm who knows where now, I guess I might as well play along. You seem very nice, so let's do it." She made the right decision.

"I think primarily we have to look into why you felt it necessary to take refuge in there at the very time your guests and your fiancé were waiting for you to make your entrance and the ceremony to begin. You were already in your wedding gown. You were just minutes from becoming a bride. Why did you flee at that critical moment?" Jeffrey asked as he held her gaze through the mirrored glass. It really was a most disconcerting phenomenon not to see himself in the glass, rather just this young woman in a blood spattered wedding gown sitting there staring back at him. He hoped this little session would be as therapeutic for her as his had been with the wonderful old woman, now still in there somewhere, in another room or space in time.

"I was suddenly scared to death," the girl blurted out. "I like this man, my boyfriend, but I don't really know him. I mean the wedding, after, all that, I wasn't sure I could go through with it. What if it was awful? My parents made it all seem so sordid for so long. They made me see the priest for instruction so many times. All the things nice girls just didn't do were made to seem so sinful, degrading, and then suddenly it was time to get on with my life and do the very things I'd been taught weren't nice. It was very frightening and I just lost it. I heard the priest's voice in my ear, 'You must not endanger your immortal soul, my dear. Carnal knowledge with someone to whom you have not been committed by God is a grievous sin.' My father was always so overbearing and insistent as I got older. 'I hope you are still a virgin. No man wants to have anything to do with a girl who would come to his marriage bed damaged. I can tell you what they call them. Sluts, that's what!' And mom wasn't much help either. When I first got my "friendly visitor" as she called it, she said, 'This is all very normal, if annoying and embarrassing, but it's part of this life. You'll have to deal with it just as every young woman has to. Now that it's started the boys will be drawn to you. You'll have to be constantly on your guard that you never let any of them near your private parts until after you're married. And that won't be for quite a long time yet. You have quite a battle in front of you, just as I had.' For something that she said was normal, it didn't seem normal to me at all. When I stopped to really think about what was going to happen after the wedding, I panicked. It all seemed suddenly wrong. Then I heard mother's constant lament in my ears over and over.

'I've put up with your father's infernal demands all my life. It's something you have to do. It's an awful price to pay for my precious children, but I did it for you.' I don't know if I can do that. She never seemed happy to me, and yet all she would ever say was that all she wanted was for me to be happy. Isn't that sad?" Tears began anew as the girl thought about how unhappy her mother had always been.

"I'm not physic by any means, but I thought the problem just might be something along those lines. I've had to deal with such things as well, but that's of no consequence here and now. What is important is that it may not be too late to remedy it all. I don't know your boyfriend or how serious he was about you, but if he was about to walk down the aisle and you hadn't gotten to know him in any physical way, I'd say he was very serious. I'm very surprised to hear a story like yours in this day and age. I think it's rare. I can relate to everything your parents and your priest put you through. But a friend of mine told me never to buy a pig in a poke," Jeffrey told her with a wink.

"What's a poke? Why would I want to buy a pig?" The bride didn't get the metaphor.

"I mean don't buy a piece of equipment without testing it out first. It may not perform well. You may be very dissatisfied with it. My friend did just that and it caused her a lifetime of pain and distress." Jeffrey tried another oblique approach. He wasn't all that comfortable with such matters either.

"But I don't want to buy any equipment. And if I did, and it wasn't right, I'd march right back there and return it for a full refund or else. My mother was very good at that," she insisted, still missing the point.

"I'm talking about your boyfriend. His equipment. You know. What you were so petrified of after the wedding was over and you had to, as your mother put it, 'deal with it.' She said she'd been dealing with you father and his equipment all her married life. And was very unhappy about it. That's why you fled into that mirror, wasn't it?" Jeffrey was sure she got the picture now, without using words he'd never used before; words he'd been warned would bring about severe punishment if he were to use them.

A sudden intake of breath from the girl in the mirror let him know he had hit the mark this time. She put both hands up to her cheeks and shook her head side to side, tears dried, eyes wide.

"Oh, you're absolutely right. But I can't do that! I mustn't. I'll be a slut, just like my father warned. My fiancé won't want me then. I'll be damaged goods. I might have to go into a convent and become a nun. Will convents take sluts?" she asked, as if Jeffrey would certainly know. This poor girl had definitely led a sheltered life. But then who was he to judge. He'd been a hot house plant himself.

"I'm sure nothing so drastic will be necessary. But, if I were you, and the therapist is not supposed to give specific advice, but then I'm not a therapist, I'd seriously consider revisiting the scene of your wedding, and giving your boyfriend's equipment a test drive." *I can't believe I just said that!* "I can't say how much time has passed since that day, but if he's still unattached, hasn't moved on without you, you might just have that wedding after all. If, for some reason, the love you felt for each other doesn't translate well to the physical, then at least you will know for sure. You will not have to enter a convent. You will not have any difficulty finding a replacement. You will not be required to wear a big red "A." That particular punishment is obsolete, thank goodness. There will be someone for you without doubt. You are much too pretty to languish away as an Old Maid. Contrary to your parent's views, you will still be very much sought after."

The girl turned a bright red at Jeffery's complement. But she still had a confused look in her eyes.

"Why would I have to wear a big 'A'?" she asked.

"It was something from long ago. A Puritan thing. Our strict religious ancestors thought it appropriate for anyone who tested out equipment when not married to it. The "A" stands for Adultery, and it's all tastefully described in *The Scarlet Letter* by Nathaniel Hawthorne," Jeffrey explained.

"Oh. I never read it."

"I'm not surprised. I'd never have read it either if I hadn't had some very good teachers in school. As it was, I had to sneak around to get through it. My Mother would have burned it, had she ever found it. Seems you aren't the only one who had some rough times growing up." Jeffrey let her know she had not been alone.

"I was sent to a private school. I'm sure they would never have allowed anything like that to be read in any of my classes." She took a great gasping breath. "You've been very kind and a little confusing for me. But, I think I'll give everything you've said some serious consideration. I guess I can't stay in here forever. At least I don't think I want to do that. I'm so very tired and I don't think I have another tear left. I need to get some rest. Thank you so much, Jeffrey, for all your help. I'm going to have a nice nap and sort all this out later, when I wake up." She went into another room, turning out the lights as she left.

Jeffrey was once more sitting in front of his mirror in his pajamas, staring at himself and the reflection of his own sitting room.

IN THE MORNING, Jeffrey could hardly believe the night before. Had he done the right thing? Who was he to dare give advice to a complete stranger and under such weird circumstances? He hoped to visit again with the old woman. He was anxious to let her know what he'd learned about the strange refuge in which she now resided. He would have to get through the day somehow. So far, the mirror seemed only to function in the middle of the night.

Should he go and see Mr. Finnegan? Tell him about what was happening with the mirror? Probably not a good idea. He would only think him deranged. Better to wait awhile and see what happened next.

The middle of the night couldn't come soon enough for Jeffrey. But it was not at all what he had expected or hoped for. Instead of humming, soft piano music, or distraught sobbing, he heard distant laughter. It wasn't a mirthful laughter. It was a familiar laughter. His skin prickled as he recognized his Mother's laughter. It was that teasing laughter she'd always used to taunt him. A laughter that said, 'I know something that you don't, and I'll never tell.' He had always hated it when she did that. Something particularly degrading or embarrassing had usually followed.

The light was coming in under his door, but he didn't really want to get up and open it. He didn't want to see what might be reflected from the mirror tonight. He heard a door open and shut. The laughter became louder. She was probably in the room that he would see reflected back at him now. He remained immobile. He held his breath. Maybe she would go away, although he knew she wouldn't. She never had before. She'd always been relentless, why should she be any different now, even if she was dead.

The laughter stopped. Maybe she had changed. She had gone away. She couldn't do this to him anymore. She was dead! Then he heard that sound! His Mother's foot. STOMP!! Once she stomped her foot, all hell broke lose.

"Jeffrey? I know you're in there. Don't hold your breath. It doesn't fool me one bit. You'll just pass out and kill a few more brain cells. Lord knows you can't afford that. You've barely got enough as it is. Too bad you got more of your Father in you than me. No wonder you're such a loser. Jeffery? What are you doing? I know what you're doing! Are you touching yourself again? How many times do I have to tell you not to do that?! You'll burn in Hell for sure. See if you don't. Don't make me come in there and tie your hands behind your back young man!" His Mother was on a roll.

"Go away Mother! You're dead!" Jeffrey countered.

"Dead am I? We'll see about that. Don't make me come in there. You'll be very sorry if you do." It wasn't an idle threat. She'd had the lock removed from his door in order to gain surprise entrance whenever she felt it necessary. And many were the times he'd fallen asleep with his hands tied behind his back. She couldn't do that any more, could she? After all she was dead, and he was a grown man, even if she never ever thought so. Jeffrey waited for the door to fly open. Waited to feel the rough bindings being tightly wound around his wrists. The door remained closed.

"Jeffrey! Do you hear me? Answer me this instant!" she screeched.

"Go away Mother. I'm sleeping. Don't you dare come in here," Jeffrey threw out the challenge, hoping she would not take him up on it. The door remained closed. He heard some rapid footsteps and the slamming of a door. Then silence.

"Mother?" he called softly. Then, "Mother?" more loudly. He received no answer, only the normal creaking of the old house his Mother had left him. He did not like what had just happened one bit. How had his Mother gotten in there? She'd never purchased the mirror. She'd been dead for twenty years. She couldn't have sought refuge as the other two woman had. What new wrinkle was the mirror showing him now?

Jeffrey had great difficulty getting back to sleep. Nothing more came from the adjoining room. Where were his two newly acquired friends now?

No amount of conjuring produced them. Apparently the mirror was not subject to summoning. Where was his Mother, and what was she planning now? Jeffrey lay in dread of just what that might be.

𝒥𝔼𝔉𝔉𝓡𝔼𝒴 faced the next night with the mirror with great trepidation. He went to bed late. He read for hours, putting off the inevitable moment when he would no longer be able to fight the urge to close his eyes and sleep. That moment crept up on him without warning as his eyelids drooped shut and the book he had been reading slid off his lap onto the bed next to him.

He was awakened by soft, lilting piano music and a voice he was thrilled to hear. The old woman was in her bedroom playing and singing surprisingly well a tune which Jeffrey immediately recognized. Though the voice was not Celine Dion, the song was *My Heart Will Go On.* Jeffrey sprang from his bed and threw open his bedroom door so forcefully that it banged loudly against the wall.

"Heavens! Jeffrey, is that you?" the old woman called out as the music and singing stopped and she rushed out of her bedroom into the light of her sitting room. "What a noise! What happened? My. You look awful," she noted as she approach the mirror and saw how distressed Jeffrey looked and the dark circles under his eyes.

"I'm so relieved to see you. I must come and talk with you. I've learned some very disturbing things," Jeffrey informed her as he rushed toward her.

"Of course, you may come in, but what has happened so quickly? You've hardly left. I woke up shortly after our last talk, couldn't sleep, came out here to read for a bit. I was just entertaining myself before going back to bed when I heard that thud." Indeed, she was still in her apricot dressing gown with the angora trim.

"I'm, afraid it's been several days since I left you here on the outside. I've learned some very enlightening news and some very disheartening." Jeffrey quickly filled her in on the fate of the Hollywood producer and his impact on the bride-to-be, who was unknowingly sharing the mirror's quarters. He imparted the news about his Mother last.

"Jeffrey that's absolutely dreadful. I'm very uncomfortable sharing space with a dead woman. And a very distasteful one at that. She has no right to pursue you from the grave. How on earth did she ever get in here? What is she up to? What is the mirror doing anyway? I guess I don't know everything about this amazing thing, whatever it is. I'd sure like to find out, but I haven't a clue how to do that. How awful for that poor bride. To be splattered with blood all over your wedding gown just as you're about to go down the aisle, and in such a violent and senseless way. I do feel for her. I'm very sorry to hear about the producer as well, even though he was self-absorbed and a drunk. This mirror must have bewitched him somehow. How tragic for his wife. What she must have felt when she discovered him sitting there in front of the mirror with half his head gone and his brains scattered around the room. But worst of all, that unfortunate bride, to witness it first hand. And to have his blood and brains come right through the mirror all over her wedding gown, it's a wonder she didn't lose her mind! Whatever can I do to help?" she asked as she put her hand supportively on Jeffrey's shoulder.

"I think you already have helped. I used some of the advice you gave me to help that confused girl decide what she should do next. I hope I did the right thing. I've never done anything like that in my life before. But, she seemed calmer and assured me she was going to give it all some consideration. I'm hoping she will come out of there and return to her fiancé to give it all another chance," Jeffrey confessed.

"Wouldn't that be wonderful," the old woman agreed. "But what about your Mother?"

"I haven't a clue," Jeffrey had to admit. "I'm not sure there's anything I can do about her. But one thing I'm pretty sure of. And that is, that now that she's in there, she can't get out. I dared her to come into my room last night and she couldn't. She was furious, I could tell, and there's no stopping Mother when her ire is up. But, I think she was powerless inside there. I don't know why or how she went in, but now that she's there, I think she'll regret it," Jeffrey espoused, hoping against hope that he wasn't wrong.

JEFFREY continued to hold out the hope that his Mother was imprisoned in her new home, that whatever her plans had been, they had backfired on her. Though she might invade his space from within her prison, she would not be gaining access to the house that she had left him. She did indeed invade from within her prison the next night in the wee hours.

"Jeffrey! Wake up, you miserable twit!" awakened him with a start. "Come out here and face me, you insufferable little coward. Just like your Father. Run from everything. Avoid confrontation. About as much backbone as a jellyfish! And don't you dare be playing with your tally whacker again tonight. It's a wonder it hasn't fallen off by now. Lord knows I tried to break you of the habit. You got that from your Father too. Always sneaking off to the bathroom. I knew what he was doing in there, but better that than

bothering me with it. Jeffrey! Come out here this instant!"
She was really getting angry.

"Mother, I'm not playing with my tally whacker. I'm
trying to get some much needed sleep. Go away and leave
me alone!" Jeffrey all but shouted at her.

"I'm not going anywhere until you come out here and
confront me face to face. I can keep you up all night if I
have to. I've done it before. You know I have. Is that what
you want?"

*Oh God. She's going to mount one of her midnight
marathons,* Jeffrey thought to himself. He groaned inwardly
as he reluctantly dragged himself out of bed and made his
was slowly to the door. What was she going to look like?
Would he be confronted with some horrible, decomposing,
casket-escaped monstrosity? Perhaps the sooner he got this
over with, the sooner she would leave him alone. He opened
the door and there was his Mother, with her nose pressed
up against the inside of the glass. She looked her normal
self, as she did just before she'd died, except now her nose
was flared out on the glass by her pressing against it, giving
her the appearance of Miss Piggy. All he could think about
was "A Pig In A Poke." He began laughing uncontrollably.
He couldn't stop. He'd never seen his Mother in such a
ridiculous light and it was just a Kodak moment! She
stepped back from the mirror, her nose regaining its normal
proportions, but Jeffrey still could not stop laughing. Tears
were beginning to roll down his cheeks and his stomach
hurt.

"Jeffrey Holmes! You stop that irreverent laughter this
minute! You ungrateful little lout. What on earth do you
find so amusing?" and she stomped her foot.

Even though Jeffrey knew she couldn't do anything following the warning stomp, he ceased his laughter and wiped his face. She wasn't such a fearsome spirit after all. Actually she looked rather frail and pathetic standing there in the reflection of his sitting room. She certainly had stored a lot of verbal invective, but perhaps that was all that was left of her.

"Here I am Mother. What do you want?"

"Come closer. Let me get a good look at you. Turn on some lights. It's dark in here," she complained.

"Yes, well, you always did like things in shadow. Never more than one light on in one room at any time. What a penny pincher," Jeffrey now taunted her.

"You watch your mouth young man. Remember who you're talking to. When you pay the bills, you can do as you like. When you're in my house, you follow my rules." She thought she was laying down the law.

"But Mother, I do pay the bills, and I will do as I please. You seem to have forgotten that you're dead."

"How dare you speak to your dead Mother in that tone of voice!" she spat back, trying to regain her sense of control and dignity. "Step up here. Let me see how my wasteful son turned out." Jeffrey stepped in front of the mirror, but outside arm's reach, just in case. His Mother looked him over from top to bottom.

"Turn around. Slowly." He did so hoping to avoid any further nasty outbursts. "You're quite a disappointment, Jeffrey. None of that my fault. You've got your Father's weak eyes and stooped shoulders, although you don't seem quite as bent as I remember. Get a more flattering pair of glasses and a hairpiece. Lord knows you can afford a good one, instead of all this crap you've filled my house with. You ought to get more exercise. You're getting very pudgy, just like your Father. What a lard ass he turned out to be! It's not attractive Jeffrey. And Lord knows you're unattractive enough as it is. Get out of my sight. Go back to bed! Play with your dirty old tally whacker for all I care." And she turned abruptly and went into Jeffrey's bedroom. Jeffrey rushed into his room, but of course, she wasn't in there. She was in Jeffrey's other bedroom. The one in the mirror. For all Jeffrey cared, she could stay there forever.

GLORIOUS morning sunshine was streaming into Jeffrey's bedroom window before he ever stirred. Memories of the previous night's confrontation with his dead Mother were still fresh. They had not faded like some dream, gone almost the moment one opens one's eyes. This was quite different. This was something solid, no dream. The only questions in his mind now were how and why? How could a dead person do what, as far as he'd been able to ascertain, only living ones had done? And what could have been her reason for going in there in the first place? Was it just for a new vantage point from which to torment him? Hadn't she tormented him enough before she'd died? Jeffrey was certain he would find out whether he really wanted to or not.

He would have to get through today and see what tonight might bring. He hadn't anything particular to do until he walked outside and saw that the first blush of spring had arrived. The beds he'd recently cleaned out were loaded with new growth, many clumps of perennials already had flower spikes and the bulbs had buds ready to pop as well. He had a sudden urge to get his hands in the dirt. He made a most unusual trip for him. He went to a local nursery and loaded up his car with flats of bedding plants. His Mother had always filled the bare spots in between her perennials with dozens of bedding plants. He didn't know what had sparked his desire to have some instant color in what had been his Mother pride and joy. He should have rather wanted to pour gasoline on everything his Mother had worked to maintain and set it alight. She had had more interest in her garden than she'd ever had in him or his Father.

Her recent taunts about him being lazy, wasteful, and ungrateful had stung as much as ever, but perhaps she had been right. He never had helped out doing anything growing up. He certainly had never had any appreciation for money. He had always been able to spend what he wanted. It wasn't important where it came from. And he never ever said Thank You. True, his Mother put him through hell with her warped sense of right and wrong, do's and don'ts. Some of the punishments for infractions had been painful and degrading, but she believed she was doing what was best for him. Too bad what was best for him had cost him a normal life. The old woman had been appalled when he related some of his Mother's worst methods to her.

"Wounds like that go deep and take ever so long to heal," she'd said. "But you still have a lot of life ahead of you. You must find a way to let all that go and start over. I know you can do that." Why she had such confidence in him, he had no idea. But today, planting all these beautiful flowering plants, he thought, might be a step in the right direction.

He worked throughout the day, and by late afternoon the transformation was amazing. Not only did the house look a lot better, he felt a lot better. He was just finishing a late lunch when the doorbell rang. He couldn't remember the last time his doorbell had rung. No one ever came to his house. Neighborhood children avoided it like the plague. Mailmen just left their bills and departed. Whoever it was probably had the wrong address.

He opened the door to see a rather plain woman of indeterminate age, certainly not young, perhaps his age, carrying a satchel and smiling at him as if she knew him. Her hair was limp and hung down to her shoulders. A little grey here and there. She was very conservatively dressed with sensible walking shoes.

"Can I help you?" Jeffrey asked

"Good afternoon, sir. My name is Penny Loudon and I would like to have the opportunity of introducing you to a great array of personal care and beauty products..." but she didn't get any further before Jeffrey stopped her.

"I'm sorry. My Mother has passed on and I'm not married, so there really isn't any reason for you to waste your valuable time here." He was going to close the door in her face when she smiled even broader and continued on as if he hadn't said a word.

"Oh, but these products aren't just for women. We have loads of wonderful things just for men. I have dozens of male customers, some married, others not, but they all love these products. I wish you'd at least give me the chance to show you some of the things I know you'd really like." Jeffrey was temporarily stunned. She wanted to come into his house and try to sell him products she said were just for men. Jeffrey had never had anyone try to sell him anything special just for him. He bought shaving cream and aftershave at the market, that was it. Selling shaving cream and aftershave door to door seemed odd. But there was something about that radiant smile on that plain face that caught his attention.

"Very well. But I don't have a lot of time. I want to get the rest of these plants in the ground this afternoon," he told her as he held the door open and led her down the hallway to the kitchen where his lunch dishes were still on the table.

"Oh, I'm so very sorry. I didn't mean to disturb your lunch. I thought it was late enough people would have finished lunch by now," she apologized.

"It's perfectly alright. I had just finished. I just haven't cleared the table yet. I was about to have a second glass of iced tea. Would you like some?" Jeffrey wasn't sure why he felt so at ease. Normally, he would never have let this person into the house, let alone offer her a glass of iced tea.

"Yes. Thank you. That would be very nice," she accepted. Soon they were both sitting at the kitchen table drinking tea and talking as if they knew one another.

"I couldn't help but notice the beautiful gardens around your house. I passed by here several days ago and everything looked rather dead and bedraggled. You have accomplished a great deal in a short time." She drank more of her tea as she opened her satchel and began to spread products and information in front of him. "I'll just put out the things I think will interest you. You don't need to look at any of the other things unless you want to. You can just sort of look through those while I set out a few other samples so you can see first hand what's available." Then she continued to pull small bottles and tubes from side pockets in her satchel, setting them in a row along one side of the table.

Before Jeffrey knew it, he'd agreed to purchase two out of three of the care products for men that Penny had spread out on his kitchen table. He'd never considered anything like that in the past. His buying habits had always been limited to household items and furnishings.

"I think I have all these items at home. They're so popular that I try to keep some in stock. I could probably deliver them tomorrow, if that's alright with you, Mr. Holmes," she informed Jeffrey, as she packed everything back into her carry case.

"Please. Just call me Jeffrey. No one calls me Mr. Homes. And tomorrow would be just fine with me." Indeed, no one did call him Mr. Holmes. He never went anywhere for anyone to call him anything, except his forages into the used goods trade. Most of those people knew who he was, but seldom called him by name. They gladly accepted his money, but his name was of no importance to them.

"OK, Jeffrey. I'll see you tomorrow then." And she was gone.

Jeffrey finished planting the last of his bedding plants, thinking all the while of Penny, and how nice she'd been, and how much he'd liked having her at his kitchen table sharing a glass of iced tea.

He got himself ready for bed feeling light and expectant, but without a thought of the mirror in the next room. Not tonight. He had other things on his mind. Penny. After she'd left, he'd gotten all his gardening done and he'd fixed himself a light supper, he began to survey the house in which he lived, and its contents, from a new prospective. As he walked from room to room visually picking out some of his favorite things, he mentally asked himself again, why he had crammed his house so full of so much stuff that quickly lost the attraction that had precipitated his buying it in the first place. All these things that initially had so excited him, sooner or later paled and left him relatively cold and unfulfilled. Then he'd be off looking for yet one more thing to rekindle that spark of excitement. The excitement never translated into contentment. That was what was missing.

He was annoyed when he was awakened in the middle of the night by light coming in under his door and dry croaking sobs. It wasn't the older woman. She was most upbeat and positive. It wasn't the young woman. The sound was much older, much more desperate and somehow familiar. It was his Mother. He'd heard that sobbing before. A long, long time ago, when he'd been small. He'd heard it after his Mother had just done something to hurt him or degrade him, and it had disturbed him greatly. But he had never known what to do about it. He suffered his punishment or degradation in silence, convinced at the time he must have been extremely wayward and bad to have received such treatment.

Jeffrey listened in silence to his Mother's dry sobs. Then they stopped. He heard footsteps. Then the door to his bedroom, the mirror's bedroom, closed and he went back to sleep.

He awoke with great anticipation the following morning. Penny was going to bring him a dozen care products for men. He was going to take care of his borderline middle-aged skin that she'd warned him was just as vulnerable, if not more so than a woman's skin, to dryness and aging.

"If you don't take care of it now, it will be too late once you reach retirement age, or thereabout. And you have many years to go before you get there."

He was going to use several products on his hair. One would help regrow some of the hair he'd lost. She said he should have started using something years ago. He would never have the full head of hair he might have had if he'd thought about taking care of the problem earlier, but he would regain some of it. He was going to moisturize and volumize what hair he had, so it would appear fuller and thicker.

He'd chosen several scents for men that Penny had recommended. They were earthy and masculine, not the flowery, perfumey kind that women wore. She guaranteed people would notice him and be attracted by the aroma. Something about pheromones, which she said were very important if one wanted to be noticed. Jeffrey had never particularly wanted to be noticed, but Penny made being noticed sound a little exciting. He would feel like a new man she'd assured him. Suddenly, feeling like a new man seemed an excellent idea.

He waited for her outside. He spent hours admiring yesterday's accomplishments in the garden. Penny was right. The house had never looked so good. In fact it would look even better with a fresh coat of paint. Maybe he'd change the colors. The present ones were very faded and peeling. Maybe he'd even do it himself. It would get him out of the house and all those things vying for his attention. An attention that was waning rapidly for some unknown reason.

Then her car drove up and she was carrying a large shopping bag up the walk. He ushered her into the kitchen once more and offered her a glass of tea as she removed each item he'd purchased, going over what it was and how to use it again. She provided him with written instructions as well. He paid his bill and was showing her back to her car when he suddenly had an outrageous idea.

"Would you like to have dinner with me?"

"Excuse me? What?" She was obviously taken off guard.

"Would you like to have dinner with me?" Jeffrey repeated. "I almost never go out and tonight I feel like going out. It wouldn't be much of a night out if I went to dinner alone. We could go into the city for a celebratory dinner. The prospective new me! I know a really great place my Mother used to go to, if it's still there." Jeffrey looked at her, waiting for the inevitable, "Thank you, but no." Why would this woman want to go out to dinner with a loser like him? She was just a saleswoman, after all. She'd made her pitch, reeled him in, and collected her money. Now she could drive away, having achieved her goal.

"Why, yes. Thank you. That would be very nice." He couldn't believe his ears. Had she said yes? She had said yes! She was going to dinner with him. He had a hundred things to do before then. She said he could pick her up at the address on her business card and they agreed on 8 p.m.

Jeffrey rushed into the house to try and find the number for that restaurant his Mother had always gone to when she was down. It was very expensive, but she had always insisted on quality and ambiance, whatever that was. Ambiance wasn't something Jeffrey had ever been concerned about. But tonight ambiance seemed appropriate. And expense, of course, was of no concern. He made reservations and went to get ready.

He took all his new products to his bathroom and used every one, carefully following all the directions. After he'd finished his shave and shower, done more with his hair than he'd done in years, moisturized his skin, and used a light application of the alluring pheromones, he carefully selected his attire for the evening.

As he stood in his underwear in front of his more than ample closet, he realized everything in there was old and out of date, and hadn't been cleaned or worn in ages. He'd look like an old bum with nice hair and good skin, smelling of pheromones. They probably wouldn't even let him in the restaurant. Now what could he do?

He looked at the clock and saw he had little time to decide. If he were lucky, he'd just have time to dash to a clothing store and have them dress him head to toe. He didn't have any other options. Either go looking like a street person, or risk being a tad late picking Penny up by buying a whole new outfit. He rushed to the clothing store.

The salesman was most helpful, once Jeffrey had explained his predicament, and walked him quickly through an off-the-rack fitting of shirt, tie, trousers, sport coat, as well as a new pair of shoes. When Jeffrey looked at himself in the fitting mirror, he hardly recognized the man looking back at him. He still needed a really good hairpiece. He didn't like bald anymore. And a more becoming pair of glasses would be next on his agenda, if not contacts. All in all though, he didn't think he'd have any difficulty keeping his reservations at the restaurant with Penny.

They were only five minutes late arriving. Their table was off to one side at a window with a great view of the city skyline. The appointments were tantamount to one of Mr. Finnegan's recreations at Lost & Found. Candles glowed softly in the center of exquisitely arranged and fragrant flowers. No wonder his Mother liked coming here.

Penny also glowed in the candlelight. She'd pinned her hair up and it also reflected the candle glow. She wore very little makeup, but was adept at highlighting what nature had given her, making her look much more attractive than she had as she rang his bell just yesterday.

The dinner was suburb, the service impeccable. They dined leisurely, getting to know each other and enjoying each other's company. Jeffrey didn't know where his composure and self confidence was coming from, but was grateful that it had come from somewhere. He'd pictured himself stammering, sweating, dropping his silverware, spilling his food, making a complete fool of himself. But he was relaxed and doing none of those things. When they had finished dinner, he didn't want the evening to end.

"I've enjoyed this evening so much, I don't want to end it so soon. Would you like to have a nightcap and continue our conversation a little while longer?" Jeffrey posed, knowing that now she would surely be ready to go home.

"I think that's a great idea," he heard her say.

There was a lounge just across the street from the restaurant, another place he'd heard his Mother talk about. It was very high class, with soft piano music and an excellent female singer, who sang nothing but old classics, one of which he recognized as one the old woman in the mirror had been playing on the piano prior to one of his visits after discovering it's miraculous properties.

They laughed and talked like they were old friends. Before they knew it, it was closing time. Jeffrey hadn't been out this late in his entire life. Penny had to confess that she hadn't either. Jeffrey was very pleased with himself when he dropped Penny off at her address. He was bold enough to hope he'd see her again, and she had said definitely.

He was elated, exhausted, and ready for bed when he entered his sitting room. He was not thinking of, or prepared for, the outburst that greeted him.

"There you are, you thoughtless imbecile! Where have you been? What time is it? I've been calling you for hours. How dare you ignore me! What cheek, staying out to all hours, worrying me to death!" His Mother stood squarely in the mirror's frame when Jeffrey switched on the light. He didn't need this right now.

"I've been out to dinner Mother. Can't I go out to dinner without your approval?"

"It's a little late to be coming in from dinner isn't it? I don't know exactly what time it is, but it has to be later than dinner. Your clocks don't work very well anymore, Jeffrey," she rebuked him.

"My clocks work just fine Mother. It's the clocks where you are that are out of kilter. Things are a little different in there. I'm sure you've noticed a few oddities." He wasn't about to let her get him rattled tonight.

"What are you wearing? You look like a magazine ad. You're too old for such foolishness, Jeffrey. And you smell like you've been in the woods. What is that?"

"I bought some new clothes, Mother. And I also bought some personal care products for men," he informed her.

"You horrid little toad!" she shouted. "Buying those disgusting products for men. Lubricants and creams for dirty minds and dirty purposes. I thought I'd taught you better than that!" she spat.

"There's nothing dirty about it, Mother. They're just to make your hair look better and help your skin from drying out and falling off."

"Why would you ever think about those things?"

"Someone came by selling those products and I thought I'd try some, that's all," he explained.

"And why would you get all dressed up in new clothes to got out and eat?" she asked, suspiciously.

"I had a date."

Silence. She looked at him in silence. She opened her mouth to say something and shut it again. Nothing came out. For the first time in his life Jeffrey saw his Mother speechless.

"Why would anyone want to go out with you?" she asked, when she finally found her voice.

"I don't know, Mother. But they did, and we had a wonderful evening. Dinner at your favorite restaurant and then drinks and conversation across the street at the little lounge you always talked about."

His Mother just stared at him in disbelief. A few tears welled in the corners of her eyes, and began to run down her withered cheeks as she turned and slowly went into the bedroom without further comment.

What a strange reaction, Jeffrey thought. He was much too tired to think about any of that now. He undressed, slipped into bed, and slept dreamlessly until morning.

For the next few weeks, Jeffrey's life was like nothing he'd ever experienced before. His relationship with Penny Loudon grew, and he all but forgot about his previous obsession with acquiring more and more possessions with which to cram his house, as well the mirror, that remained silent and as normal as any mirror might be. That would soon change.

Penny visited the house whenever she could. They learned a great deal about each other and it only served to deepen their interest in the other. Penny found Jeffrey's house intriguing, imposing and a bit bewildering. She went from room to room, examining all Jeffrey's "treasures," asking questions about many of them, to which Jeffrey found he had no answers. He had long ago forgotten some of his purchases. He hadn't a clue where he'd gotten it, or what significance it might once have had. She found some things which she thought fantastic, others quite bizarre.

It was inevitable that eventually she would discover the mirror. She stood in front of it, looking it over with some interest before giving her opinion on the piece.

"This is truly an imposing piece of work," she began. "But, there's also something sinister about it. I can't put my finger on it, but I don't much care for it. It reminds me of something from *Snow White*. You know, 'Mirror, mirror.' Except this one isn't on the wall. This one has feet and it's on wheels. Guess you'd have to change things a little. Maybe, 'Mirror, mirror, that rolls on claws, who's the beauty without flaws?' Something like that. What do you think?"

"I think you're enchanting," popped out of his mouth before he could stop it. Penny blushed a deep red.

"Sit down," she ordered him as she recovered. "I want to ask you something." They both sat down and once they were settled, she looked directly into his eyes and asked, "Why have you filled your house with all these things? Everything bunched so close together you can hardly tell one from the other. I've never seen anything like it in my life." She continued to stare at him, waiting for Jeffrey's response. Jeffrey pondered the question he'd asked himself many times, trying to come up with the definitive answer.

"I was searching for something," he began. "Something that gave me pleasure. Something that made me happy. Each and everything in here did for awhile. But they were just things and they gave nothing back. Soon I was out searching for the next thing, which in time would join all the rest in failing to provide what I was looking for. But I think I've discovered my mistake. I've think I've found the answer. What the search was all about."

"And what would that be," Penny enquired.

"You," Jeffrey said, simply. What followed was a blur for both of them. A kiss. An embrace. Suddenly they were in Jeffrey's bedroom. Clothes were on the floor. They were on the bed. Their union was quick and passionate. And as they faced each other when it was completed, it was with great joy and fulfillment. The second time was much slower with deliberation. Each exploring every part of the other's body and finding it pleasing. No pig in a poke here. This poke was torn open, ripped apart, and no pig was secretly hidden within. Everything revealed was to the other's liking.

When Penny left Jeffrey's house that afternoon, they both knew their lives would never be the same. Jeffrey began to entertain all the ways in which he would change his life, and Penny's. A future he'd never considered was now a distinct possibility. In fact, there were limitless possibilities. He went to bed with all of them swimming in his head.

"Jeffrey, you filthy boy! What have you done? I know what you've done!" His Mother's strident voice awakened him. He definitely did not want to see her tonight. She'd been silent for so long, he had just about convinced himself that she had gone for good. Apparently, he had been wrong. He got up and trudged reluctantly into the sitting room to find his Mother standing there with her face close to the mirror. She wasn't pressed against it. No piggy face tonight. Nothing to engender so much as weak smile.

"Good evening, Mother. It's nice to see you again, too," he said, calmly.

"Don't be sarcastic! It's not becoming. You've been very wicked. You've disregarded everything I sought so hard to teach you. You've thrown it all back in my face, so sinful and evil you've been. Don't think I don't know what you've been up to. You've rutted with that street tart! You let your baser nature completely control you. Vile actions were the only possible outcome! I warned you about all that. How many times did I warn you about that?" she continued to berate him.

"I've lost track of the times, Mother. But here's the thing. There's nothing vile about what I've done. It's perfectly natural and I'm glad I did it. It has changed my life. For your information, I intend to marry Penny Loudon. She is a wonderful and respectable woman and we deserve to have some happiness together before we're as withered and misguided as you were before you died, and remain to this instant. I insist you leave us alone. I can divest myself of this mirror with you in it, if I have to." Jeffrey let his speech take hold, watching his Mother's reaction.

She suddenly sat down and appeared to implode, so small and insignificant she became. Her head in her hands, her shoulders began to shake. The dry sobbing that Jeffrey had heard so many times before commenced. He let her be. There was nothing he could do. He couldn't go to her, put his arms around her shoulders and tell her everything would be alright. The mirror wouldn't let him into his own sitting room as it had into the others. And apparently it wasn't going to let his Mother out.

Why did she go in there in the first place?

"I had to check on my boy," his Mother said, as if she'd heard his silent question. "I had to see that you were alright. I tried so hard to keep you safe. Your Father didn't give a damn about anyone but himself. He was all about the money. He'd have bankrupted us if I'd let him. And you? Well, you were an unfortunate annoyance. He'd have been just as thrilled if you'd never happened. Lord knows I tried to avoid it. But, there you were and I had to protect you from a wicked and depraved world, that eats people up and spits them out like so much road kill. And I had to make sure you'd be taken care. You and I, both of us. We'd have gone to the poorhouse sure as anything if I hadn't intervened. Your Father was a sick man, Jeffrey. And his sickness was money. Why he always needed more and more was beyond me. He started gambling to get more quick. How he loved a "Double or Nothing!" Instead he began losing. It made him nasty and angry. It made him gamble even more. I swear, it would have killed him, if I hadn't killed him first."

"But dad died of a heart attack," Jeffrey reminded her. He'd witnessed his Father's collapse and being rushed to the hospital. He'd seen the death certificate with his own eyes.

"You better believe he did. And I gave it to him!" Jeffrey couldn't believe his ears. What was she talking about?

"What do you mean, you gave it to him?"

"You'll find some lovely foxglove in my garden. Your Father just couldn't hold his foxglove."

Flashes of a dream came to Jeffrey, as he stared unbelievingly into his Mother's eyes. The Queen Mother. The King Father. The sinister, dark, oily smudges swirling around the room. The crystal bowl filled with a deadly punch. The King Father slumping to the floor. The Queen Mother's words echoing in his mind, "See how it's calmed your Father? See how it's calmed your Father? See how it's calmed your Father?"

As he continued to stare, her sobs began anew. "I kept everything I could from you, so many things. I couldn't tell you about what I'd done to your Father. I couldn't tell you about the other things either. It wasn't something a little boy should ever know about. I wish to God I'd never had to know about them. If I hadn't, I know I wouldn't have been so awful to you. All those terrible things I said and did, all because I was trying to protect you. Trying to protect you from what I thought you might become."

"Mother, I'm a grown man. You don't have to protect me from anything anymore. What else is it that you've kept from me and tried to protect me from?"

She dried her tears and looked pathetically at Jeffrey, the suffering evident on her face and in her eyes. "I had two brothers," she began. "Twins. A devilish pair they were. Depraved beyond belief. They did terrible things to me, and laughed about it in my face. They made me do awful things to them. I didn't want to. They were quite capable of doing even worse things to me if I did not comply with their twisted desires. I fled when I was old enough to. I've no idea what happened to them. I hope they rot in Hell!" She paused again to get her breath. "I'm so sorry. I think I was much too harsh on you. I attempted to stamp out anything I saw developing in you that reminded me in the least of my twin brothers, my tormentors. You must forgive me. You are so much more than I ever hoped you'd be. And you did it in spite of my harsh treatment and misguided principles. Can you ever find it in your heart to forgive me?" she pleaded.

Tears were now streaming down Jeffrey's face as he stood helplessly in front of his mirror. "You should have told me this long ago, Mother. What a different life we might have had, you and I together. Of course I can forgive you. I'd have done so without question had you shared this information with me as an adult. I've been an adult for a long time. When I was younger, I wouldn't have understood. But once I became an adult, you should have come to me. I wish you had."

"Please, Jeffrey. Get me out of here," she begged.

"I don't have any control over this mirror, Mother. I don't know the reason some get in and others can't. I don't understand why some can walk back out and others can't. I wish I could help, but I don't know how. I'm sorry."

"It's all right. I'll deal with it. I've dealt with worse. You're going to have a wonderful life, I know it, you and Penny. Maybe I'll have grandchildren. Tell them about me. Make me sound like I'd have been a fantastic grandmother. Good night, Jeffrey." His Mother walked into his/her bedroom, and he never saw her again.

JEFFERY proposed to Penny and she accepted, as he knew she would. He vowed to give her the biggest, most elaborate wedding her imagination could possibly conjure up. He did not fail in that regard. They planned for themselves a lengthy honeymoon. Jeffrey had decided not to paint the house himself after all. Rather, he'd have it painted while they traveled. He also vowed to Penny that his obsession with filling his life with things was at an end.

"I want you to go through the house and select those things which you truly like and would want to keep. We'll pack those things away. The rest I'll make arrangements for someone to auction off while we're away."

Penny chose a number of very fine paintings, a few pieces of glassware, Jeffrey's infamous bowl not among them, some silver pieces, and a few dozen eclectic objects she found interesting. The rest would be gone when they returned. The antique mirror would be numbered among everything to go at auction. They would refurnish the house inside its new paint job when they returned, and begin their new life together.

𝒯𝐻𝐸 𝒩𝒪𝒯𝐼𝒞𝐸 in the paper announced the giant estate-type sale at the Holmes mansion. Horace Finnegan read the details with great anticipation. He was there to preview the merchandise and list those items he particularly wanted to get his hands on. He was impressed with many of Jeffrey's items. If he could manage to bid and obtain those items, he would make a killing on resale. He'd attended enough of these auctions to know that everything went for pennies on the dollar. He was also overjoyed to find the antique, full length mirror among the objects to be auctioned off. For that particular piece he might be willing to bid a little extra.

The day of the auction drew many more people than Horace had expected. However, the bidding was slow and he managed to get everything on his list for less than he would have paid had the bidding been more lively. He returned to his shop most pleased with himself. He had all his purchases delivered to his store. His rubbed his hands together at the prospect of the money he was going to make and the adjustments he planned to make to that antique mirror. He was anxious to examine it more closely to see why it enthralled people so. He would never make that killing, and he would very soon discover how enthralling that mirror could be.

When the merchandise arrived, he placed everything except the mirror in one corner of his workshop for cleaning and pricing. He then turned his full attention to the mirror. He examined it from top to bottom, back and front. He still was in the dark as to what the attraction was to this mirror. He looked at his reflection in the glass. He was about to walk away, when he noticed something. His reflection was somewhat more enhanced than it had been a moment ago. Horace Finnegan held no misconceptions about his appearance. He knew he was ungainly, even frightening to some people. But now as he stared at himself, he saw a softening of the edges that had always plagued him. He thought he looked better than he'd ever seemed to before. Was that the secret of this infernal mirror? He stepped closer and noted the luminous sheen over the surface of the glass. He reached out and touched the surface, feeling a vibration and pulling back quickly. Was this part of the secret? A most intriguing mirror. He touched the mirror again. The vibration was still there. The surface had a spongy quality to it. He pressed harder and saw a puckering of the surface and a distortion of the reflected image in the area where he was pressing. He pressed even harder, and to his amazement, his fingers slipped into the mirror and disappeared. Unlike Jeffrey, he could not see his fingers, but he could feel them. Horace smiled a wicked smile. This was the secret!! He would be fabulously wealthy! He pushed yet harder and his arm disappeared. Horace stepped boldly into the mirror and disappeared. The mirror reflected Horace's workroom as it had been a moment before. All his purchases were there in the corner awaiting cleaning, pricing, and the killing he would make on resale. He would not be making that killing. There was no Horace in the reflected workroom. There was no Horace in the mirror. Horace had simply vanished.

The headlines in the local paper read:

LOCAL PROPRIETOR OF LOST & FOUND ANTIQUE
STORE MISSING.PROPERTY IN FORECLOSURE.ALL
MERCHANDISE UP
FOR AUCTION.

The headlines in a Hollywood tabloid read:

WIFE OF PRODUCER FAMOUS FOR BOX OFFICE
FLOPS BREAKS
LONG SILENCE. TELLS OF HUSBAND'S OBESSION
WITH
CURSED MIRROR BEFORE HIS TRAGIC SUICIDE.

The headlines in a Midwest newspaper read:

ELDERLY SOCIALITE FEARED DEAD FOUND
ALIVE AND WELL.
HUSBAND, WHO COMMITTED SUICIDE, ONCE
SUSPECTED IN
HER DISAPPEARANCE.

The headlines in the same Midwest newspaper read:

RUNAWAY BRIDE RETURNS. FIANCE ELATED.
WEDDING RESCHEDULED.

THE AUCTION for the merchandise at Lost & Found attracted mobs of people. The money raised would go toward the foreclosure proceedings. The bank wanted what was due. There was a lot of merchandise to dispose of and the creditors were hopeful they would recoup their losses. The auction was going well. The auctioneer was announcing the next item.

"Item number 6348, an antique, full length mirror on swivel and wheels.

How much am I bid?"

THE LAST ROSE OF AUTUMN

ALMA THORNDIKE was dead, only no one knew it yet. That is no one except Barney.

~~~~~~

CLYDE AND FREDA THORNDIKE were thrilled with the birth of their first child. Freda had had some difficulty with pervious pregnancies. Any complication one could have with a pregnancy she'd had. The litany of her procreative maladies included an Ectopic Pregnancy, Placenta Praevia, Pre-eclampsia and a Still Birth. Both parents were relieved and ecstatic that this, the latest fetus, had outsmarted the obstetricians, presenting herself with great aplomb, perfectly formed, perfectly healthy and screaming her lungs out. Freda immediately named her Alma after her grandmother, little Alma's great grandmother, now ninety-eight and still screaming her lungs out. The only difference between the elder Alma and the newborn was that great grandma was a bit loony. Her elevator never reached the top floor and hadn't in some time. In addition she was as deaf as a doorknob. Consequently she screamed everything at the top of her lungs. She was incapable of discerning the difference between her loss of hearing and other people hearing her. Since she couldn't hear herself, she assumed no one else could either. Thus, she cranked up the decibels. Everyone heard her, even the neighbors two doors down. It was just the volume of sound coming out of this tiny mouth that instantly reminded Freda of the sound machine that lived under their roof at home.

The Thorndikes were of an old school that deemed it proper and obligatory for family members to care for their elderly on their own, if it was humanly possible. So Alma senior would probably spend the rest of what little life was left to her in the care of her granddaughter and her grand son-in-law. She wasn't that much of a burden to her caregivers. No round- the-clock warden was needed to keep her safe and secure. She just needed a very structured environment to maintain the precarious balance between a solid reality with which she could usually relate, and any deviation from the routine, with which she could not cope. The unexpected, or unplanned, sent her to a lalaland the family quickly learned to recognize and address with alacrity. Any delay, and Alma was off and running, and it was anybody's guess where she would end up. There was a little bottle of pills prescribed for her, just for such occasions.

Freda would say to Alma, "Time to come back from Neverland granny," as she popped her a pill and a generous swallow of water, always laced with a splash of bourbon. Alma had always liked bourbon and would take her medicine much more readily when she thought she was getting her favorite "tonic." The doctor said it would be perfectly alright when it was that diluted. Freda did keep the bottle well out of Alma's reach. She had been known to swig considerable amounts as a younger woman. Should she find the bottle when unattended now, she might not be as temperate as she ought, given her advanced age and mental liquidity. She might just drain the whole bottle. That would definitely have been a no-no.

But this isn't about Alma, Sr. It's about the newborn Alma. Alma, Sr. would join her ancestors soon. Although she was usually quite confused and forgetful, there would come a day when her mental fog lifted sufficiently enough for her to watch where Freda put the hooch. She would recall that hiding place with the next retreating of her mental clouds, retrieve what she craved surreptitiously the minute no one was watching, and help herself to her final "tonic." The only downside to her final libation was, that she had become so accustomed to Freda popping her the pill before her treat, she helped herself to more than a couple; the prescription setting conveniently next to the bourbon. No one had ever suspected she could reach that high. No charges were ever brought, but Freda would forever feel responsible for her grandmother's thirst-quenching departure.

Little Alma was only six month's old when great grandma made her exit. In fact, the new edition was responsible for Freda's momentary lapse. Between the elder's screaming and the newborn's wailing she often couldn't decide which to attend to first. The baby had gone down for her nap and she usually slept peacefully for hours. Freda thought she could safely concentrate her attention on granny for several hours at least. When the baby awoke screaming fifteen minutes afterward, Freda ran to get her without the slightest notion that The Fog would lift so suddenly; that granny could move so swiftly, reach her desired goal with such ease, adding the extra pills to the mix while she was at it. When Freda returned with the baby after a diaper change, granny was sitting nonchalantly, smiling, and rocking back and forth in her favorite chair. No one had any inkling she was rocking herself to death.

Granny was laid to rest with sufficient solemnity and now the auditory disruptions of the Thorndike residence would be cut in half. Even the neighbors were pleased. Not that they hadn't liked old Alma. She was, for the most part, a likeable old woman, but she had been a disruptive force that had been impossible not to notice, short of constantly wearing earplugs. Of the baby's crying they were much more tolerant.

Remarkably, after Alma's funeral, Little Alma's outbreaks of screaming and wailing decreased dramatically. Freda thought that with the baby's arrival at the house the two Alma's fed off each other. Often Freda would go to the baby first and that would cause granny to holler louder. She wasn't used to waiting for what she wanted. The baby heard that high pitched keening and upped the ante. Granny couldn't hear the baby's cries, but she certainly knew no one seemed to be coming to her aid and doubled her protests. Now a relative calm might just prevail. Granny was in the ground and baby ceased to make a sound. No more wailing.

Little Alma seemed quite content to suck on her fingers, if no bottle was in evidence.

Alma soon became a model child. Her sweet disposition was much appreciated after the many years Freda and Clyde had coddled Freda's demanding, often demented, grandmother. Alma grew quickly into a bubbly toddler with an inquisitive mind, an engaging smile, and a love of the outdoors and all the creatures that lived there.

The backyard was a universe in itself for Alma to explore. Freda sometimes worried Alma might chose to investigate too closely something which would cause her harm. After all, spiders and bugs of all kinds were out there somewhere and Alma seemed to find every one. Freda didn't even want to think about snakes. She'd never seen one, but somehow she suspected Alma would find one with ease.

"She's going to be a real little tomboy, that one. Don't know's I've ever seen a little girl get so much entertainment out of a ladybug and a caterpillar. She's not the least bit afraid of anything. And look how that ladybug just sits there on her finger, staring at her while Alma stares back," Clyde said. "I'd swear if I didn't know better that they were having a stare down!"

"Well I'm worried she's going to pick up some dreadful and poisonous spider and get bitten," Alma countered. "I've seen what a spider bite can do. My dad got bit on the leg once and he was never right after. A little piece of his leg turned black and they had to cut it out. His leg bothered him the rest of his life."

"Freda, I don't think we have any dangerous insects out in our yard," Clyde tried to allay her fears.

"But what about..."

"But what about snakes?" Clyde cut her off, knowing his wife's antipathy to anything without legs. She thought about rattlesnakes and copperheads a lot. "We don't have anything that could hurt her out there. The most she's apt to come across is a small garden snake. If I know Alma, she'll have that little snake wrapped around her little finger. I just hope it's me she runs to show it to. You'd probably faint!"

"No probably about it! I can't help it. I'm just deathly afraid of snakes of any kind, no matter how little and beneficial. You know very well I grew up with 'The Snake of All Snakes.' Pastor used to scare the pants off me describing how devious and deadly that ancient reptile was. 'The Deceiver,' he used to call it. Ever since I get cold chills and break out in a sweat when I even think about it." Freda had a major problem with snakes.

Alma would, of course, find the largest garden snake for miles around right there in her yard. She would indeed charm the snake, as it had never been charmed before, and run to Freda with it wrapped around her little finger, her hand, and her wrist.

"Look, Mommy! See this most interesting creature I found in the yard. Isn't it just the beautifulest?" she asked Freda to no avail. Freda had passed out cold in the grass at the bottom of the porch steps. Alma wasn't about to let Mommy miss out on this momentous occasion.

"Mommy! Mommy! Wake up and look at this most beautifulest thing. I think it likes me too. Look how tight it holds onto my hand. Look at its little tongue. I think it's saying 'Hello.' What do you think?"

Freda gained consciousness just as Alma displayed her snake close enough to Freda's face for her to see that little tongue darting in and out. Freda promptly passed out again.

~~~~~~

AS ALMA GREW, she continued to perplex and frighten her mother with a plethora of nasty pets. While Alma just adored worms and bugs, her mother was constantly startled by finding these strange and nasty creatures most anywhere in her house. Freda got no support from Clyde. In fact he was secretly amused by his daughter's choice of friends. She couldn't have pleased her father more than if she'd been a boy. Freda didn't much like her daughter behaving like a tomboy, but she had little success breaking that propensity. Alma had no interest whatsoever in dolls. Never liked dressing up in anything fancy or frilly. She preferred boys jeans and a flannel shirt. There would be no tea parties in the back yard under the ample shade of their huge maple. Freda's purchase of the table and chairs, the tea set, and enough dolls to attend the expected tea, were for naught. Alma wasn't to be found under the tree, serving her guests tea and crumpets. The table was set. The guests were in place, awaiting their afternoon treat. But Alma was far above them in the maple tree. She was studiously observing a great fat caterpillar as it industriously worked its way through its afternoon treat; a nice juicy leaf.

Carefully removing the leaf so as not to dislodge its occupant, she came down from her lofty perch with her prize. She was sure her mother had never seen anything like this before and that she would be suitably impressed this time with such a find. Finally planting her feet firmly on the ground at the base of her favorite haunt, the maple tree, she couldn't wait for her mother to see the beautiful new friend she'd made.

"Mom! Mom! Come quick!" she hollered as loud as she possibly could, while checking to make sure the fat caterpillar was still obliviously finishing up what was left of the succulent, green, leaf material between the more substantial veins. He was indeed most industriously occupied.

With Alma's shriek ringing in her ears, and expecting to find her daughter lying under the maple with blood running copiously from yet another injury, Freda burst from the house nearly bowling Alma over as they each rushed toward each other. She stopped on a dime when she caught sight of the ghastly thing Alma was proffering for her approval.

"Yuck! What on earth have you found now? That's the most disgusting thing you've come across yet. Put that down right now. You have no idea what horrible diseases it might be carrying." Freda would never adjust to her daughter's propensity to "befriend" bizarre creatures and crawly things of any kind.

"But mother, look how beautiful it is. Look at all the colors. And when it's done eating, it will spin itself a cocoon and come out again an even more beautiful butterfly. Oh. Wait. It might be a moth. Most of them are not quite so pretty. But just look at the colors!" Alma was not about to give up on mother. She'd have her appreciating nature's creatures, even the creepy ones, or else.

211

BY THE TIME Alma was old enough to start school, Freda had still not adjusted to her daughter's fascination with all things "icky."

"I hope *your* daughter starts acting like a normal child once she's exposed to other normal children," she informed Clyde.

"And why is she *my* daughter? I don't see what the harm is in her being interested in living things." Clyde found his daughter's choice of playmates more acceptable than Freda, and Freda knew it. She felt Clyde wasn't steering Alma forcefully enough toward "little girl" pursuits. She thought Clyde was more than tickled to have his daughter acting like a tomboy.

"I wonder what her classmates are going to think of her? Kids can be very cruel. Anyone as different and headstrong as Alma is bound to get noticed and that may not be a good thing."

Clyde only waved a dismissive hand at the notion there'd be any problems at Alma's school.

~~~~~~

ALMA CERTAINLY did get noticed. Her classmates had never experienced anyone who seemed to attract every manner of creeping, crawling thing. Her teacher had never seen anything like it either, and she wasn't too pleased to have her classroom invaded by Alma's "friends."

"Alma, you'll have to take that bug and put it outside. I can't have the classroom in chaos over that insect. Most of the students don't want to have anything to do with it, and I must say I agree. Take it outside or put it out the window, please." Miss Crandall waited patiently as Alma reluctantly put her latest interest out the window. "Now maybe we can get back to our lessons without further interruption!"

Poor Miss Crandall had no idea that her day was going to be one giant interruption. A sudden scream, and several girls sitting in close proximity to Alma jumped from their seats, retreating, placing some distance between them and Alma's desk.

"Miss Crandall! There's a mouse under Alma's desk!" one of the girls shouted out at their very perturbed teacher.

"Miss Thorndike, why have you brought a mouse to school with you? Such behavior cannot be tolerated. I'm afraid I'll have to inform your mother!"

"But, Miss Crandall, I didn't bring any mouse to school. I don't know where it came from. I didn't even know it was there." But now that she did, she reached down and put the mouse in the palm of her hand, where it sat quite contentedly, it's gaze on Miss Crandall.

Alma was totally unaware of Miss Crandall's inordinate fear of mice. When she saw the filthy little rodent staring directly at her, she fainted dead away, hitting her head on the edge of her desk as she went down. Everyone was screaming. Some were running for the door. The commotion was not unheard by the school principal, Mr. Downsworth. He came running from his office as several students ran out into the hallway in front of him.

"What is the meaning of all this noise? Why are you running out into the hall?" he asked the first child.

The frightened first-grade girl just pointed to the classroom she'd just left and, nearly in tears, said, "There's a mouse in there and Miss Crandall is dead!"

Mr. Downsworth rushed into the room to find boys and girls in a panic, running every which way, bumping into each other. No one seemed to notice him at all. Only one child was seated at her desk, quietly looking at him with her hands folded in front of her. Then he noticed Miss Crandall crumpled on the floor next to her desk. She was very pale and still. A small pool of blood had formed under her head. He was in a panic. He had no idea what to do, and fled immediately out the door, making a beeline for the school nurse's office.

~~~~~~

~~~~~~

MISS CRANDALL was not dead, but she was admitted to Grant Memorial in very serious condition. She'd suffered a hairline cranial fracture and a very long, open gash in her scalp, the excessive bleeding from which had sent Mr. Downsworth into his hurried exit, looking for Nurse Violet. His quick action proved fortuitous for Helen Crandall since Violet Mallory had known just what to do. The ambulance spirited the unconscious teacher away, while Violet and Mr. Downsworth were left to calm the panic and return order to her classroom. Once all the students had been rounded up and herded back to their desks, it fell to the now frazzled principal to look into the cause of the morning's disruption. Downsworth wasn't a fan of anything but the strict progression of order in all things, particularly those at his job as administrator of Elm Hill Elementary. Leaning forward with menace, and looking over his heavily bifocaled glasses, he plunged into ferreting out the cause of this most unacceptable tear in the fabric of his day.

Clearing his throat in a most threatening manner, and directing his gaze squarely upon Alma, he began the inquest.

"Miss Thorndike, it seems we have the unfortunate matter of an unauthorized mouse to contend with! What have you to say on your behalf?"

"I can't contend the mouse. It wasn't even my mouse," Alma replied weakly, not quite sure what "contend" might mean.

"Excuse me! What do you mean you can't contend the mouse?"

"Well, I didn't contend it. It just showed up under my desk." She didn't know what else to say but added, "I'm very sorry about Miss Crandall."

"And well you should be, young lady. Miss Crandall lies unconscious at Grant Memorial as we speak. She's in very serious condition. We're all very lucky she wasn't killed. And all over your mouse!" He had to place the blame securely on someone. These things just didn't happen. He'd heard through the proverbial Grapevine that this child was weird. He was not a fan of weird children either.

"But, Mr. Worthless, it wasn't my mouse. I never saw it before. It just appeared under my desk," she pleaded.

"It's DOWNSworth! And since many of the students saw you with it in your hand when Miss Crandall succumbed, I cannot but assume your complicity. I must inform your

parents of your gross infraction of school policy." Although
Elm Hill Elementary hadn't any "No Mouse" policy per
say, he was sure he'd find something with which to root
out a trouble maker before more damage was done, and left
summarily to phone Alma's parents.

"Now you're in for it!"

"You're going to get what for, for sure!"

"Did you see her pick up that awful creature?"

"Way to go, Alma! Mouse Power!"

This from her fellow classmates. Some were grossed
out. Some wanted to see her punished. They didn't like her.
She was strange. One boy was obviously enamored of her
pluck and tomboy bravado.

Alma was mystified. Although she didn't understand
exactly what was happening, she felt something bad was
about to occur, even if she had done nothing wrong. Why
Miss Crandall had fallen, she had no idea, but she knew
enough to know Mr. Worthless, ah, Downsworth, was
blaming her for everything. And her mother was not going
to be pleased.

Freda had never come to grips with her daughter's
unusual behavior, and this might just push her over the
edge. Clyde, on the other hand, had accepted Alma's being
different, indulging her, her unicity.

THE FALLOUT from "The Mouse Incident," as it came
to be known, was unlike anything that had ever happened
at Elm Hill before.

Mr. Downsworth campaigned vigorously for expulsion, due to the serious nature of the consequences involved. Miss Crandall was hospitalized for many weeks, leaving him a teacher short and twenty students under the tutelage of a Miss Frampton, an ancient reptile of a woman whom Downsworth abhorred. She was authoritarian to a flaw, mean-spirited, and, he felt sure, took pleasure in the students' discomfort. In short she was very much like Mr. Downsworth himself. So much for not recognizing one's self in others.

The other students' parents were onboard Downsworth's train.

Freda was beside herself. "Didn't I tell you we'd have problems with *your* daughter?"

"Freda, they're making *our* daughter the scapegoat for an unfortunate and probably unavoidable incident. Alma didn't take any mouse to school with her. Lord knows that old building is probably crawling with mice. That one got into her classroom has nothing to do with her. Her teacher's reaction was unfortunate, but certainly not Alma's fault."

"Then why are all her classmates so anxious to report her sitting there holding that vile rodent in her hand? Except for that Boyd child, who has portrayed her as some kind of heroine for Mouse Rights. What a nut job he must be!"

"You know that would be her natural reaction to any animal she might encounter. Just because she happened to pick it up, you can't charge her with malice aforethought toward Miss Crandall. Has everyone lost their minds? She's just a six-year-old child, not some bad seed from the nether regions sent to wreak havoc on an unsuspecting grade school!"

"I have a very bad feeling about this. Everyone seems bent on getting her ousted from school permanently. What will we do then, huh? What will we do then?"

~~~~~~

ALMA *WAS* EXPELLED from school. In light of Miss Crandall's injuries, hospitalization, and extended absence from work, the community as a whole, *sans* The Boyd's, felt they were not comfortable with the possibility of a repeat performance, one which might turn out even worse than its predecessor.

It was far from fair to Alma. She was devastated by her classmate's reaction to what she saw as a perfectly normal response on her part. The mouse had obviously been terrified by all the commotion it had unwittingly caused, fleeing to who knows where the moment pandemonium broke loose.

Alma was just glad the mouse hadn't been trampled to death. Of course, she felt badly for her teacher, but couldn't see how that could possibly have been her fault. Everyone else seemed to differ, shouting awful things at her and her parents at the school board meetings regarding her fate.

~~~~~~

~~~~~~

ALMA TOOK her expulsion very hard. She had been so looking forward to school and making friends there. She had been a solitary child with no one her age living close enough for her to have formed any kind of friendship. Now that hope was dashed, and she was the object of the other children's scorn and ridicule. That scorn was more the fault of her friend's respective parents than the children themselves. Although many were caught unawares by the sudden appearance of the mouse, their concerted blame of Alma and subsequent shunning were due in large part to cues they received from their outraged parents' overreaction to the whole affair. The Elm Hill Elementary would soon forget Alma, but Alma would never forget Elm Hill. She would carry the injustice she'd received there with her in the back of her mind, and it would color her response to others, her ability to form any kind of lasting, trusting relationships, from that day forward.

~~~~~~

"DON'T LOOK so glum. Alma is going to be fine. She may very well use her gift, or calling, whatever you want to call it, as a basis for her whole life's work," Clyde counseled.

"More like obsession!" Freda spat back. "We're all the object of dirty looks and cold shoulders because of her love of animals."

"So it's obsession. Many very successful people have had their lives changed and enhanced by their obsession. Don't count her out just because of one silly misunderstanding."

"Silly misunderstanding! Her teacher is still in the hospital in serious condition because of this misunderstanding!"

"So now you're joining everyone else in town in convicting your own daughter of something that was not, and I repeat, NOT, her fault?" Clyde was quick to rebuke his wife.

"No. That's not what I meant. I certainly wasn't expecting anything like this and I just don't know where to turn." Freda approached her husband and put her head on his shoulder and sobbed.

"It's alright. You know, she may very well become a veterinarian or a biologist. She has a bright future ahead, I'm sure. Forget all those other people so quick to judge. I think she might need some comforting. She's not come out of her room today. And we need to decide what to do next. We have to look out for her now. We can't let this incident set the tone for her academic life. She's much too bright not to give her all the encouragement possible, and quickly. Go on up and give her a big hug. I'm going to look into our options for her. We'll find the right place for her where she'll be appreciated for who she is."

ALMA WOULD NOT get the opportunity to attend that facility where she'd be appreciated for being herself. Freda would find Alma restless and feverish. Her condition would deteriorate and Freda and Clyde would face a much more pressing and serious situation than that silly classroom mouse or finding the perfect venue for her education.

~~~~~~~~~~~~~~~~~~~~~~~~~~~~~~~~~~~~~~~

FOR MANY CONTRACTING the dreaded virus, there were no symptoms at all. They were the lucky ones. For others, it began with a vague flu-like complaint. A general feeling of unease, fevers, and a sore throat was as far as it ever went. Treatment of the symptomatic complaints was all that was needed. They, too, were the lucky ones. For the unlucky ones, their symptoms progressed to aches and weakness in their extremities. Their virus had migrated from their digestive tract, which was often as far as it got, to their nervous system. There it attacked the nerves and nerve endings, causing profound weakness and then paralysis. Sometimes it was just the legs. Sometimes also the arms. Some people experienced an aseptic meningitis, causing a stiff neck and sensitivity to light. But in the worst case, it attacked the mechanism that regulated the diaphragm, enabling the host to breathe. It left the unfortunate victim in a state of respiratory arrest. Alma's was the worst case. And she had polio.

~~~~~~~~~~~~~~~~~~~~~~~~~~~~~~~~~~~~~~~

~~~~~~~~~~~~~~~~~~~~~~~~~~~~~~~~~~~~~~~

POLIO IS NOT something one hears about anymore. With the advent of Jonas Salk's vaccine, the threat of this once unstoppable killer and disabler declined rapidly. Prior to 1955 that was not the case. In most parts of the world, polio has been vanquished, but it still lies in wait in third world countries with inadequate health care facilities.

~~~~~~

WITHOUT THE BENEFIT of Salk's yet to be discovered vaccine, Alma's condition rapidly deteriorated, requiring she be rushed to Grant Memorial, there to take up residence with her alleged victim, who was just beginning to show signs of improvement. Alma had no knowledge of where she was, or that Miss Crandall was, indeed, very close-by.

Unfortunately for Alma, she now was suffering from the worst case scenario, with the virus attacking the nerves controlling her breathing. The only remedy was to place her quickly into an iron lung.

For practical purposes this once necessary life saver is now rarely seen except in museums of medical history. We now intubate patients and place them on relatively small respirators, much less frightening and intimidating for the patient, as well as family.

Unfortunately for Alma, she didn't have the benefit of yet to be developed medical technology either. And so she would find herself within this monstrous iron cylinder, lying on what looked very much like a long cookie tray. The end of the cylinder at her head had apparatus to make as good a seal as possible around her neck. The foot end had a large diaphragm with a metal armature which worked like a bellows, pushing into the chamber, and then retreating.

When the armature withdrew it created a negative pressure, acting like the patients real diaphragm, expanding the chest cavity as air flowed into the patient's lungs. When it reversed, the positive pressure forced the chest cavity to contract, forcing air back out of the lungs. The patient's respirations were thus maintained for as long as necessary.

When Alma began to recover, she was completely disoriented and confused by her confinement in this machine. At first she was terrified. She didn't understand what was happening and, although the nurses were there to console and explain her treatment, it took some time for her to calm down.

Freda and Clyde spent as much time as possible at her side, the incident at the school forgotten in light of the current crisis. Alma would spend weeks entombed within this giant iron monster, and although it would save her life, her life would never be the same.

When polio strikes a child at a time when they are still growing and developing, that growth and development is derailed. There is deformity of vital bones and uneven muscle growth. The victim is often left with lifelong paralysis and disability. Braces may assist and physical therapy may regain some lost function, but all too often the end results are devastating. Alma's results would be so.

AS ALMA'S VIRUS seemed to be losing its grip enough for her to begin to regain some spontaneous respirations, Miss Crandall was also on the mend. She too had some minor paresis, which was being seen too, but she was up and about enough to stop by Alma's room. Even though this girl had frightened her so badly with the mouse that she'd ended up here, she was heartbroken when she saw Alma lying pale and dependant on that awful contraption. Alma was sleeping peacefully, as her iron lung breathed for her through the night. That visit would mean the world to Alma later, even though she was not aware her teacher had been to visit her.

~~~~~~

ONCE ALMA had been successfully weaned from the confines of the iron lung, it was time to begin exhaustive sessions of physical therapy. Alma was able to make considerable progress with arm mobility, but her legs would not co-operate. Even with braces and crutches, she was barely able to get around. She would spend most of the next year in a wheel chair. Anxious to go back to school, she was unaware of the magnitude of the firestorm that had resulted from her teacher's injuries. While she was in and out of consciousness, learning to deal with her imprisonment in that terrifying machine, learning to breathe again on her own, enduring endless therapies, and finally able to return home, she had to face the sad and distressing fact that she couldn't go back to school. Even after all she'd suffered, the community had not forgotten what a strange child they had deemed her to be and still felt she was. No one seemed inclined to show her the least bit of compassion. No one, that is, except the very person who'd been injured in the whole affair, Miss Crandall.

No amount of intersession from her on Alma's behalf would budge the obstinate board or school administrators. Mr. Downsworth was one of the most vocal in opposition to any concessions regarding the Thorndike's errant child.

Miss Crandall was ashamed for the community as a whole and went out of her way to apologize to Freda and Clyde.

"I hope you will accept my offer of assistance. I cannot get anyone to see reason down at the school. After all, it was I who ended up in the hospital, not any of them. And that was really entirely my own fault. There was no way Alma could have been aware of my inordinate fear of small rodents. My problem to deal with not hers. I believe her story that the mouse was just a drop-in. We do have mice problems at times in that old building. I understand that she is very fond of all things small and helpless. We probably could use many more like her. The reason I've come is to offer my services in any way I can. I understand it may be some time before Alma will be able to return to any formal schooling and I feel she shouldn't have to wait for that to get started. I would like to offer her some tutoring whenever it would be alright with you. I feel so badly about what the community has done, I have to do something to help make it up her."

Freda and Clyde were overwhelmed with her generous offer, and thus resumed Alma's formal education. Freda and Clyde worked along with Miss Crandall to try to bring Alma up to speed. She was now very much behind all those classmates who she had once looked forward to getting to know. She would never know any of them now.

By the time Freda and Clyde were able to arrange for a private school for Alma, those classmates had forgotten all about her. Their parents had not. And they privately thought Miss Crandall had lost her mind for placing herself in harm's way again, by actually tutoring the girl who had so viciously attacked her with the infamous mouse. For whatever reason, the parents had embellished the incident to reflect the irrefutable culpability of a child "who would come to no good."

Miss Crandall was not the least concerned for her safety. Due to her selfless act of atonement, Alma was now in great shape academically to continue her education. However, it was painful to watch Alma desperately trying to get along physically. Alma was in poor shape to manage on her own, needing a great deal of assistance. Her legs remained uncooperative. She had also grown, but her legs had not. It was now an undeniable fact that she would have very noticeable deformities. How much function she might regain was still undetermined, but Alma was determined to make it as much as she possibly could. She had come to hold her teacher/tutor in great regard, and credited her, along with her parents, for seeing her through what had been enough to crush someone with less resolve. Because of the many hours spent teaching her what she should have mastered by that point in time, had she not been so rudely detoured, plus making every effort to see that she would even be ahead of those her age, Alma would be forever grateful.

THERE ENSUED a number of years of intense dedication to academics, coupled with relentless sessions of physical therapy and exercise. Alma was determined to get her body back into as good a shape as her mind. Her mind was, indeed, quick and retentive. She forewent all attempts at camaraderie directed her way in order to concentrate on absorbing every morsel of information thrown out to her.

She had not forgotten her classmate's response that unfortunate day when a certain mouse appeared under her desk. They had all been most eager to throw her to the wolves. She had no intention of risking a repeat performance.

Unfortunately, her body did not respond as readily as did her mind. No matter how far she pushed herself, the hours of punishing, repetitious bending and stretching, her legs were not going to grow into anything approaching their expected size and shape for her age group. In fact, her legs would become more and more noticeably deformed as the rest of her body matured normally.

Eventually, Alma would resign herself to the reality of her deformity and disability, but she would never give up pushing herself to the limit, attempting any and everything, never counting herself out until she had at least given it all she had. Then, and only then, would she place an endeavor in the realm of unattainable for her.

Clyde and Freda were amazed and very proud of Alma's accomplishments, despite the recalcitrant muscles and damaged nerves that left their daughter so much shorter than she should have been, and plagued by the slow side-to-side gait that made her stand out in any crowd. But Alma had learned how to manage without her crutches. It took her years of practice and many a fall before she sallied forth without them. However, they were not gone for good. She still had them on reserve for those occasions where she was unfamiliar with the surroundings and might actually find them necessary. She tried to keep such situations to a minimum.

~~~~~~

AS MUCH AS ALMA enjoyed her time at school, she treasured her summers at home with her parents. Even though formal classes were suspended, she still spent a great deal of time reading and preparing for what would come with the next year's study.

Miss Crandall was the only visitor she saw while at home. She never failed to encourage Alma to stay ahead of her peers, read works beyond her age group, delve into subjects not yet on the curriculum and prepare to surprise her teachers with her perspicacity.

Along with a more than heavy schedule of academics, Alma made sure not to let up on her physical battles as well. As part of that endeavor, she developed a growing interest in her mother's garden. If she, herself, would never be the perfect, beautiful young woman she'd striven to be, at least she could learn to produce the perfect, beautiful, perfumed blossoms that were her mother's favorite. Working in her mother's garden was not the easiest job for her. Bending and stooping were most difficult. She armed herself with a helpful garden stool which was adjustable, placing her at the exact level she needed to be for each individual plant and task.

Freda had dozens of hybrid tea rose shrubs. Each year she enlarged her collection, adding that year's prize-wining rose and any others that she found particularly pleasing. Each plant was marked by a bronze plaque on a sturdy metal spike. Many were named for their developer, others for celebrities. Freda had every color one might want and many in between. Her personal favorite was The Peace Rose. Its blossoms were large and full. The colors were a creamy white with light rose-colored, peach-colored, and lemon-colored highlights, some on the inner aspects of the petals, some on the outer. The highlights darkened ever so slightly as the petals unfurled. The perfume was heady and long lasting, increasing as the blooms matured. Alma would take immense pleasure in presenting her mother with the largest of its buds, just ready to begin its display, resting appropriately in the most delicate of crystal vases.

Alma would also keep one or more specimens in a vase next to her bed. They would be the last things she laid eyes on before she turned out her light, and the first things to greet her as the sun lit her room with its first rays of the day. There were amazing blood red blooms, buttery yellow, peach, orange and coral. There never seemed to be an end to the variety of Freda's collection.

~~~~~~

ALMA DID SO WELL academically that she was offered a scholarship, if she chose to further her education. Since she had placed so much emphasis on her studies, foregoing any kind of interpersonal relationships with any of her classmates, she thought continuing her studies would be the best, indeed the only, option. She loved the pursuit of knowledge for its own sake, and had not decided exactly where it was she was going, or what she wanted to do. She had never lost her love of all creatures great and small, but had purposely not indulged in bringing any of those creatures into a classroom. She had even resigned herself to the fact that her mother was never going to be a fan of nature, especially its less that warm and cuddly creatures. She no longer pushed the limits of Freda's endurance by offering her close up looks at specimens Alma found fascinating. She would keep her fascination to herself.

Her continued interest in the natural world seemed to direct her toward collegiate studies in biology. Freda and Clyde were hopeful that once she began college, she would begin to form some relationships other than those with her textbooks. They realized her great reticence to open herself up to others stemmed from her deformities and disabilities, as well as the cruel and thoughtless treatment often directed her way by mean and ignorant classmates. It was no wonder her distrust ran so deep. The stigma of polio sometimes translated to aversions of all kinds. Some poor misinformed souls thought they might be infected by contact with Alma, and kept their distance. Freda and Clyde were optimistic that the older, more well informed academic community would treat their daughter more kindly.

AFTER SPENDING a relaxing summer working among Freda's prize hybrid teas, Alma was actually excited about beginning college. Miss Crandall, now very grey and getting ready to retire, visited her to bolster her confidence and counseled her to make positive attempts at broadening her horizons by letting her guard down a little, forming some lasting friendships.

"Take some advice from an old maid. I was never a physically attractive woman, and I knew it. I let that color my thinking and my life to the extent that I now find myself a very lonely old woman. I withdrew from everything but work and I regret it now. Don't let that happen to you. While you may have physical disabilities, you are a most attractive young woman."

"Oh, Miss Crandall, I...,"

"Let me finish," she cut her off. "You *are* attractive. Don't let you legs rule your body. Lord knows you've put enough work into pushing them to their limits. Accentuate your positives. And, my dear, you have plenty. There's absolutely nothing wrong with the rest of you. Take a closer look in the mirror. You have the face of an angel. And a mind like a steel trap. If anything intimidates the opposite sex, it might be your mind. I'm sure there's a brilliant young man out there who will appreciate you for who you are and not give a whit about the unfortunate state of your legs. Keep an open mind to all possibilities. And enjoy everything about the journey you're about to begin. You're only young once. I wish I had a second chance. Now I really must go before I get maudlin or cry. Do think about what I've said."

"Thank you so much for everything. I really will try." And Miss Crandall was gone. Alma wouldn't see her again.

She would die only weeks after her retirement. Alma then began to think even more seriously about what her teacher and mentor had advised on that last visit.

~~~~~~

FOR THE FIRST TIME Alma was very much on her own. Gone were the small very structured classes of private school. Lecture halls were immense affairs packed with hundreds of students. She was adrift in a sea of humanity, everyone with their own goals and agendas. For the first time she felt inconspicuous. It was a welcome feeling. No one seemed to take any great notice of her diminutive stature. Wearing long attractive skirts camouflaged the deformities about which she'd been so self conscious. Only the telltale side-to-side swing of her gait gave hint at an underlying abnormality. She felt freer than she had ever felt in her life. In a more relaxed frame of mind, Alma then set forth to remedy the long avoided, even dreaded, fostering of a friendship, perhaps more.

~~~~~~

ALMA'S BIOLOGY CLASS was held in one of the campus's largest auditoriums. The seats were arranged in a semicircle around a center podium with a large wraparound screen behind it. The aisles were steep, with each descending row of seats placing those student's heads at knee level of those behind. Alma had difficulty getting in and out of the lecture and planned to arrive early to attract the least attention, and leave last for the same reason. She could see that there were still many obstacles, with which she would have to find a way of dealing.

The upside of this biology course was that the laboratory portion was held in a most comfortable facility, easily accessible, and she would be partnered with another freshmen. It would be the first time she would have the opportunity to try her wings at connecting with another student, developing a rapport. She was apprehensive, nervous, and ready to walk away when her lab partner arrived.

One look and she almost swooned. Stepping up to their station, and unceremoniously dumping his armload of textbooks into the cubbyhole under their counter, was the most attractive man she'd ever laid eyes on. He was tall, slender, with a swimmer's build, broad shoulders tapered to a narrow waist. He was well muscled, but not overly so. She could not help but notice how well he filled out the tight jeans he was wearing. His hair was honey blonde and slightly curly with an ample lock hanging over his forehead. His eyes were cornflower blue and danced with light.

"Hello," he said, giving Alma the biggest smile, filled with perfect movie star teeth. "I think I'm going to be your lab partner for the term. I'm Gavin. Gavin Fowler. And you are?"

"Alm-," her voice cracked. Clearing her throat she gave it another try. "I'm Alma Thorndike. You'll have to excuse me. This is all so very new to me and I have to admit, I'm more than a little bit intimidated."

"Don't be," came his quick reply. "No need to be. We're all pretty much in the same boat. I believe almost everyone taking this class is a freshman. I say let's make the very best of it. What say you?"

"I think that's a very calming idea."

Thus began what would become a relationship Alma had never thought possible. Gavin took an instant liking to her, and she couldn't fathom why. He treated her as if she were the most normal person in the world. It was like she had no handicap, no disability. He was completely accepting of her just as she was, no questions asked. She had to wonder if he wasn't a little bit curious about her diminutive height and strange swaying gait, but he didn't seem enough bothered by it to ask.

The second person to befriend Alma was her new roommate, Sally Bigelow. Sally was everything Alma wished she could be. Tall, willowy, with strawberry blonde hair that seemed to float like waves around her shoulders. Sally's eyes were hazel with green flecks and she too sported teeth of white. She was as inquisitive as Gavin was not.

"So, Alma, what's with the fancy gait? You trying out for some new dance?" Alma could tell she was not being smart, but she was very direct; no beating around of the bush. "You're just about the cutest little thing I've ever seen."

"I had polio when I was six and it left me with severely limited growth in my legs and years of paralysis. I'm a permanent shorty and I think the walk is as good as it's going to get." Never had she been so forthcoming, and especially to this, as yet, stranger.

"Well doesn't that just suck? But you know what? You're a testament to the human spirit. I've heard of some unfortunate people like you, and they never got this far. You must have had tremendous support through it all."

"Yes. Yes, I did." Not for the first time, but with an intensity she'd never felt before, Alma realized that she *had* had the most spectacular support in her parents and Miss Crandall. She also had to give credit to all the teachers that worked so hard with her in the excellent private schools she'd been privileged to attend. "I was very fortunate. And I was very obstinate. I vowed that polio was not going to get me down no matter what!" She kept her fear of forging any kind of friendship with anyone her own age to herself. Sally might think that strange and now Alma was striving to move away from strange and toward normal.

AS ALMA ADJUSTED surprisingly fast to her college experience, she also quickly formed a bond with both her roommate, Sally, and her lab partner, Gavin.

Sally turned out to be a no-nonsense, call-them-as-you-see-them, brutally honest type individual. Alma was often taken aback by some of Sally's off-the-wall but insightful remarks. She soon learned that Sally didn't have a mean or judgmental bone in her body.

"You know, Alma, you could use a makeover. You're so damn cute, but you're hiding it all with the severe clothing and hair styles. Have you ever used make up? You know you wouldn't need much at all. Your skin is like alabaster and flawless. Just a hint of color here and there would be spectacular. Just say, 'To Hell with that old polio!' You really deserve better than you've got so far."

"Oh, I don't know, Sally. I've always done everything I possibly could to deflect any attention away from me. I certainly attracted more than I wanted whether I liked it or not. Now that I'm sort of feeling comfortable in my own skin, I just don't think I'd be up to doing anything that would make me stand out any more than I already do. I try to hide my ungainly walk with long full skirts. It's really difficult to disguise my height. I once thought of elevated shoes, but I know I'd fall and break my neck for sure."

"Well, I think you ought to at least give it a try." Sally was a very forceful girl and would end up chairman of any committee she found herself on, and would become one the freshman class office holders with ease. She was ingratiating and always left anyone with whom she had contact certain that she had heard every word they'd said, and that their thoughts and opinions mattered.

Gavin, on the other hand, mystified her to a great degree because no one had ever related to her on such a personal level, so quickly, and with such ease. She fought the feelings that insinuated themselves into her psyche the moment she'd set eyes on him. How dare she ever entertain such thoughts, given his gorgeous good looks with his unaffected personality, and her own perceived notion of unattractiveness and inadequacy.

"Good morning Alma. You sure seem upbeat today. Something interesting or exciting to share?" Gavin greeted her as she'd been in animated conversation with the two girls across from their station.

"Not really exciting, just maybe different." Alma had been seriously considering Sally's advice and had asked her what she should do, or who she should see to begin any kind of transformation. "My roommate, Sally, has been after me to update my wardrobe and get a new do. Nothing that would interest you, I'm sure. Just a girl thing."

"*Au contraire,* don't think men don't notice such things or have no interest. We do. We just do our best not to show it. It's part of the male mystique. Don't let anyone know I've told you that. I don't relish divulging secret male contrivances and conniving. It might be viewed as a sell out. Uncouth. And I certainly want to remain as couth as possible, especially with you."

"So you don't think it would be silly for me to take Sally's advice?"

"Certainly not. Fashions and hair styles change. Nothing wrong with going with the flow. Even us guys do it."

"I've never seen any guys that have changed their hair style and dress noticeably," Alma seemed unconvinced.

"That's just the point. We have to do it in a manner that seems we haven't. That way we maintain our steady, stalwart demeanor at all times, seeming not care about such things, while we secretly do. Mums the word," he said as he placed his index finger in front of his mouth.

Alma could feel her heart beat quicken. As he unhurriedly donned his lab apron and grabbed a pair of gloves, Alma caught his masculine scent. It was not cologne or any artificial scent. It was obvious that he was freshly showered. His hair was still slightly wet. But it was not the scent of any shampoo or hair product either. No deodorant smelled anything like the essence that now tantalized her olfactory senses. She leaned closer to him as she also reached for a pair of gloves. The aroma was definitely all Gavin.

She would need all her powers of concentration to keep her mind on the experiments and projects before them. For the first time a class was going to offer her a challenge she'd never had before.

~~~~~~

ALMA CONTINUED to consider making some changes in herself. She began to notice the other girl's hair and clothes; things that had never concerned her before. When she compared that with what presented itself in her mirror, she had to admit she appeared dated. She looked like a younger Miss Crandall. Not that there was ever anything wrong with Miss Crandall, but she had been an elderly woman.

Alma had never paid much attention to being youthfully attired. She hadn't much frame of reference. She had only paid attention to her mother, who had always been very conservative, and her mentor, who'd been on the far side of middle age when struck down by the infamous mouse. Now she was faced with the decision to "stay the course," or "opt for a change." She wanted badly to be more attractive, particularly in Gavin's eyes, but she was deathly afraid of seeming to be too forward and brazen, bent solely on snaring her prey. Then she had to be brutally honest with herself. She'd like nothing better than to snare Gavin Fowler.

~~~~~~

WHILE SHE WAFFLED over what to do, she received word that her mother was very ill. She would be needing surgery and Clyde felt Alma ought to be there. The administration did not see any problem with her absenting herself from classes to be there for her mother, especially with her past sterling record.

Freda's surgery went extremely well. They were able to remove the cancer and were relatively certain it was early and had not spread. Nonetheless, Alma was frightened by her mother's pallor and weight loss. She hoped the doctor's assessment of her mother's condition was correct. Freda did seem much more animated after surgery. Her appetite was much improved and there was none of the nausea and vomiting that had been plaguing her for months.

Once at home, Freda continued to improve and Alma felt reasonably secure returning to classes.

~~~~~~

IN ALMA'S ABSENSE, a situation had developed that would change the course of her life forever.

~~~~~~

"ALMA, I'M SO GLAD you're back," Sally greeted her with a hug. "It's been awfully quiet while you were gone.

I'd turn around to say something or ask you a question and there would be your empty desk. How's your mom?"

Alma felt a warm feeling of belonging at Sally's heartfelt welcome. Life could be good enough to embrace even her, despite past snubs and slights.

"She's really doing very well according to her doctor and the surgeon. They think she sought treatment in time to remove all the cancer without any signs of spread. She looked very ill when I got home. I've never seen her so pale and she'd lost a great deal of weight. But she perked up immediately after the operation. Her color was much better and she began to eat like she always did, and mom had a good appetite. I used to wonder why she didn't put on weight with all she ate. Maybe because she's always been a very physical person, always on the go. She works in her garden like a field hand. You should see her rose garden. I even worked out there whenever I could. It was good therapy for me."

"So, you think she's going to be alright?"

"I sure hope so. Cancer can be such a sneaky, evasive affair," Alma qualified her optimism. "They'll monitor her very closely and time will tell."

"Now that you're back, you've got a lot of territory to catch up on. I've never seen so much information dished out at such a furious pace. It surely isn't like high school. It's all I can do to keep up. I don't know what your classes were like, but mine have been grueling. And I refuse to fall to the old adage that blondes are dumb!"

"You're far from dumb. Anyone can tell that very quickly. I'm sure you'll be fine. And I know I have my work cut out for me. I guess I'll have to make the rounds and find out all the assignments I missed. Maybe I can get some make up notes from the lectures, too."

~~~~~~

ALMA WAS PARTICULARLY anxious to return to her biology lab where Gavin and his easy, breezy personality would once again make her day. She would soon have to make the decision on whether or not she wanted to remake herself, and actively encourage Gavin to see her in more than the light of a lab partner. He already treated her as if she were more than that, but then he was more than cordial to everyone. She longed for him to specifically seek her out other than the scheduled time they spent together diligently pursuing their lab assignments.

When Gavin saw her, his face lit up, and that disarming smiled beamed down at her, making her knees weak and her heart flutter. Certainly her inner turmoil must be transparent on her face, in her eyes, in the catch in her voice.

"Well, there you are! I can't tell you how boring this place has been without you. I've had to do all my work alone. I much prefer the two-man approach. So glad you're back! How's the family?"

"I'm relieved to be back, and sooner than I might have been. My mom's doing great, from all appearances. The surgery went well." Alma was touched at his concern for her family. They really hadn't discussed much of a personal nature. He'd never even broached the subject of what she felt was a glaring disability. Her height and obvious halting gait didn't seem to be of any consequence to him. This gorgeous lab partner of hers was simply perfect. How could she possibly have been so lucky as to have drawn him out of all the others now busy working in the room all around them?

"I saved everything I thought you might need once you got back. I have some lecture notes and all my paper work on the experiments we've done while you were gone. I hope they'll be enough for you to catch up. At least for this course."

Alma nearly cried. She hadn't even had to ask, and here he was offering everything she'd need for the class. Most guys wouldn't have been nearly that thoughtful.

"I… I can't thank you enough. You have no idea how much this will help me out. Now I only have to worry about my other classes."

"No problem. Glad I could help."

ALMA HADN'T A CLUE how quickly her euphoria would turn to despair. It would all come crashing down around her ears so quickly she would lose all sense of reality. A true psychic break was just around the corner. Everything would start to unravel when Alma took her lunch break.

AFTER LEAVING the biology lab with copies of Gavin's lab procedures and lecture notes, Alma spent the rest of the morning trying to gather as much missed information from her other classes as she could. Unfortunately, no one in her other classes had been as thoughtful as Gavin. No one had even noticed she was absent. It seemed she was going to have an uphill battle closing the gap in all her other subjects.

By lunchtime she was feeling the strain and had worked up an appetite. She'd skipped breakfast and regretted it now. The cafeteria was crowded with students, wolfing down a quick bite before their afternoon classes commenced. Alma was thankful she had a free period after lunch and could take her time.

She waited patiently in line with her tray until it was her turn to choose from the array of foods on ice and on the steam table. She chose a chicken salad sandwich from the cold case and a bowl of steaming mushroom soup from the hot entrées. Grabbing a glass of iced tea, she turned to look for a seat. She was hoping to spot either Sally or Gavin. She suddenly realized they were the only two people she'd really made any contact with since beginning college. Two months and only two people in the hundreds of students milling all over campus for her to approach, with whom to share her lunch break.

Quickly scanning the room, looking for either of them or an empty table, she suddenly spied both. Over in the far corner, Gavin was just rising from his seat as Sally rushed up with her tray. Taking her tray from her, he expertly placed her food next to his, deposited the empty tray on a stand within reach, and resumed his seat next to her, giving her shoulder a squeeze along with a kiss on her cheek.

Alma froze. She felt lightheaded and her tray was suddenly very heavy. Her appetite had vanished in a flash. Without realizing what she was doing, she took her tray full of food directly to the nearest tray stand, deposited it there and left the cafeteria before Sally or Gavin noticed her. She needn't have worried. She glanced back over her shoulder as she exited to see that they were engrossed in animated conversation, their eyes on no one else but the other.

Alma could hardly make it to her dorm. Tears were streaming down her face and everything was blurry. Instead of a leisurely lunch with her roommate or Gavin, they would be spending their lunch together and she would be sobbing in her room.

Alma's nightmare was not over yet. She simply could not summon up enough energy to even think about any afternoon classes. She was unable to focus on anything. The only two people with whom she'd developed any rapport had just trampled on her heart. She had misconstrued Gavin's attention as something other than a genuine concern for another human being. She'd read more into it than had been intended. Why had he been so very nice to her? How could such thoughtfulness be just that and nothing more?

Alma had no point of reference with which to judge Gavin's actions. It seemed she was totally lacking in points of reference. She hadn't had a friend in her life other than her parents and Miss Crandall. No compassion had been shown her by a judgmental citizenry. An inconvenient mouse had made her an outcast before she even had a chance. An inconvenient virus had ruined her chance for a normal life. Just when she'd thought it was possible for her to enjoy all the things everyone else had been enjoying their whole lives, she saw all that disintegrating before her.

She was certain Sally had not purposely moved in to take Gavin away from her. There was no premeditated malice involved. Alma had mentioned how nice her lab partner was, but had kept any more detailed information to herself. Sally didn't even know his name. Alma had kept that to herself as well. Now she wasn't sure why. That didn't make seeing Sally leaning up against Gavin any less painful.

Alma also did not have any way of knowing that Gavin treated everyone just as he'd treated her. There wasn't anything particularly flirtatious about anything he'd said or done. She had just interpreted it that way because she desperately wanted it to be so.

Hours later she was still sitting there when Sally returned from her last class.

"Alma, what on earth is the matter? You look terrible. Please don't tell me it's your mother." Sally sat down next to her and put a comforting arm around Alma's shoulders.

"No. It's not my mother. Well, maybe partly. I don't know. Maybe it's just stress over the whole thing. I just…I just…" and Alma dissolved into tears again.

There was a knock at the door. Sally went to see who it was.

"There's a phone call for Alma Thorndike," the dorm monitor from the front desk announced.

Alma got up and slowly left the room, wiping away the fresh tears. Sally decided to accompany her down to the front desk.

The phone was lying on the counter and Alma picked it up, putting the receiver to her ear.

"Yes. This is Alma Thorndike." And then her face went as white as a sheet and she began to slump to the floor. Sally caught her, propping her against the front of the counter, taking the receiver from her as she did.

"This is Sally Bigelow, Alma's roommate. She's not feeling at all well just now." Then she, too, knew why Alma was lying on the floor, propped against the counter. "Oh, but that can't be. Her mother just had surgery and is doing so well. Alma just got back from home."

"She was doing very well. We were all very encouraged. But this afternoon, as Mr. Thorndike was driving her home from her doctor's appointment, they were struck by a drunk driver and both her parents were killed," the voice at the other end made it final. "I'm so very sorry to have to be the barer of such awful news."

"Yes. Well, thank you for calling. We'll... I'll see to Alma now," and she hung up.

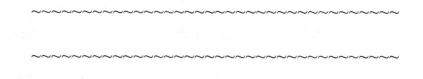

WHEN SALLY hung up the phone, Alma lay dazed and pale, her back propped against the counter front, her legs stretched out straight in front of her. Sally dropped to the floor beside her and, putting her arm around Alma's inert form, pulled her towards herself so that Alma's head rested on Sally chest. Alma immediately stiffened and drew back.

"What are you doing?" Alma's tone left no doubt she was not happy about Sally's proffered shoulder.

"I just wanted to try and comfort you. You seemed totally in a daze. I can't imagine how anyone can cope with such a tragedy. They told me what happened. Oh, Alma, I'm so dreadfully sorry."

"That's very nice of you, but I don't need your pity!" Alma spat back. "I've been coping fairly well without any support from someone like you."

"But, Alma, this must be devastating. And what do you mean, 'someone like me'?"

"Someone who waits until I'm out of the picture, and then swoops in and steals the one person I'm interested in. The first guy who's ever shown any interest in me, and treated me as if I were totally normal." Alma knew she was being needlessly unkind, but she was unable to stop her tongue from giving voice to the first thoughts that had come into her head, as she had stood there with her tray in her hands, crushed to see her roommate and Gavin more than casually together.

"What are you talking about? I don't go around planning to steal other girl's boyfriends, especially not my roommate's boyfriend. Besides, I didn't even know you had one. There must be some mistake," Sally was obviously mystified by Alma's outburst.

Alma was on a roll now, and she couldn't put on the brakes. "I saw you with my own eyes just hours ago, cuddling up to Gavin in the cafeteria."

"Gavin! Gavin's the boy you told me about? How was I supposed to know that? There must be several thousand eligible, good-looking guys wandering around campus. We just happened to bump into one another a few weeks ago. He never mentioned you. I guess I didn't mention you either, but it certainly wasn't a premeditated act to steal him on my part. I'm sorry if you think it was"

At that, Alma dissolved into shuddering sobs and allowed Sally to once again offer her shoulder. After Alma had settled down a bit, Sally helped her up and they went back to their room.

"What are you going to do now?" Sally asked Alma as she crumpled onto her bed.

"I have to go home. There's so much to do, and I don't know what it is. This can't be happening. I'm losing my mind here. I can't even think. I've got to pack. You can help me gather up everything." She got up and like a zombie marched toward her closet.

"You're going to pack up everything?" Sally asked, wondering if Alma was still not too clear of mind.

"Yes. I won't be coming back this time."

"But why not? You can't just chuck everything. This is your whole future at stake. You're going to need everything you get here more than ever now."

"No! I was very foolish to delude myself into thinking I could be just like everyone else. I'll never be. All those suggestions you made about my changing my appearance, those changes won't alter who I am. I must have been an idiot to think I could truly interest anyone like Gavin. As for any further studies here, well, I'm so far behind already. Another absence for who knows how long this time, and I'll never ever catch up. I've never been a quitter, but I think now I quit." Alma began tossing things right and left out of her closet onto her bed and the floor. "Help me get all this stuff packed up. I'll have to see about getting back home as quickly as I can."

"Alright, but I think you're making a mistake to walk away now," Sally answered her, as she retrieved Alma's suitcase from the closet shelf where she'd had to put it for Alma months ago. "Aren't you at least going to attempt to say goodbye to anyone?"

"No. I can say goodbye to you when I leave the dorm. The only other person would be Gavin, and I can't. Not after…well, I just can't." And with that Alma put what little energy she could muster into preparations for her to leave as soon as possible.

~~~~~~

ONCE SHE HAD MADE her decision, she vowed there would be no turning back. In order to forestall any such vacillation, she hurriedly packed, with a great deal of help from Sally, then sat down to write her intensions to withdraw from any further academic pursuits in letter form. She personally delivered her letter to the Dean of Students office. He happened to be in at the time and wished to speak with Alma directly. His secretary showed Alma into his comfortable office and departed.

"Miss Thorndike, I'd like to personally convey my condolences on the tragic deaths of both your parents. I know you must hurry home. There must be many things to attend to. I hope you have some assistance in that quarter. But, I really must caution you to slow down just a little, and think about your future as a whole. Once all the unpleasantness of two funerals and adequate time for you to grieve over your tremendous loss are over, you're going to have a great deal of life to fill thereafter. Do you really think it serves you best to let all this go? Your scholarship may not be renewed if you curtail your education immediately. I just want to be sure you've thought this out well in advance. It's only been a matter of hours since you heard of your parents' accident. Do you truly want to do this?" He looked out at her over his glasses with a kindly and concerned expression on his face.

"I know it's been sudden. But I do think it's for the best. I seem to have gotten myself into a situation that has gone way over my head. I don't think I have the stamina I used to. I've never given up before. But there's a first time for everything. I always did so very well in school, but college has turned out to be quite another animal. I think I've reached my limits."

"Very well. If you're absolutely sure I can't persuade you otherwise, then I wish you every good fortune whatever you do. Do try somehow to make this a new beginning of some sort, once everything settles down there at home."

With that, Alma's academic career ended and a new and sadder chapter began.

~~~~~~

ALMA SLEEPWALKED through the double funeral of her parents. She was fortunate that there wasn't a whole lot she was required to do. Both Clyde and Freda had made all the necessary arrangements in advance. The mourners were few. Alma barely knew any of them. A few hushed condolences. Several tentative hugs. The cemetery lay behind her, an empty house ahead.

Clyde and Freda's lawyer informed her that her parents had made sure she would be well taken care of should anything happen to them. The house was hers, free and clear. There was a large trust fund that would be more than enough to meet her needs while she contemplated her future. Alma had already finished that contemplation before the last shovelful of dirt closed over her parents' caskets. She would have no future.

A future was something normal people had. She now knew she was not normal and never would be. Her break from any kind of meaningful reality was complete. She had a roof over her head and plenty of money in the bank. What more could she possibly want?

Returning home alone, she opened the door to the nothingness that stretched out in front of her. There would be no after service buffet. No one would be coming by to offer her any comfort.

She thought of Sally once more and then put her out of her mind. There was no reason to keep in touch. She hoped Sally would be happy with Gavin, if that was in the cards. She knew it wasn't in her deck. The house was silent. She would keep it that way. Solitude would be her refuge.

Unplugging the radio and the TV, they would sit there for years gathering dust. No records would be played on the stereo. CD's would appear on the scene without Alma's slightest awareness. Music would never come from the house again.

Alma would spend her time reading and working in her mother's garden. She devoured books by the dozens, reading everything she could get her hands on. Though she became a wealth of knowledge, no one would ever know. She talked with no one. She spurned any conversation with anyone when she shopped at the grocery store.

Her exercise consisted of vigorously enlarging and cultivating Freda's hybrid tea rose garden. Eventually, there would be no more room in the backyard for another plant. For all the care she lavished on the roses, she skimped on everything else. The house soon looked uninhabited and shabby. The paint was pealing, but she took no notice. The roof didn't leak. The furnace worked. She was content with several window A/C units. She barely looked at her refuge of solitude when she exited or entered on necessary errands. It was impossible to be aware that behind the more and more ramshackle façade there was a garden of great beauty, as lovingly tended as everything else was blindly ignored.

~~~~~~

THE YEARS passed and were not kind to Alma. She could have cared less. She had no interest in her appearance. Grey hair formed a frizzy, uncombed halo around her head. She never wore anything but gardening clothes, often stained with dirt, torn by thorns. She was a frightening sight.

Children learned to give the house a wide berth. They were sure she was a witch. Even adults in the community gossiped about the strange reclusive old lady, even they were somewhat leery of.

Alma was blissfully unaware of the consternation she engendered in the children or the wariness of their parents. She had no interest in any of them. Her roses and her books were her world.

She had never revisited her once-consuming interest in all things great and small. In fact, she even rebuffed all attempts any of those creatures might make to encroach on her solitude. She chased away any stray cat or dog. Bugs were just predators to her precious roses and they were summarily dispatched with an effective insecticide. Birds came and went. She paid them no heed, as long as they did not get in her way. She certainly wasn't about to feed them, encouraging their continued and constant presence. Nothing was going to penetrate her wall of isolation. Until Barney.

~~~~~~

THE SUMMER had been mild and with adequate rainfall. Her roses were in full and glorious bloom. She took a few of the choicest buds into the house each day, placing them around the house in crystal vases, allowing them to open slowly, releasing their powerful perfumes. That such a drab and unkempt interior could smell so wonderful was a paradox. It was the only beauty in Alma's world and she reveled in it.

As she toiled one afternoon, pruning back errant branches, mulching around each plant, applying the life-giving, bloom-boosting fertilizer that supplied her with never-ending blossoms from early spring until frost, she noticed a squirrel, sitting at the base of her maple at the foot of the yard. She was not pleased to see it. The last thing she needed was a pesky squirrel, digging holes and burying nuts in her rose garden.

"Shoo! Go away!" she shouted at it. The squirrel just flicked its tail a few times and stared back at her. It didn't budge an inch. Alma got with up with difficulty. Her legs were not co-operating any longer, despite the exercise they received in the garden. She flailed her arms menacingly and shouted louder.

"Shoo! Get out of here! Go away!" The squirrel sat up, as if to get a better look at the crazy person waving their arms in the air. But he did not move from the spot. Annoyed, Alma saw she was going to have to be more explicit. She began to trudge toward the offending rodent, being careful of all the thorns around her. Even so, she snagged her jeans on a branch and nearly went down.

"Now look what you've done. You've made me tear another pair of pants and I may just be bleeding underneath. You'll be sorry if I ever get my hands on you." The squirrel waited until the last minute before Alma was upon him to scamper quickly to the first branch of the maple, out of Alma's reach. No amount of shouting or flailing would scare the squirrel from its vantage point above Alma, as it continued to examine her like it was trying to figure out what this strange woman was doing.

Alma finally got tired of waving her arms to no avail. Her shouting wasn't intimidating this bold rodent in the least. They commenced a prolonged stare down. The squirrel was the first to blink. It just stretch out on the branch, closed its eyes, and appeared to go to sleep.

"Of all the cheek! How dare you lay down and take a nap when I'm talking to you." The squirrel did not move a muscle. Alma was reduced to returning to her gardening, incensed by the rodent's impudence, but unable to rout him.

As she spent the short half of the afternoon at her tasks, she glanced often to the lowest branch of her maple tree, to find the errant squirrel peacefully asleep.

~~~~~~

FOR THE NEXT few days Alma continued to see her inquisitive rodent at the maple tree, waiting for her when she came out of the house. Her movements never phased it, unless she tried to scare it off. Then it would merely retire to its favorite branch beyond her reach. It became too much effort for Alma to continue interrupting her work for a stupid squirrel. She decided to ignore it. Eventually it would grow tired of watching her and go elsewhere.

She was mistaken. Not only did it not go elsewhere, it began to narrow its watching distance considerably, a little bit at a time. The squirrel knew Alma could never move fast enough to get to it, and Alma knew the squirrel knew it. She was at a loss as to what to do about her unwanted visitor.

One day when the squirrel was only six feet from her, sitting calmly on its haunches, intently studying Alma, and seemingly very interested in what she was doing, Alma stopped short, put down her tools and let her guard down.

"And just what do you find so fascinating about an old woman and her roses?" she asked it, not expecting an answer. But answer it did. A series squeaks sounded as if the thing had understood exactly what she said. Of course, that wasn't possible, but the conversation continued never the less.

"Is that so? Well if you're that interested, why don't you just help instead of just sitting there?"

A few more squirrel words were offered before it came even closer, approached the shrub Alma was working on, and began pushing mulch up around the base of the bush. Alma was flabbergasted. She was utterly speechless. Her isolation wall crumbled and she wanted to reach out and hug the furry little beast now helping her mulch her roses. How could this dumb animal possibly understand what she said, and be doing exactly what she'd just been doing herself? It had certainly observed her doing the same thing enough times, but squirrels were not particularly known for their intellect. But there he was doing it. She now referred to him as he.

~~~~~~

FOR DAYS AFTER, Alma began to look forward to seeing him. Sometimes he did things that looked like he was helping, other times he was just a playful squirrel. But he was not just a squirrel any longer. He was her squirrel. And as such, he needed a name. Thus, he became Barney.

On Alma's next trip to the grocery store, she would be shopping for two. In the pet aisle she put a bag of field corn in her cart. A large bag of unshelled peanuts was next. She'd never had to feed a squirrel before, and he must be eating fine on his own because he was a very healthy looking specimen, but she felt he deserved to be rewarded for all his help. If it truly was help. Well, he needed a treat even if it wasn't help.

Alma took to having her lunch in the yard with Barney. The conversation was decidedly egocentric. Barney hadn't much to offer on the socio-economic scene. Politics were not his forte either. But he did chatter on about a great many things that Alma was sure were very pertinent to squirrel society and ethics. He did not hog the conversation though. He listened intently to Alma's thoughts and ideas. Alma now had a forum for everything that had ever bothered her. She could vent on all the injustices that had come her way. She could expound upon the egregious insults visited on her by thoughtless or ignorant others, or just rail against fate for her lot. It was very therapeutic. She felt better than she had in years.

~~~~~~

BARNEY GREW BOLDER with each passing day, and soon he was waiting on the porch, just outside the door, when Alma came out to start her day. After several days of being thusly greeted, she greeted him with a treat as soon as she opened the door. Barney was most appreciative and his physique was beginning to show it. He was a very happy, very plump, very kept squirrel.

~~~~~~

THE WEATHER was gradually turning cooler. A touch of fall was in the air. Alma and Barney had become great companions. Then one morning, as Alma opened up the kitchen door, Barney came rushing into the kitchen like he belonged there, hopped up on the table and waited expectantly. Alma already had his treat in her hand and he let out a little chatter, letting her know that he expected it immediately. And he got it. From then on it was understood that Barney would get his treat, at table, in the kitchen, as Alma was having her breakfast. Breakfast and lunch were now officially on the calendar.

~~~~~~

AS SEPTEMBER merged with October and cooler temperatures became more frequent, Alma suddenly realized that autumn would soon be in full swing, with even cooler days, colder nights and the inevitable first frost. Often, the very first frost had been a killing affair. Her roses had been wiped out in one night. Then her gardening was, for all rights and purposes, on hold until spring. With her then spending all her time indoors, what would become of Barney? She rationalized, and rightly so, that Barney was a wild animal. He'd lived most of his life outdoors, fending for himself. He probably had hidden ample stores from all the food he'd been receiving the past months. But that didn't allay her fears about how long, and cold, and friendless this coming winter was going to be without Barney by her side most of the day. Barney would most likely build himself a nice comfortable nest to hibernate in through the winter months. He would surely not forget her. He'd be there in the spring to help her get her roses going again. She would have to cope as best she could. She'd do a lot of reading. That would occupy a great deal of her time. But she would sorely miss Barney's presence.

~~~~~~

IT WAS TWO WEEKS later that the weather really began to look ugly. Alma had been gathering every bud each day, filling the house with their fragrance as they opened. She didn't want a single blossom to be killed by that inevitable frost, now very near. On the last morning before the killer frost, one that broke all records, she had her usual breakfast with Barney, before they proceeded to the garden. She would just have time to spread a heavy covering of mulch for the winter. Then Mother Nature would be in control and Alma would retire for the winter.

Barney seemed to intuit that something was up. He was extremely fidgety the entire day. He hardly took time to sit down and have his lunch before he was up and cavorting around the yard, making a great deal of noise. Alma had no idea what he was so upset about.

Once the last of the mulch was distributed, Alma spied one last bulging rosebud. It was going to be one of her favorites, a blood red, "Mr. Lincoln."

She left Barney running frantically around the yard, taking the last rose of autumn with her into the house, and closing the door for the last time.

~~~~~~
~~~~~~

ALMA FOUND an appropriate cracked glass bud vase for her prize, filled it with water, and placed the rose lovingly in the vase. She put the vase on the kitchen windowsill, where it would get the most light. She would watch it slowly unfurl its deep velvety petals over the next several days. She thought. But as she turned to contemplate what to fix for dinner, she had a sudden agonizing pain behind her eyes. Her vision became a field of black spots, growing in size until there was nothing but black, and she was falling.

~~~~~~

THE ROSE on the windowsill was opening its dark red heart to the light of day. The fragrance was already permeating the entire kitchen with its heady perfume. Alma's heart was still beating, but she was in no state to enjoy her prize rose, sending out its essence to a nose that was not going to smell another rose ever again. The stroke had left Alma completely paralyzed and unconscious for most of the night. With the dawn she regained enough cognizance to realize that she was in terrible jeopardy. She was nowhere near a phone. No one ever came to her house. There was no reason for anyone to come looking for her. She might lay on the floor for days, even die there, and no one would know.

Outside, Barney was at the kitchen door, waiting for Alma to come out, but somehow knowing there was something wrong. She would not be coming out. Barney was hungry and it was time for his breakfast. Alma should have let him in by now. After several hours, he gave up his vigil at the door and went out to the street. It was a very quiet street with little traffic. Occasionally, residents would go for a walk, or a jog around the neighborhood. They usually tried to ignore the eyesore where Alma was now in dire need of medical assistance.

Several matrons from one street over had begun a walking regime in order to lose some weight, and perhaps improve their overall health. They were passing Alma's house, which they privately thought was a disgrace. That such a once elegant home should be allowed to sink into such a state of disrepair seemed almost criminal to them. They were about to go by without looking too closely, they'd already done that before, when a loud chattering attracted their attention. There on the walkway leading up to the house was a fat little squirrel scolding them fiercely. Then he suddenly stopped and ran to the side of the house, turned around and looked at them. They just stood there amazed and puzzled by its odd behavior. The squirrel ran back to the walkway and repeated his scolding and retreated once more to the corner of the house. The women decided to keep their distance. They were well aware that wild animals often carried rabies. This squirrel could possibly be rabid. They continued their walk and forgot about the squirrel.

~~~~~~

SOMETIME DURING THE NIGHT, Alma slipped back into unconsciousness and by morning she was close to death. Barney was at the door once more, and this morning he was frantic. Wasting no time waiting for Alma to come out, he took up his surveillance post on the front walkway. He had to wait a long time before the same two women came down the street on their daily walk. He started his racket before they had even gotten to the house. They heard the noise immediately and slowed as they approached, still wary of such strange behavior. Barney repeated his desperate plea for help three times before the women once again moved off, shrugging their shoulders, wondering what was wrong with the crazy squirrel. No one else appeared for hours. Finally a mailman started his rounds. But he had no mail for Alma, and he too ignored Barney's antics. Barney gave up and returned to the back porch where he curled up and went to sleep.

Alma died during the night. In the morning Barney somehow knew he had to get someone to pay attention. He also knew is was too late for Alma. How he knew that was a mystery, but he had to get someone into the house. He jumped up on the outside sill and peered in at the dim interior of the kitchen. He could see Alma lying on the floor. She was not moving. She was not bringing him his treat. She was not having her breakfast. The last rose she'd cut was fully open on this third day, showing its full glory to no one but Barney. He became frantic, pawing at the window, chattering as loudly as he could. There was no response from his friend.

Back to his post he went. He was feeling a little tired. He hadn't eaten or drank in three days. Nevertheless, when he saw the two women coming down the street, he ran out to greet them, chattering frantically and running back to the house. Back and forth he went, time after time, until one of the women finally thought perhaps she'd made some sense of his actions. He certainly wasn't trying to attack them.

"You know, Mave, I think he's trying to tell us something. He just keeps running back there like he wants us to follow him. You think he's dangerous?"

"Rhonda, if he were, wouldn't you think he'd have tried to bite us by now. This is the third day we've been by and watched his little show. There's a crazy old lady lives here. Everyone avoids her. Maybe she's in trouble."

"Maybe we should go have a look," Rhonda replied as she altered course to skirt around the house, Mave in tow, following Barney now in the lead.

At the back porch, Barney took up his post directly in front of the door. Mave and Rhonda paused to have a look in the window. Mave was the first to spot Alma lying motionless on the floor and let out a shreik.

"Oh, my god, Rhonda, there's the old woman on the floor. Quick, try the door."

The door opened immediately. Alma had never had the chance to lock up for the night before the stroke had thrown her down on the kitchen floor.

"Mave, call 911. I don't think it's going to do any good though. I think she's been dead for awhile."

THE PARAMEDICS were quick to arrive to find a bizarre scene in Alma's kitchen. Mave and Rhonda were sitting calmly at the kitchen table. Alma was lying motionless on the floor. Curled up and motionless on her chest was Barney. The team quickly determined that both Alma and the squirrel were dead. Alma was already cold. The squirrel still warm.

"What's the deal here?" asked one of the paramedics.

"Why don't you tell him, Mave. It's just too strange for me to even believe."

"Well, believe it or not, for three days that squirrel has been trying to get our attention every time we walk past the house. Today he was particularly vocal and persuasive, leading us around to the back where we found the door unlocked and this woman dead on the floor. Once the door was open, the squirrel ran in, curled up on her chest and never moved again," Mave finished with a flourish, pointing at the tableau at their feet.

"No way," said the medic.

"I don't care if you believe me or not, that's what happened," Mave said with complete confidence.

"We'll have to take her to the ER. They're not going to believe this either. What shall we do with the squirrel?"

"I think you should take it with her," Rhonda said. "After all, if it hadn't been for the squirrel, who knows when she might have been found?"

The paramedics did just that. They took Alma and Barney and the bizarre tale Mave and Rhonda told back to the ER. Left behind on the windowsill was the last rose of autumn, now dropping its fading crimson petals into the kitchen sink.

THE ENTITY

The interstellar craft sped through the vast blackness of deep space at incredible speed. The sole occupant reposed in comfort within a bubble of protective superplasma in a state of suspended animation. The entity was aware of being, but nothing more complex than that. The suspended state would continue until the craft was within several light years of its destination. At the appropriate time, the bubble of plasma would dissipate and the entity would assume manual control of the craft for the final approach and landing on the targeted world. This was to be another routine reconnaissance mission. The entity had been on many before. Once an interesting avenue of expansion and conquest had been delineated, it had investigated the possible object of exploitation surreptitiously before, reporting back to its superiors on the suitability of such a target's being considered for a full force attack. Its superiors abhorred wasted time and effort on unworthy ventures, especially when such distances needed to be factored into such a campaign. The entity enjoyed this work tremendously. Great weight was given to its evaluation once returned from its scouting missions. It had been responsible for some very huge acquisitions and massive submissions of other unsuspecting worlds. It was looking forward to yet one more.

As the craft sped past Lorodak, a star we would not even be aware of for eons, not even halfway to its intended destination, a malfunction of the hyperdrives caused an ominous thrumming and instant dissolution of the plasma covering the entity. It was immediately aware of a grave situation that needed its attention quickly and expertly. A rapid systems review revealed the craft had somehow been damaged, perhaps by something extremely small but deadly. A minute fractoid spinning aimlessly through the intergalactic void could have been the culprit. The craft was supposed to be programmed to detect and avoid possibly dangerous bodies in its path, but this particular obstruction seems to have been so minute as to have escaped detection until it was too late to avert the collision. The injury was not even as big as a pin hole, but had punctured the starship in the most vulnerable of places. It could have entered and exited at hundreds of other locations without disrupting the craft's progress. However, a direct pass through the hyperdrive chamber meant a considerable loss of power and perhaps maneuverability, if the breach could not be sealed immediately. It was the most serious injury that could be inflicted on the almost invulnerable scouting machine. Before the entity could even think, the craft was losing speed and off course. It was now passing through a relatively new and emerging system of stars its superiors referred to as

The Amalgam. It would soon become what we would term The Milky Way. There was little of interest in this infant formation and no visit had been envisioned or authorized here. The sudden course change had thrust the now crippled craft on a path slicing directly across this evolving system. Alarms were sounding as the craft lost speed exponentially and veered off any course programmed into its memory banks. A small yellow star was gaining prominence on the ship's forward view screen. A preprogrammed disaster response message was informing the entity of the impending changes in the craft's mission.

"EMERGENCY! EMERGENCY! LOSS OF HYPER THRUSTER CAPABILITIES!"

Even as the message played over and over, the craft's computerized disaster avoidance system was feeding co-ordinates into the data banks, preparing the manual overdrives with the necessary information that the entity would need when the automatic drive systems relinquished control to its capable expertise.

"EMERGENCY LANDING DATA COMPLETE. EMERGENCY LANDING DATA COMPLETE. RELINQUISHING AUTOMATIC CONTROLS. PILOT ASSUME MANUAL NAVIGATION. PILOT ASSUME MANUAL NAVIGATION."

The entity was well aware of the gravity of its situation. Never before had such a catastrophic event marred any of its previous missions. The information it was seeing, flashing before it on the diagnostic screens, was dire indeed. The repairs that would be required upon landing might not be possible or plausible. There was the remote chance that it would be marooned on this emergency landing site. That possibility was not comforting, although it was well fortified to survive almost any eventuality. Other scouts had disappeared over the history of their race and not been heard from for eons, only to eventually turn up with great discoveries and new conquests not on the Old One's agenda. The fact remained that repairs would have to be instituted before, and if, the mission was to continue. The recorded voice droned on, as cool and calm as could be as the entity awaited the moment it would need to assume control of the vessel.

As the computer-mechanized data systems frantically searched for a likely emergency landing site, the entity studied the damage control reports still being displayed in front of it and steeled itself for assuming control of the ship. It had done this many times on training sorties, but this would be the first actual application of those experiences.

"SITE CHOOSEN. SITE CHOOSEN," the automated voice program was now informing it of the targeted destination. "PRESENT SPEED AND DISTANCE OPTIMAL. PRESENT SPEED AND DISTANCE OPTIMAL. DISENGAGING AUTOMATIC CONTROLS. ASSUME MANUAL FLIGHT. DISENGAGING AUTOMATIC CONTROLS. ASSUME MANUAL FLIGHT."

The entity was able to ascertain from schematics at hand that the destination would be a small planet in a system revolving around the yellow star that had been growing in size as the craft sped toward it. The entity would be landing on the third planet from that star, after passing some rather large and foreboding worlds which the ship's cognitive sensory banks had deemed most inappropriate.

Manual control was turned over to the veteran pilot and the craft sailed past a small reddish orb, heading directly for the more inviting and larger planet coming into view. The surface was shrouded in dense cloud-like cover and occasional flares of fires below reflected upward on the planet's darkened side through that cover. The entity chose to enhance a landing program which would enter the dense atmosphere at the upper point of the planet's rotation where obvious volcanic activity was minimal. The craft was becoming more unstable by the minute as the propulsion chamber's damage was reaching a critical point. Then the small scouting vessel was plunging into the billowing grayness of this foreign atmosphere. The craft pitched and yawed as the entity strained to maintain control. Forward speed was being compensated for as efficiently as the undamaged reverse propulsion units could manage, but it did not appear their function was going to be adequate enough to allow the now tumbling ship a smooth touchdown. Rather, it was going to be an extreme event and the entity just had time to deploy the emergency life preserving encapsulation measures before the craft hit the surface with a sickening thud and bounced several times before coming to rest upside down at the bottom of a steep ravine.

The entity was rattled but unhurt. It did not take long to ascertain the seriousness of the present situation. Repairs to the ship were not going to be possible. Although an automatic tracker signal had engaged, it was unlikely to ever be detected on the home planet, and if it were, a rescue mission would take quite a long time, if it were ever sent at all. They were a very pragmatic race and not prone to wasteful efforts rescuing one lone scout in the middle of a galactic nowhere. It did not distress the scout, dispassionately examining the situation it was now facing. Making the most of any scenario was drilled into its consciousness from its inception. An expert evaluation of the atmosphere of this evolving planet revealed a noxious mixture of gasses not conducive to exploration or exploitation, at least not now. But the mixture was promising.

The entity pushed its cognitive pattern retrieval abilities to the limit, and, as expected, all reports came back negative. There wasn't anything out there which held the slightest interest. The entity was not surprised, nor dismayed. It had lots of time in which to wait. It had waited before, although perhaps never as long as it might be required to this time. It would program an encapsulation mode to see it through as much of this new world's birth throws as it deemed necessary, reinvigorating itself at a much later date. It was already ancient anyway. It was in no rush. It could afford to wait.

When the entity next emerged from its self-induced suspension, many changes had taken place, as it had been sure they would. The noxious atmosphere had mellowed. It was still poisonous, to be sure, but less so. The volcanic activity continued, but had also diminished in volume and intensity. It pushed for cognitive retrieval and was not surprised to again find nothing. However, everything it did sense was encouraging. Given more time it was fairly certain this world had potential. Another suspension cycle was instituted.

Upon a second awakening, this new world was coming to life. The retrieval waves were not empty any longer. They did not report any awareness, but they were vibrating with living things. The entity perceived small creatures, both animate and inanimate, but it was still a world lacking any purposeful direction. Everything seemed on its own, not only unaware of otherness but selfness as well. Back into suspension it went.

The third awakening thrilled the entity with progress it had know would come. Now the air was pleasing and the temperatures had moderated. The mantle of this young world was becoming stable and supportive of its new life forms. The entity intuited they were many and diverse. Thousands were also huge, some fleet, some lumbering, but all aware of each other. There was a pervading hunger in the air. Rage and violence permeated its senses. The entity was well acquainted with those. These creatures were acting purely on instinct and their brains were small and inadequate for the type of awareness it was looking and hoping for. But, this may well prove to have been a fortuitous accidental inconvenience after all. Yet one more brief suspended interlude should yield the answer.

Though the interlude was brief for the entity, it encompassed the end of the era of dinosaurs, and the rise of the new masters of the planet, the mammals. A particular mammal had risen to prominence and now thought it dominated its world. This relatively new species was in for a rude awakening. Homo sapiens, as we know it, was about to learn that there was another, which had lain in wait, hoping this exact kind of creature would eventually emerge. When this other awakened, it would not be disappointed.

The minute the entity slipped from its epochal repose, and pushed for awareness retrieval this time, its senses were immediately assaulted with a myriad of conflicting signals. It smiled. Well, what would pass as a smile for its kind. Anyone witnessing such an expression would never have described it as a smile. In fact, anyone witnessing it would quite possibly have died of a heart seizure on the spot, so grizzly and ghastly was this alien's glee.

It was more than pleased with what had occurred while it had rested. The entity was instantly aware that these were thinking, feeling, extremely cognitive beings, both of themselves and each other.

It was also pleased to note that along with this new found awareness, the old rage and violence of lesser species was not diminished. Rather, it had been enhanced and refined. It now approached what the entity catalogued as an art form. It was delightful. It was exactly what this ancient star traveler had been looking for in the first place when fate stepped in, in the form of a tiny piece of space matter, crippling its ship and imprisoning it here eons ago.

The question now was how to proceed. It was well aware that the immediate environment had turned cold, bitter cold. It perceived itself alone in this vast, now frozen landscape, and that was probably a good thing. At least it was for the present. Perhaps later other arrangements might be undertaken. For now it was a perfect place to observe, familiarize itself with all the nuances of this amazingly complex new species, plan a course of action afterward. It had many options.

It had the capacity to remove or at least drastically ameliorate the inherent rage and dissention within the ranks of these poor creatures, but what would be the fun in that? It had never exercised those powers before. It didn't expect to do so now. The other option, of course, was just the opposite. It could use, expand, deepen, and hone all that pent up fury and anger to a boiling point that would turn this entire planet into a seething caldron of enmity. After all, it had been so very long since it had had any fun.

As it slowly and painstakingly analyzed this strange species it discovered a few surprises. Others had visited during the last suspension. They had come at a time when this new manifestation was just developing its communication skills. The rudimentary languages were far enough advanced to include some nebulous references to events ill understood at the time. They had not as yet developed any method of written word by which to document their history, thoughts or beliefs. They had left some interesting pictures behind which gave some insight into what had occurred in the murky past. In fact there were a few brave souls even now who espoused the opinions that the entity now knew to be facts. It would not push too hard at these individuals. It certainly didn't want them to be aware of its presence, and it was possible they might become aware of its intrusion into their mental processes if it probed too deeply. These were highly intelligent individuals, quite possibly so because they had received slightly more of the DNA left long ago by "the others." It would not do for the entity to delve any further into their psyches. Not now anyway. It could easily reveal itself and take control of this entire planet with a snap of its fingers. At least what passed for its fingers. These few individuals could become the leaders of this new planet, should the entity decide to assume supreme control. They would pledge their allegiance to it with a gloating, "I told you so!" to all the nay sayers who branded them as kooks and fools.

There were so many other psyches to be investigated first. This species seems to have evolved as a peculiarly dependent phenomenon that based the very bedrock of their belief in things poorly understood, not fully known or knowable, but rather on things perceived and believed based on myth, word of mouth, and tradition. There was the wide held belief to this day that the entire race had sprung from two individuals who had appeared out of nothing and nowhere, formed by a omnipresent spirit that was initially known as YHWH. Sometimes this deity was referred to as the "I AM THAT I AM." As millennia passed, the names by which this spirit would be known multiplied exponentially and took many sidetracks and metamorphoses. Each new name would spawn yet a new belief system, one for which its adherents were more than willing to kill any who did not embrace their particular interpretation of documents whose authorship was suspect, and written based on the many myths and words of mouth passed down through generations of superstitious ancestors.

One of the first to emerge, which prevailed in a number of forms even now, was that of a "Chosen People." They felt they had been singled out as special, and had carried a box that housed the Spirit that had "chosen" them everywhere they went. This box contained laws written by the very Spirit that made them special. Indeed the box went before them wherever they went and protected them from those who did not believe in the Spirit in the Box. Those who disbelieved dropped dead before the box. But now they no longer had the box or the written words that had been in the box. It had disappeared millennia ago, along with the protection they thought the box had afforded them. The history they had written for themselves alluded to the visitation of the Others, but couched in such an allegorical fashion as to blur the true events. It also detailed a long history of approval and disapproval, blessing and punishment, peace and war, independence and slavery, meted out to them according to the pleasure or displeasure of the Spirit in the Box. Nothing seems to have changed with them except the fractured and varied sects now extant trying valiantly to move on without any tangible evidence of their past, save their own slanted stories and their tradition. All around this group, many other belief systems rose and fell, some small bits and pieces of them finding their way into the Chosen One's records without them even being aware of where it had originally come from.

From this group arose yet another. It came out of that group, but was rejected by the majority of that group, even though the basis for the new beliefs were delineated within the old group's documents. The entity shook its head, or what passed for a head, at the perfidiousness of this species. The box was gone and had now been replaced by the Son of the Box, who died and came back again. Those who still followed the box killed those who followed the Son of the Box, and vise versa. The battle raged for centuries as new written documents by proponents of the new belief superseded the ancient ones. Many new accounts emerged and were carefully culled in order to approve only those that met with the standards of the leaders of the new belief. Those found unacceptable or not following a rigid screening process were destroyed or suppressed. Everything would soon have to be approved by the one person who spoke for the Son of the Box. He had the supreme authority to make policy and bless or punish the adherents of this growing belief. Then there was a sudden rift within the new system. There was dissention among the ranks as to who had the final and infallible word to speak for everyone. The group split in half and now two supreme leaders spoke for the half over which they held sway.

Later still, one arose who challenged the Son of the Box as spokesman for the box. Yet another term emerged for the same Spirit that had inhabited the box, Allah, and great dissention ensued among already established groups over this new name for the Spirit that was the same, and sprang from accounts held in common, and written by ancestors also in common. The entity was greatly entertained. Now a whole other group of people flocked to follow this challenger. The animosity between these groups escalated until the planet's soil ran red with the blood of the faithful. The entity chuckled at the carnage that ensued. All that killing over such ill-understood and documented events. It tickled its sense of irony.

All the while, for millennia, this strange race labored under some fairly serious misconceptions. For one, they believed themselves to be the center of the universe as they knew it. Literally everything revolved around them. Their world had been the lynchpin of creation, having appeared first before any other thing. Their perceptions were also a bit skewed. According to the ancient writings, myths, and oral traditions, their specialness was sacrosanct, but their vision was flat. They believed their world was flat. Goodness reigned above the flatness and Evil dwelt below it.

There were a few more enlightened souls, probably those with an extra helping of The Other's DNA, who recognized their finite place in the scheme of things, and even built their monuments in alignment with the stars. They were well aware of rotation and revolution, seasons and the phases of the moon. Had these early seers been know to any of the other schools of thought and belief, they would immediately have been branded as pagan demons out to destroy the faithful with their tales of astrology and other such nonsense. They would have been heretics plain and simple. But those learned ancients vanished, leaving their disappearance a mystery.

There was also afoot, far to the east, yet other more temperate, non-violent, contemplative mindsets. They were Esoterics bent on meditation and left the entity bored with their sedentary, introspective pursuits. It craved more demonstrative and destructive schools of thought.

But the entity was not up to speed yet. It had not yet come full cycle to the present day. There was still much more to learn. There ensued a long period of dark days which enthralled the entity no end. Poverty, pestilence, hatred, and murderous zealots reigned supreme. A very few learned ones who read and wrote, held sway over everyone else. They told the faithful what to think and believe. No one had access to the precious writings except a select few. The enmity between the factions of beliefs had ample time to brew and fester. They fought each other incessantly.

Then there dawned a day of new enlightenment when suddenly art and music began to flourish. More rational and intelligent, less superstitious and ignorant minds prevailed. Science took hold where superstition once ruled. The old ideas of the world's centrality and flatness were questioned, and those who espoused those ideas were indeed branded as heretics by the old school leaders who were loath to give up any of their control over their subjects, who had allowed them to ensconce themselves in their positions of power in the first place.

A new process by which almost anyone could obtain copies of written documents dismayed those who'd always kept such things from public view. Suddenly dozens of brave souls appeared on the horizon with all kinds of new interpretations and translations of those previously hoarded documents and they withdrew all their support from the old schools, forming their own, causing much friction, hatred and more bloodshed. The entity felt things getting interesting once more.

Just when it appeared this new species was on the road to a more promising and productive future, ruled by science and logic, there were still those who continued to concoct the most bizarre fabrications that, once established, were accepted as fact. There were, in the traditions of this increasingly confusing collection of creatures, numerous accounts of strange and outrageous beliefs. One involved an old man who traversed the globe on the very night the Son of the Box was supposed to have been born. He traveled in a cart with skids, soaring far above the ground, pulled by a team of antlered flying beasts, and carrying loads of presents. His job was to distribute these gifts that very night, mostly to the young, but also many expensive and elaborate things to older ones as well. He did not knock on doors to deliver these presents, but rather had to go down chimneys to do so. The rest of the year this white haired old guy supposedly lived very near where the entity was conducting his investigations into this world. Preposterous, thought the entity.

There was also a large furry animal with long ears, who made his rounds on the day the Son of the Box had come back. He delivered baskets of candy to little ones, hiding them so that they would have to search to find them.

The entity particularly liked the little flying person who came at night when a little one had lost a tooth. If they put it under their pillow as they slept, the little flying person would come and take it away, leaving little round flat metal objects, or sometimes pieces of paper with pictures and numbers on them. The small ones derived a great deal of pleasure from what they found under their pillow the next morning. Who were these creatures and what kind of mental deficiencies were they suffering from? The entity was totally at a loss.

These people seemed drawn toward items of faith that disappeared as soon as they were found. Yet another new sect sprang up in a fairly new western nation. Golden Tablets were involved but were quickly whisked from public scrutiny, buried at the request of an emissary from the Spirit of the Box, while the founders of this new faith wove their web and snared anyone whom they could convince to follow them with yet another tome deemed "truth beyond reproof." This new belief espoused its followers to take many wives and father many children. Their leader had many dozens of each. More distrust, hatred and bloodshed erupted between this new group and all the old ones. The entity was enjoying its romp through the history of this strange new world.

It was disappointed to learn that it had just missed a world conflagration in which it would truly have loved to have gotten involved. A piss ant, mustached, painter somehow managed to subvert an entire country with his mangled thinking, killing millions of Followers of the Box, as well as others he considered to be inferior, sparking a conflict that raced around the globe. Before it was through, an eastern ruler joined him and awakened a Sleeping Giant that arose with a might not previously experienced in history, unleashing on the ruler's unsuspecting subjects a devastation beyond belief. The entity almost swooned in ecstasy over the brink to which this planet had almost brought itself. It was so deeply sorry it had not been there for the dawn of that new age of fear, of self destruction. What might it have done to promote that very thing? But it had missed that opportunity. It needed to rush ahead to the present to see what new mischief it might involve itself in, what new fright might be afoot.

And yes there was light. A new light taking shape from a most unexpected source. There was a man; tall, rich, bearded, and malcontent. He held a most prominent chip on his shoulder for the People of the Box. He was receiving assistance from the Sleeping Giant in a military campaign against invaders from the north, but secretly loathed the Sleeping Giant. This giant was in bed with the People of the Box, and that was unforgivable. It was a land ruled by laws he did not aspire to or approve of. It was a land of excesses. It was a land that looked down on the usurpers of the ultimate authority of the Son of the Box, of which the tall man was a major voice and gaining audience with each passing day. His Prophet was a distant relative of the Son of the Box, but claimed to be superior. Something about a barren old woman convincing her husband to sleep with her handmaiden to father an heir had gone terribly awry. Ancient history was molding the Modern. It was this wealthy malcontent's goal to destroy the People of the Box along with their friends, the Sleeping Giant. He would see to it that his beliefs became the only ones acceptable on the entire planet. He was a dangerous and vicious person. The entity immediately related to him.

The entity found itself in the present. Waves of deep seated hatred and animosity were growing ever higher and more turbulent as plans began to be formulated to strike a devastating blow on an unsuspecting world. It was underestimating this tall, rich, bearded, malcontent. He didn't like that, and everyone would be sorry. He had visions of massive explosions, mass casualties. He had no compunction in killing innocent women, children, elderly, irregardless of what they believed. No one in his way was safe from harm. He was engaging himself in a final, all out war for his particular belief, his particular interpretation of his particular writings above all others on the planet. It was quite possible this man was insane. It was also possible he was just overly ambitious. Perhaps he was just suffering from a brain tumor. Whatever the circumstances, he was a most dangerous and determined individual with a growing legion of followers more than willing to kill themselves, as well as as many others as they could manage to take with them, all for the privilege of a state known as Martyrdom. For the sacrifice of their life, they would be met in death by a plethora of virgins, intent upon doing their bidding. That promise seemed an irresistible reason and attraction to commit suicide by his faithful. This truly was an unfathomable but fascinating race.

The entity now knew what it would do. It would align itself with this pitiful man and use him beyond his wildest dreams. After all those millennia of slumber, it was finally going to have some fun.

This pawn would be completely unaware that he was being duped. The entity cared not a whit for the tall man, only what it might accomplish under his guise. This world upon which it had been accidentally deposited was in for a treat.

FEAR IS A BIRD

THE ACTION

MYRA WAS AN EXTEREMELY superstitious person. Part of her problem was her European background. Her mother had been raised in a very mountainous region of the Balkans where superstition was a way of life. She, in turn, instilled in her daughter an almost religious adherence to good luck charms, harbingers of bad luck, and all sorts of silly traditions "proven" to ward off evil. All of them, upon close scrutiny, could be chalked up to being nothing more than Old Wives Tales.

However, emigrating from a place where stories of werewolves and tales of vampires ran rife, to the sophisticated bustling city of New York, it was only natural that she brought every piece of baggage with her. She was also not adverse to adding to that baggage whenever she discovered some new and heretofore unknown harbinger of bad luck.

She was just as quick to adopt any new good luck charm or potion to ward off every conceivable evil.

She was a treasure trove of eclectic lore of all kinds. She would then be most remiss if she did not instruct her son in every nuance of her craft, for so she saw her ridiculous and ponderous body of knowledge.

Myra Karpinski could not wait until her son was old enough for her to begin instructions in the art of avoiding and warding off evil, attracting good luck, and making the most of the world around one by adhering to the advice of every preposterous Old Wives Tale she could cram into an otherwise fairly empty head. This could not be good for Joseph Karpinski.

Before Joseph had even thought about school, he was already on his way to a serious psychosis. Unfortunately, he internalized every word of advice his mother spouted. And she spouted volumes. She would quiz him on some of her favorites to make sure he had heard and remembered what she'd told him. She was most displeased if he had not absorbed her "lessons." Punishment was imminent should he flounder. He soon learned not to.

Starting school was traumatic. No one else seemed to know anything, and when he informed them what he knew, they laughed. In fact, some of the bolder and bigger boys would ask him to repeat some of his knowledge for a group of students they had rounded up just for that purpose. The laughter would be multiplied many times over from everyone in the group.

Joseph could not understand their ignorance. He was mystified by how they could be so cavalier with Fate. How could they tempt bad luck to come and find them. They would surely be sorry.

After only several weeks at school, one of the mockers was very sorry. During recess, a lively game of dodge ball was in progress. There were some workmen doing some paint work on the exterior off to one side. When a particularly forceful volley of the dodge ball bounced in the wrong direction, flying right toward the oblivious painters, Jim Bitterman, Joseph's most vocal critic, dashed to retrieve it. The ball flew under the workmen's ladder and into the street. Jim Bitterman flew after it. Running into the street without ever looking, he was struck and killed by a surprised motorist who was unable to stop in time.

Joseph had his moment of, "I told you so!" If Jim had only listened and heeded what Joe had told him, he'd still be alive. If he had not rushed headlong under the painter's ladders, taking a more circuitous route, the car would have passed before he dashed into the street. His mother's voice rang in his ears, "Never walk under a ladder!" Joseph never would.

Walking to school each day was often a virtual minefield. There were so many snares out there just waiting for you to trip them. Even the sidewalks could get you if you weren't careful. Not stepping on any cracks wasn't that easy a task. Some of New York's sidewalks seemed to be more crack than not. It was very tricky. One day he nearly knocked himself unconscious, looking down to avoid the cracks, and walked straight into a telephone pole. He had a large lump on his forehead but he hadn't stepped on a single crack. His mother was very proud when he told her about it, as she put the ice pack on his forehead.

As he got older there seemed to be an ever increasing volume of do's and don'ts with which to deal. He was hard pressed to keep them all in mind, while at the same time retain everything he was supposed to be learning at school. As he slipped into adolescence, there was one little problem he seemed to be having a great deal of difficulty with. Myra had been very adamant about this one.

"If you do that, you'll go blind! You know what that is?" she asked Joe one day when she noticed a conspicuous wet spot on his trousers where there shouldn't have been one.

"You won't be able to see," answered Joe, hoping it would end there. But, of course, it didn't.

"Don't be smart! I can see that wet spot, and I don't think you've wet your pants. I'm sure by now you know about what little boys do with their pee-pees that they shouldn't. I'm telling you, don't do it. Just remember what happened to Jim Bitterman! I really don't want to have to revisit this subject again. Am I being clear?"

"Yes, mama." She had been very clear, but he still couldn't stop himself. He became so frightened of going blind that he dropped into the school nurse's office several times a week to have her check his eyesight. It was always 20/20, but who knew when that might change if he was unable to curtail his guilty pleasure. In order to facilitate just that, every time he felt the urge, he would put his hand on a hot stove. After enough burned fingers, he got himself under control and the school nurse was glad she no longer had to check his eyesight and change bandages on fingers he seemed to always be burning. If she ever made the connection, she remained silent. She never questioned Joseph's explanations as to how he burned his fingers.

She did worry that perhaps she had a potential arsonist in the making. However, playing with matches was something a lot of little boys did. By the time she thought about delving deeper into the problem, Joseph had stopped burning his fingers.

Of course, Joseph would never play with fire. He was not about to become a bed wetter. The hot stove was an acceptable alternative; it didn't threaten him with the potential bed wetting and it worked wonders for him.

Along with a more than healthy dose of negatives, Joseph was also supplied with a plethora of positives. Good luck was as much to be sought, as bad was to be averted. Joseph could always feel confident and protected by the things he wore, or carried in his pockets. Myra was not about to send her son out into the world unshielded from the forces of evil that lurked everywhere.

Joseph never left the house without his rudraksh bracelet. It was something most people noticed, unless it was winter and Joe was wearing long sleeves. Not too many young boys wore bracelets, and certainly not ones that ugly. A string of gnarly, knobby, dried nuts did not make much of a fashion statement, but Myra insisted it was a powerful tool to ward off most anything. He also kept, in the deep recesses of his pockets, an acorn, a feather, a rabbit's foot and a pressed four-leaf clover. He was indeed armed for bear.

Once Myra had started the ball rolling, there was no stopping it. Joseph was the quintessential proof of one of physic's laws of motion.

The Law of Inertia: Once an object is in motion, it tends to remain in motion.

Joseph was inertia personified.

THE REACTION

MYRA'S EARLY ATTENTION to Joseph's proper education set the tone for the rest of his life. It virtually condemned him to a difficult, even bizarre, up-hill battle to ever attain or enjoy any kind of normal existence.

As he continued to add more and more things to his litany against bad luck, and quest for good luck charms, those around him found him most difficult to relate to. They tolerated him and kept him around primarily because he was such an oddity. He was, for some, a form of entertainment. One never knew what outrageous statement might fly from his mouth next, all said with conviction and complete sincerity.

When his idiosyncrasies became more than anyone could deal with, people simply faded away, to be replaced by fresh new faces who were, at first, intrigued by his oddities. It was almost like a private sideshow, with the main act unaware he was performing, and for free.

Joseph ended up with a loft in The Village that drew a crowd just to stare in awe at Joe's unique decorating theme. It was a good luck museum. Everywhere one looked was something related to good fortune or warding off ill fortune.

Joseph had become an avid fan of the horseshoe. He had quite a collection. Everyone had been worn. Each now resided in its own frame. They had been polished and affixed to the backing with the prongs pointing upward, thus holding all the good luck within their grasp. Joseph never thought you could have too much good luck.

There was also an extensive array of pressed and framed four-leaf clovers. He ascribed to the slightly altered adage:

"A bird in the hand is worth two in the bush." In his case he believed that: "Dozens of four-leafed clovers on the wall were worth one in the pocket." Joseph's reasoning wasn't the most logical. He could thank his mother for that.

There were feathers. If one didn't know what was really going on, one might think a large bird had exploded and the feathers stuck everywhere. Actually most people rather liked the feathers. Many were very pretty. They were tastefully displayed. And everyone was assured that no birds were harmed in the mounting process for such an extensive exhibition.

Joseph had also reached back thousands of years for a symbol of luck much admired, the reproductions of which were artfully placed throughout the loft. If scarabs were good for ancient Egyptians, they were certainly good for Joe. He had brass scarabs, porcelain scarabs, glass scarabs, and wooden scarabs. He had added a scarab ring to his attire.

Despite his unconventional, sometimes maddening, obsession with all things relatively esoteric, he never seemed to lack an entourage. That group was mostly attractive young women, with a smattering of good-looking men. Did I fail to mention how handsome Joseph Karpinski was? Forgive me. He was more than handsome. When that X met that Y, Mother Nature created one of her finest specimens.

Joseph's only problem was that he was so engrossed in his obsession, that he'd never given any thought to his physical appearance whatsoever. Not surprisingly, Joe was not a fan of mirrors, since mirrors could get broken and he certainly wouldn't want that. The solution was not to have any. He shaved with a small, round, shatterproof mirror that reflected only a very small portion of his face, the area he happened to be shaving at the time. So he was not aware of the effect he had on the opposite sex, and the occasional member of the same sex. He only knew that he was popular for whatever reason, and that pleased him.

He found he liked entertaining very much, defined by him as having people over for dinner, or having a party. He was still unaware of himself as part of the entertainment.

After meeting a particularly smitten and beautiful young woman at lunch one day, he doubled his circle of "friends," probably more like "on-lookers," but we won't quibble. Between those he knew and those she knew, it was a very considerable circle. Joseph was very pleased. He was always up for imparting his vital information to the ignorant or ill-informed. Let the entertainment begin.

The dinner party was scheduled for a Saturday night when everyone was free from work, and up for some good food and lively conversation.

There would be Joe and Brenda Kraft, his "girlfriend," plus six other couples. A dinner party for fourteen was the most ambitious undertaking Joseph had ever embarked upon. He certainly was not going to cook for fourteen people, and Brenda, his "girlfriend," said she didn't cook, period. He called a caterer. Everything he wanted would be prepared for fourteen and delivered to his loft. He decided on a cold buffet with champagne. The trays of food just fit into his refrigerator, everything in stackable containers. The champagne was cooling in a chest of ice. He was looking forward to a pleasant evening.

Brenda arrived shortly after the food had been delivered and helped Joe set up for the buffet. The caterer had supplied him with a long collapsible table and a tablecloth.

There were also an ample supply of sturdy but disposable dinnerware and utensils. Joe had purchased his own glasses for the occasion. He really hated plastic or paper beverage ware.

He let Brenda select CD's from his cabinet and, along with some she brought with her, they had an entire evening's worth of music without a repeat. Once the CD changer had been loaded and the music begun, people began arriving.

While Brenda and Joe had been busy setting up the table and arranging for the music, it had begun to rain. The very first couple to arrive stood at the door slightly damp and carrying an oversized umbrella for two. Brenda took their coats and was going to take them into Joseph's bedroom when Joe let out a scream.

"NOooo!"

Brenda's head snapped around to see the man opening the umbrella and setting it on its side. She knew where this was going.

"Never, NEver, NEVER, open an umbrella inside! How could you be so thoughtless? I thought everyone was at least aware that that is definitely taboo," Joe reprimanded the offender severely as he snatched the umbrella from the miscreant's hands. He went into the closet for the all important umbrella stand and, placing the dripping weapon in it, he put the stand by the door, out in the hallway. "We don't want to risk any repeat performances like that," he said as a second couple approached the door, also carrying a dripping umbrella.

Brenda backtracked to take two more coats, then took them to the bedroom muttering under her breath as she went, "Get out your umbrella holder, it's going to be a drippy night!" She was doing Betty Davis as Margo Channing as best she could. "Not an auspicious beginning to the evening. What else is going to happen to set him off? I hope I forewarned everyone well enough not to take Joe's comments personally. I told them he's eccentric, but I don't think even I know the depths of his eccentricities." She put the coats on the bed. "Here goes nothing." She went to answer the door, finding two more couples already making good use of the umbrella stand, thank goodness.

Joe was animatedly giving the grand tour to those who had never had the pleasure of seeing this one-of-a-kind loft. They were seemingly giving it the attention it deserved, with the right amount of interest frozen on their faces. Brenda made another trip with coats as the doorbell rang again.

"It's alright. I'll get it," Joe hollered at Brenda, as he disengaged himself from his tour group and headed for the door. The couple did not look familiar, so they must be two of Brenda's friends.

"Hello, I'm Joe. Won't you come in. Let me take your coats," he said as the man handed over his overcoat. The woman just stood there. "Where's your coat?" he asked, looking up and down the hall, as if someone else out there had already taken it.

"Oh, I don't have one," the woman answered.

"You don't have a coat?" Joe asked incredulous.

"Of course, I *have* a coat. I'm just not wearing one."

"Do you think that's wise? You know you'll catch pneumonia going out in the rain and the cold without your coat."

"I'll take my chances," she fired back, a little miffed that this person she was meeting for the first time was giving her advice before she even got in the door.

Joe could not believe that anyone could be so foolhardy, but was not able to pursue it as the couple brushed past him to greet Brenda.

Couples continued to arrive and things seemed to be going well. Everyone was mixing and getting to know one another. Only one couple was missing. As soon as they arrived the buffet would be put out and the champagne opened.

When the doorbell rang and Joe went to answer it, there was just one young lady standing in the hall.

"Can I help you?" Joe asked her, thinking she had the wrong apartment.

"Is this Joe Karpinski's apartment? Brenda gave me this address."

"Yes. I'm Joe. Are you alone? I thought there'd be two of you."

"My boyfriend got sick, but I decided to come by myself."

Joe had a sudden thought that there was trouble somewhere. Something didn't seem right. He couldn't quite put his finger on the premonition at the edge of his thoughts. He just stood there staring at the woman.

"Are you all right? Is something wrong?" she tried to see around him but he was very tall and she was very short. He blocked her line of sight into the space beyond. She could hear people laughing and talking.

Joe glanced over his shoulder and then it hit him.

"You can't come in!" he said, looking a little pale.

"But Brenda invited me. I don't understand. Where's Brenda?" As she attempted to move forward, Joe closed the door behind him and stepped into the hallway.

"Brenda's inside, but we can't go in just yet. It would not be a good thing right now. But I think we can fix that. Come with me," Joe told her as he took her hand and started down the hall pulling her with him to stop at the door at the end of the hall. He knocked at the door and it was opened quickly.

"Joe, what are you up to?" the older woman asked.

"I'm having a little get together and I'm short one person. I've got a great buffet to set out and some champagne. Can you come and join us?"

Ranada Holtz was well acquainted with her kooky neighbor down the hall. She knew he was rather strange, but basically harmless. It would be unlike her to turn down a free buffet with champagne, even if it was at Joe's Museum of Goodness and Luck.

"Sure, Joe. Thank you. I was just going to go out to get something anyway. Just let me grab my purse."

Joseph breathed a sigh of relief as they proceeded back to his loft and went inside. Now there where fourteen, just as it was supposed to be. He'd never factored in a missing person due to illness. And an evening with thirteen people would have been flirting with disaster.

"There you are! Where did you go?" Brenda asked as the threesome came in.

"I decided to go and invite Ranada over. Apparently we had one cancellation due to illness, and I wanted to keep the number at fourteen," Joe said as he took the last coat into the bedroom.

"I see he's true to form. How do you stand it?" Ranada whispered into Brenda's ear as he left the room.

"I don't know. It's starting to drive me crazy," Brenda had to admit.

Now that all the guests had arrived, Brenda and Joe began to set out all the trays from the kitchen. Brenda noticed the Joe was fine leaving the room on his own but made sure he was right with her if she left. The pattern was beginning to make sense, at least she knew it made sense to Joseph. Personally, she was beginning to get annoyed. If Joe was so fearful of being the thirteenth person in the room, he should have invited a few less, or a few more, people.

The food looked wonderful. The champagne was opened. The finishing touch was lighting the candles. Myra's mother, Joe's grandmother who he'd never met, never had a meal without at least one lit candle. Myra had done the same and passed on the habit to Joseph. Dimming the lights, once the candles were burning, threw the loft into a soft golden glow.

Everyone started in on the buffet. Conversation dwindled as meats, cheeses and fruits were devoured. A tray of French rolls was soon diminished as sandwiches were made. Everyone helped themselves to macaroni and potato salad. The champagne flowed and Joseph was feeling more confident about the evening when someone inadvertently knocked over the salt shaker. Joe saw a feminine hand with bright red nail polish reach out to right it. Everyone one knows that just setting a salt shaker upright once some salt has been spilled is not sufficient enough. He dashed to the girl before she could leave the table to let her know the egregious error she would be making by just walking away. He could not remember her name, but that was of least importance now.

"Excuse me. Are you the one who just knocked over the salt shaker?" he asked the startled woman.

"Yes. I'm sorry, but I put it back. I haven't broken anything have I?" She looked confused about the menacing look she was getting from her host. She'd been warned about strange outburst and seemingly silly request that might come out as demands, and to just go along.

"I just thought I should let you know the risk you would be putting yourself in, were you to just walk away as you were doing."

"What kind of risk?" she asked. Perhaps she was going to experience one of those off-the-wall things Brenda had said might occur, and probably would.

"What the risk is cannot be expressed in specific terms. What might happen is anybody's guess. The question is, do you want to expose yourself to what will surely be something to your detriment? It could be something small, but then again it could be a major tragedy. Are you willing to flirt with possible disaster?"

"I... I guess not." His manner was scaring her. "So now what?"

"Quickly, you have to throw some salt over your left shoulder!"

She just stood there staring at Joe with her mouth open, about to say something, but nothing was coming out.

"Do it, if you don't want to place yourself in jeopardy!" he all but shouted at her.

She was momentarily frozen by his loud, and she thought funny, instructions. Everyone stopped to look and see what was going on. This was definitely one of Brenda's warned "outbursts," so she decided to comply. She threw some salt over her left shoulder.

"You have no idea the grief you may just have saved yourself," Joe told her, pleased he had been able to help.

"Try not to do that again. But if it should happen again, remember to throw some salt over your left shoulder. Better safe than sorry," he told her as he moved off.

"Yeah. Right," the girl said under her breath. "He really is a fruitcake."

Once everyone had served themselves and things were going really well, the unthinkable happened.

With no one at the buffet table, a candle suddenly fell over. Joseph saw it going over and immediately made a mad dash to catch it, but he was much to far away to do so. The candle toppled toward the front of the table; the flame extinguished in the potato salad. Suddenly Joe had cause to worry once more.

Rapidly wiping the candle off, securely affixing it back in its holder, and relighting it, took him but seconds. However, the candle *had* fallen over and it was anybody's guess what that might portend. Whatever it was, it wouldn't be good.

He rejoined his guests, most of whom had completely missed the drama that had just played out at the buffet table. Brenda and Ranada had not missed it. They looked at each other and shook their heads.

"Is there anything he doesn't miss?" Ranada asked.

"Sadly, it seems not," Brenda answered.

Brenda and Ranada had been admiring a ring that the last girl to arrive was wearing. Joe thought her name was Missy, Mitzy or Misty. There were so many new faces he was having difficulty with the names.

"Yes, Kevin gave it to me just last week. Isn't it lovely? Look at all the fire deep inside," Missy, it *was* Missy, said. "I've always wanted one. Kevin is just the best."

Joseph glanced over at Missy's ring and saw that it was a very large fire opal. It was truly a magnificent gem, exquisitely set, with a ring of what had to be diamond chips surrounding it.

"So your birthday is in October," Joe said; a statement of fact.

"Oh, no. I was born May," Missy corrected him.

"You can't wear that ring!" Joe pronounced with authority.

"Why not?" Missy sounded confused and a little angry.

Brenda and Ranada looked at each other again. They knew where this was going.

"No one should wear an opal if it's not their birthstone. It's very bad luck. You should have him take it back and get you something else," Joe informed her.

"I think that's ridiculous!" Missy was not about to give up her opal ring on the advice of this stranger, who'd not let her in at first, then dragged her down the hall to get someone else at the last minute. Brenda had said Joe was a little odd, but this was too much. Missy moved off to another group.

As Missy left, Joe noticed one of the other women heading toward the bathroom.

"Go with her," Joe quietly told Brenda.

"Why? You afraid she might steal the linens?" She was making a joke, but Joe didn't get it. She knew he wanted her to accompany the girl so there would be twelve people in the room.

"Just do it. Women always go to the john in two's anyway." Reluctantly, she followed the woman to the bathroom, wondering what he'd do when one of the men made the same trip. Men didn't go to the bathroom in two's.

Well, sometimes they did, but Joe wasn't one of them.

Brenda would soon find out how Joe was going to handle that problem. As soon as any of the guys headed for the john, Joe ducked into the kitchen and didn't come out until the guy returned. Brenda didn't know where Joe got all the energy to keep up with juggling so many phobias and obsessions at once.

Despite everything, the evening went fairly well. It was an interesting mix of people, all seeming to enjoy the company. No one could say there wasn't enough to eat and drink. Half the group had had just a little too much to drink.

Ranada was the first to feel herself fading. She was most definitely the oldest one present, but had fit in perfectly with the younger crowd. She acted a lot younger than she was. However, no matter how young she acted, how young she felt, eventually the truth would out. The extra years reared their ugly heads and told her, "You better get on home girl!" She went to Joe to thank him for the evening.

"Joe, I've had a marvelous time. Thank you so much for including me, but I think it's time for me to get down the hall." She should have known better. Perhaps it was because she was beginning to feel sleepy. Perhaps it was that extra glass of champagne. Her reflexes were just a tad tardy, but as soon as the words left her mouth, she knew what Joe was going to say.

"Ranada, you can't leave yet. It's only 9:30," Joe said, taking her arm and propelling her over to Brenda and the group she was talking to. Ranada immediately realized her gaff. Of course, she would not be allowed to leave *alone*. One of the couples would have to leave first before she would be able go. Joe really could be a pain in the ass with his ideas. Ranada would love to meet his mother and tell her a thing or two, but unfortunately she was dead. Ranada wondered if she had had any idea how badly she'd handicapped her son. She must have been a nutcase herself.

Mercifully, one of the couples soon departed, leaving her free to make her exit. She really had had a good time, but she was tired and normally went to bed early. It was now 10:30, which was not too bad. Joe and Brenda said goodnight to her at the door.

Once everyone had gone, Brenda decided to put into motion a plan that had been rolling around in the back of her mind for some time. She felt herself falling in love with this slightly unbalanced, terribly good-looking, physically adept, and basically thoughtful and companionable young guy. She also knew that his fears would drown her, or drive her insane, should she have to deal with them daily for the rest of her life. It was almost criminal that he had bought every crazy thing his mother had told him. She was sure there had to be a way to snap him out of the prison his mother had locked him in.

"I was wondering if you thought it might be alright for me to have a key here," Brenda asked. "I hate waiting out in the hall, and I usually find you're not here when I arrive. I'm not pushing to move in or anything like that. It would just be a little more convenient. You don't have to decide right now. Just think about it."

"As a matter of fact, I was thinking about giving you a key." Joe took out his key ring. There were three keys on the ring with his rabbit's foot. Joe always doubled his luck if at all possible. "I can't give you this one, then there'd only be two keys left. I know I have a spare somewhere, but I forget where I put it. If I can't find that one, I'll make you a copy."

Little did Joseph know how badly giving Brenda a key was going to turn out.

THE INTERVENTION

JOSEPH NEVER FOUND his extra key. It was well hidden at the back of the silverware drawer under some odds and ends of utensils he never used. He'd put it there when he moved in and forgotten all about it, except for the fact that he had one.

He had to have a copy made of the key he had on his key ring. He was comfortable doing it. He'd been dating Brenda for a sufficiently long enough time to trust her with open access to his place. He wasn't ready for her to move in, lock, stock and barrel. That would be pushing it. She'd said herself that that wasn't her intention. At least he didn't think it was her immediate intention. At some point the ultimate move would have to be contemplated, but he'd deal with that later. How much later, depended on how he perceived her acceptance of, and compliance with, his absolutely stringent directives to observe each and every one of his do's and don'ts.

He couldn't risk having someone living with him who would either blatantly or ignorantly bring any shadow of lurking Doom, or even the slightest breeze from the Winds of Chaos, into his abode. He'd gotten just a small sample of what could happen on the evening he'd hosted the buffet for fourteen.

God forbid anyone like Missy was left alone to her own devices in his apartment. She might just as well step out in front of a speeding bus for all the thought she gave to her own safety and well being. Joseph was sure she'd rue the day she blew off his stern warning not to wear that stupid opal ring. It was just a piece of jewelry to her, a beautiful bauble she had coveted and been given by her boyfriend. For anyone whose birthday fell in October, that would be just fine. Why couldn't she see the danger in it for her? He was glad his mother had been so adamant about things like that. It not only made his life safer and more prosperous, but he'd also had the opportunity to save others much grief, sometimes in spite of themselves.

"Oh, Brenda, here's the key I had made for you. I stopped off on the way home from work today to have it made. Put it on your key ring," he said, holding out the newly minted key.

Brenda took out her key ring to slip the loft key onto it. She was about to put the keys back in her purse when Joe noticed a serious flaw he couldn't let go without bringing it to her attention.

"Brenda, you really should take one of those other keys off that ring if you hope to promote any sense of harmony and balance."

"Right. Three keys on a ring. Would it really be so bad if I kept all four on this ring?" How could she not have seen that coming? But she still risked a rebuke by asking if she could let this one slide.

"If you do that, you may regret it. My mother was always very up front about consequences. No one can predict what they might be, or even if they might be, but who in their right mind would want to tempt Fate that way? Better safe than sorry. And who knows who else might be sucked into the maelstrom along with you, should that lapse in judgment cause one?" He thought he'd made his point quite eloquently without having to resort to a direct order. He might be that one who got sucked in and he'd prevent that at all costs.

"Of course, you're right," she acquiesced, but now that she had the damned key, could she carry through with her plan? Getting the key in the first place was just a ruse to see if she couldn't somehow jolt him out of his ridiculous phobias. She knew that if she was unsuccessful in rescuing Joseph from himself, she'd have to give the key back. No way could she live with his kind of insanity, much as her love for him was growing. Perhaps she shouldn't have gotten involved with him in the first place. But damn! He was so hot, and in bed he was scalding. How could such passion and expertise coexist with lunacy and downright silliness? Joseph was talking to her. She'd missed most of what he was saying while she mused over how to proceed with Operation Rescue.

"...that way we'll save time as well as money. What do you think?"

"Great. That'd be great!" She had no idea what was going to be great, but she'd figure it out later.

"For now, how about we go out for dinner? There's a new Romanian restaurant that someone at work said was terrific. I'll bet they serve some of the wonderful dishes my mother used to make."

"That sounds fine," Brenda said with feigned sincerity. Truth be known, she didn't much care for dishes that were too foreign. Wouldn't you just know she'd have to hook up with someone whose roots were in some Slavic country. They probably had "Ghoulash" on the menu. Garlic would be oozing out of every pore of everyone in the place. She didn't mind a little garlic, but she suspected some of the patrons might just be wearing more than they were eating.

Dinner turned out to be quite good and garlic jewelry seemed to be at a minimum. The live music she'd found very relaxing and mellow. She hadn't expected entertainment with her dinner.

While trying to keep up with Joseph's conversation, she was plotting in her head the logistics of her plan.

"... told him in no uncertain terms to bug off. Can't you just hear her saying that to him?"

Joseph had just asked her a question. She hadn't a clue what the answer should be. Who said bug off to whom?

"I guess that sure put him in his place," she chanced.

"He was adequately chastised!"

Thank goodness she'd gotten that one right. She had to pay more attention now and plan later.

Brenda took her time laying the groundwork for her grand scheme. She had to first establish a comfortable feel and rhythm to her comings and goings at the loft. She couldn't risk Joseph's detecting a whiff of anything unorthodox taking place before the curtain went up on Operation Rescue.

She had to carefully orchestrate the scenario that would absent Joe from the loft for the required length of time, in order for her to make the necessary "adjustments."

She'd enlist Missy's help for sure. Missy had been miffed ever since the buffet and the ring incident, not to mention the side trip before she could gain entrance to the loft. She wanted in on the action, but for a different reason than Brenda had in mind.

Ranada lived right down the hall. She'd be easily available.

Could the three of them pull it off? Maybe one more person would be better. They had to be quick. They certainly didn't want to be caught in the act.

With Missy on board and Joan, "the coatless wonder of pneumonia fame," Brenda went to talk with Ranada. She hadn't told her anything about what she'd been up too yet, but filled her in and asked if she would be willing to help.

"I don't know if that's such a good idea. I know he's a mess, but damn, it's so ingrained, I just don't know what might happen. He's lived with these neuroses or misguided notions, what ever you want to call them, for so long he might just dissociate into a blithering idiot. It might push him over the edge. It's possible he might end up in Belleview," Ranada gave her candid opinion.

"Do you really think it would be that bad?" Brenda was now concerned she might not be doing the right thing after all.

"It's a possibility. I can't predict the results with someone like Joe. I've never met anyone like him before. Freud's dead, so he's no help. I doubt you'd get Joe anywhere near a psychiatrist's office anyway."

"Ranada, I 'm falling head over heals for this guy, but I can't live with all his bullshit. My grandmother, if she were alive, would waltz up to him and throw, 'Poppycock!' in his face without thinking twice. I can't even get out of one little silly thing. I even agreed to take a key off my key ring so there'd be only three on there. Why did I do that? Two.

Three. Five. Eight. What the hell does it matter how many keys you've got on your key ring!? He actually thinks if you don't have three keys there, you're setting yourself up for possible disaster. Isn't that just crazy?"

"Just a bit. You really want to do this, don't you?"

"Yes. I really want to try."

Ranada agreed to help, still nursing her reservations.

Once the girls' rolls were laid out in detail, Brenda had to also enlist a few of the men to get Joe out of the loft, and keep him out long enough to effect the change. They would have to set the final date for the deed on a Saturday, when work schedules would not intervene. Weekdays everyone worked, except for Ranada. Evenings were just too unreliable. Joseph seldom went out anywhere on a work night except to dinner. Saturday would be the perfect time for a few of the guys to lure Joe away on some pretext. They'd make it something that would occupy them for most of the afternoon. While the men were off putzing at whatever, the women would transform the loft. When Joe returned late in the afternoon, the stage would be set.

On the chosen day, there was a game at Madison Square Garden. Joseph loved basketball and one of the guys had gotten super tickets to the Nicks vs. Jazz. They'd be there all afternoon.

Brenda had already informed Joseph that her and three other girls were going down to Atlantic City for the day, so she'd probably not be home until late. He would come home to find their surprise waiting. It would be a shock, she knew, but he'd soon see that nothing bad happened just because of silly superstitions.

The Saturday arrived and Brenda told Joe she was leaving to meet the girls.

"Enjoy the game with the boys. I'll see you later tonight."
Then she slipped down to Ranada's, where the rest of her
crew were assembled and waiting.

As soon as Joe was gone, they all trouped over to the loft
and started work. They had to invert all Joe's horseshoes.
That was fairly simple. All they had to do was flip the
frames and put them back on their nails. No one felt a rush
of good luck leaving the room as the last of the lot was re-
hung.

Next the four-leaf clovers had to become three-leafed.
They couldn't unframe them to do it, but Brenda had gotten
some assistance from a local arts and craft shop on how to
make one of the leaflets disappear, making it look like an
ordinary clover leaf. It took some time and effort for the
transformation to be almost unnoticeable. The ceiling did
not fall in on them while they worked.

The bird feathers were not alterable, so they were carted
into the bedroom and shoved under the bed.

Likewise, the scarabs could not be altered, but removing
them would be a much more immediately noticeable
absence. They just thinned their numbers a bit, stashing
the banished in the bottom of the closet.

Joseph still had his rabbit's foot key chain with three
keys on it. He would be wearing his rudraksh bracelet. He
never took it off, even in the shower. Would the shift in
balance be enough?

It would be the inverted horseshoes, three-leaf clovers,
no bird feathers and a limited number of scarabs against
the rabbit's foot, three keys and a Rudraksh bracelet. This
would be a battle to see who would finally gain the upper
hand. Once Joseph saw that nothing changed, the world did
not come to an end, and Brenda would be there right beside

him, as well as all his friends, what better support or luck could one want but that?

As a last thought, Brenda unscrewed a number of light bulbs so the loft would be more dimly illuminated on Joseph's return. Noticing things slowly might help. They surveyed their work and deemed it sufficient before leaving

It just had to work. She didn't want to have to walk away to maintain her sanity, and she refused to abandon Joe to his insanity.

THE RESOLUTION

THE GAME was a squeaker, The Nicks winning by only three points. The boys stopped for burgers and fries afterward and a lively discussion about the game. They hadn't said a word about the dirty trick that was afoot. They agreed with the rest of the group that Joe was definitely a fucking nut job, but he was also a great guy, personable, and they felt a little guilty betraying him the way they were. However, they'd lived up to their part of the deal, occupying Joe for the afternoon. Now it was out of their hands as he left them to return to his loft.

"I'm not sure when the girls will be back, but if they're not too late, we might all go out for a few drinks and dancing later," he suggested, as he got up to leave.

"Why not."

"Sounds good to me."

"I'm in," came the replies all around.

"Great! I'll give you all a call later. And, hey, thanks again for the game," and he was gone.

They sat in silence for a few minutes.

"I sure hope Brenda's little scare tactic works."

"Yeah. He'd be so much easier to deal with."

"Let's just hope it doesn't backfire!"

What an understatement that would be!

They all thought about the last remark as they finished their last beers.

The girls had gone for lunch as well, after a brief but necessary shopping spree. You had to catch the sales when you could. They sat around their big round table in the corner, sipping martinis as they waited on their food. They were just a very typical group of New York friends, enjoying what was left of the afternoon. They basked in the glory of their "finds" and what a bargain each had been. They re-examined each purchase in detail while downing the second round of "tini's." Their food had not yet arrived.

Their waiter approached the table. He was edible. If their food didn't arrive soon, they'd start on him. His trousers were so tight they could see his religion. However, when he opened his mouth, it was fairly obvious he played for the other team. And it looked like he had a lot to play with.

"Ladies, I'm ever so sorry for the delay. We've had a small power failure in the kitchen. Chef is working ever so hard to remedy the situation. He's instructed me to offer you a complimentary appetizer and a free round from the bar."

They ordered a cheese and fruit tray, and the waiter swished off to get their drinks.

"Um-um-um. To think of all that going to waste," Missy commented the moment he was out of earshot.

"Yeah. Too bad. The last boyfriend I had looked like he hadn't even passed puberty yet. I think he was still waiting for his testicles to descend," Joan added. With that comment, the table erupted into uncontrollable giggles. The martini's were definitely having the desired effect.

"The las' boyfriend I had didn't even have any tes'icles. Least I never worried about getting knocked up. Best reason I can think of for dating a man without balls," Ranada weighed in.

That comment brought on a renewed peals of laughter as the new round of drinks were delivered and Ranada administered a stealthy brush against the waiter's tight little bottom.

"Hard as a rock!" she announced, as he returned to the kitchen. Yet more laughter. They were hard pressed to start in on the food that was finally delivered, hungry as they were, they were having such a good time at their waiter's expense.

As they were finishing their food, Brenda suddenly gave a little squeal.

"My goodness! Look what time it is! The game's been over for some time, unless they went into overtime." They hadn't. "Jeez, I should have been back at the loft before now. We need to finish and get out of here."

While Ranada had been checking out the waiter's tusche, Joseph had been climbing the stairs to the loft.

He opened the door and threw his coat on the nearest chair, as he went into the bathroom to pee. When he returned, he thought the place seemed rather dark. The windows faced east, so mornings were the loft's brightest hours. With the sun in the west, and going down, the loft was at its gloomiest. But today it seemed gloomier than usual.

He crossed to the light switch and flicked it on and off several times. A few of the lights were out. The bulbs must have blown out.

He went into the kitchen to get replacements. Something didn't feel right. He couldn't put his finger on it, but there was a strange premonition that something was about to happen.

He wasn't psychic. He'd never predicted a specific event. His mother said that his grandmother had done so several times but, as far as he knew, he hadn't inherited any of her psychic genes.

He went back to the living room to replace the burnt out bulbs with that nagging feeling still hovering nearby. Putting in fresh bulbs increased the illumination incrementally with each one. As he screwed in the final one, he noticed an empty spot on the table next to that lamp. Something should have been in that spot.

A SCARAB! One of his scarabs was missing. He scanned the floor. Maybe it had fallen off. But, it just wasn't there. He had known there was something wrong and this was it.

His shock at the missing scarab was about to be ratcheted up a notch when he noticed a second one had vanished as well. Then a third!

"What the hell is going on here?" he shouted at no one.

The worst was yet to come.

He scanned the room slowly, looking, not knowing just what he was looking for. Then he noticed the walls were a little bare. Things were missing from his walls! There were no feathers hanging in their usual places. Every one had vanished.

"Someone's broken in here and stolen my things. Son-of-a-BITCH!"

Then his expression of anger turned to one of horror as he noticed his horseshoes, all hanging upside down. Bad luck! Bad Luck!! BAD LUCK!!!

He was short of breath. Something terrible was happening. He pulled his key chain from his pocket. He rubbed his rabbit's foot and palmed the three keys. Suddenly all his pocket-held protectors seemed inadequate to this situation. His rudraksh bracelet still circled his wrist. This couldn't be happening. He'd taken so many precautions. He had so many fallback's nothing could get through the armor he'd amassed as protection.

He moved closer to one of the offending horseshoes. Right next to it was one of his four-leaf clovers. But it wasn't right either. It had mutated. It was now only a garden variety three-leaf clover. No luck there! Lack of Luck!! BAD LUCK!!!

There had never been this much bad luck in his world.

Suddenly, there was a thud at one of the loft's huge windows. Joseph was feeling dizzy. His breath came in fits and starts. He didn't want to go over to the window. He was afraid of what he might see. He dragged himself toward the darkening panes anyway.

When he saw it, he froze. He couldn't get his breath. The pain in his chest was building. There on the broad outside sill lay a large bird, not moving. Joseph knew instinctively what had happened. The bird had smashed into the window, broken its neck, and dropped lifeless onto his windowsill. It was a sign of DEATH!

There was no one in the loft but Joseph. The bird had come for him. Despite all his precautions and backups, this wicked bird, this harbinger of death, had chosen his window to fly into. He took a last look. The bird was black as night.

The pain in Joseph's chest was excruciating. His vision was blurring. He was sweating like a pig. He couldn't breathe. He staggered toward the sofa but fell short, hitting the floor with a muffled thud.

The room was silent. Joseph's inert form was hidden by the overstuffed sofa that faced away from the loft's now dark windows.

The girls were enjoying their lunch. They hadn't yet noticed how late the hour had become. The martini's were exceptionally good.

Too late, they were rushing from the restaurant, the cute waiter's tusche forgotten. Too late, they hailed a cab. Too late, they rushed up the stairs to burst into the loft, finding it deserted.

"Thank goodness he's not back yet. He's probably eating with the boys," Brenda heaved a sigh of relief. But something wasn't right. The loft was much too bright. She'd unscrewed a number of light bulbs to temporarily conceal what they'd done. They were now all lit.

Then she saw his coat.

"He's been here! There's his coat. What must he have thought here by himself, finding what we did?" Brenda felt awful.

"Where do you think he went?" asked Missy.

"He didn't go anywhere," Ranada spoke up. "There's his coat. You know Joe would never go out without his coat, even in a panic or an emergency." She was right.

"Then where is he?" Brenda wondered. She called out, "Joe! Joe! Are you here!?" No answer.

She went into the bedroom. Empty. The bathroom door stood open. Empty. As she reentered the living room, she saw him. Well, not him, just one foot. One shoe protruded out beyond the couch, which hid the rest of his body.

Brenda rushed to his side. He was deathly still. White as a sheet and soaking wet. She knew he was dead. His pupils were the size of dimes. Hardly any iris was visible. Brenda knew what that meant. She'd killed him. Sure as anything she'd killed him. She'd set him free from his prison of stupid superstitions, good luck charms, Old Wives Tales, the whole damned lot. Now she'd live with a lifetime of guilt. She broke down and sobbed, big fat tears falling into his unseeing eyes.

"Brenda, come here," Ranada sounded urgent.

What could possibly be urgent at this point? Brenda thought. She got up, crossed the small space between the back of the sofa and the windows.

"Look at this," Ranada said, pointing to a splash of something on the window. "Looks like blood."

Brenda opened the window, and then she, too, saw it. She picked it up and held it in her hands. It was still warm. It was a large black bird, maybe a crow? It's head flopped around like it was no longer connected to its body.

"Poor thing. It must have flown into the window and broken its neck. Could it have picked a more inopportune time to do that? Crap! Crap, Crap, CRAP!!"

She'd totally forgotten to factor in a damned, stupid bird! She'd set the stage for Joe to scare himself to death.

Printed in the United States
135493LV00001B/259/P